No Longer Captive

Rai
Lindsay-Wallace

First Blessed Press print edition published in 2016.

Book cover designed by *Elena Kosharac*.

Book Edited by *Phillip Smith*

Photo Credit: *Kent Wallace*

ISBN: 978-0-692-54621-5

Printed in the *United States of America*.

To my very special grandchildren:
Kayla, Brianna, Lauren, Mariah and Lamad.
Nana loves you all so very much!

Contents

Acknowledgements

All glory and honor goes to my faithful Father God, Jesus Christ, my Lord and Savior and the Holy Spirit, my constant companion, for gifting me to write inspiring stories with messages of hope, healing, forgiveness and love.

To my wonderful husband of twenty-five years, Kent. You keep me smiling and laughing. Not only do we make beautiful music together in singing, but in loving. You're my heart!

Special thanks to my son, Maurice, my partner in "crime", for pushing me to a new level of writing and publishing. This book is because of you. Thanks for working so hard to make it happen. Also, to my very supportive children, who are also so gifted, Karlton, Grace and Ashley.

To my number one fan, my mom, Mary Watts. You're the greatest and I love you with all my heart. Here's another book that you can re-read for the millionth time. To Lisa and Willie, your support is faithful and unending! To my in-laws, Norris and Grace Wallace, I love you!

To all my family and friends, I dedicate this book to you. You have supported my dream of writing without fail. I appreciate all of you and love you even more.

The Spirit of the LORD *is upon Me,*
Because He has anointed Me
To preach the gospel to the poor;
He has sent Me to heal the brokenhearted,[iii]
To proclaim liberty to the captives
And recovery of sight to the blind,
To proclaim the acceptable year of the LORD.

Luke 4:18-19

CHAPTER 1

Freedom

Slam!

The final gate closed as Jonah Bates departed the place that had been his habitation for the past five years. Refusing to look back, Jonah put one foot in front of the other, feeling lighter with each step away from his past. It was liberating. The feeling was indescribable. Manchester Correctional Institution was a place that Jonah wanted to forget forever. For 1,825 days, Jonah had been stripped of his freedom. He was imprisoned by man for the wrongdoings that he had purposely committed. His rights as a free man had been taken, and he had to do and say what others told him to do and say. Because of his choices, he had been enslaved for five long, dreadful years. Jonah had endured things that he vowed to go to the grave with, only he and the *good* Lord knowing the secrets of his heart. Jonah went in to Manchester at the age twenty-four and came out at twenty-nine. He went in as an angry, bitter, violent young black man, and came out as a humbled Christian. Life had broken him, but by the grace of God, Jonah did not stay that way. He had been pieced back together, molded and reshaped by the hand of Almighty God. Jonah was a new creation. Old things passed away, and behold, all things were made new.

Today was the beginning of the rest of his life. Jonah felt like dancing and never stopping. The rhythm of his soul stirred to a triumphant tempo. His spirit tangoed to the tune of triumphant freedom.

When the Spirit of the Lord comes upon my heart, I will dance like David danced! The lyrics of a song Jonah had heard from a visiting church in prison had struck a permanent chord in his heart. Jonah was grateful. *Thank God for Your servants, who faithfully visited the prison. Truly, a lifeline had been extended to us through their commitment in sharing the Gospel of Jesus Christ. I was in prison and they visited me. I desire to go back and share the Gospel as a free man. Lord make a way. Open unto me a door that I may go forth and encourage my brothers that are still locked up. Better yet, Lord, open up a door that I may help the young boys and girls from not ending up behind prison bars.*

Inhaling the freshness of the air after a storm, Jonah felt hopeful. God had given him another chance to make things right and to live a life that was pleasing to Him—on the outside. No more bars! No more shackles! No more chains! No more torture! No more Nixon!

Nixon had been a thorn in Jonah's side from the first day of his incarceration. The big, bulky, evil-spirited man had made being locked behind bars almost unbearable for Jonah. If it had not been for Jonah finding God, surely he would not have survived the man's torment. Yet, God had a ram in the bush, even behind prison doors—Wayne Helms.

Lord, thank You for my bodyguard, Wayne. I sure do miss him. He was a father-figure to me. He repeatedly protected me from Nixon. He risked his life for mine. He taught me about You. Wayne shared his love for You with me. He led me back to

You. My Aunt Alice paved the way, and I had strayed away, but Wayne steered me back in the right direction.

Looking upward, Jonah mouthed, "I'm out Wayne! Hope you are looking out for me down here! Put in a good word for me, with the Big Guy!" Wayne had exchanged his earthly temple for an immortal temple in Heaven.

Reaching the border of the institution, looking around, Jonah saw no one waiting on him. His heart plummeted. He did not stand alone, disappointment stood with him.

Lord, please let Joel come for me.

Jonah had hoped that his twin brother, Joel, had buried the hatchet and would be waiting on him outside Manchester. Jonah waited for nearly an hour, praying that his brother had not forsaken him. In the end, Joel was a no-show.

What do you expect? You stole from him. You lied to him. You humiliated him. You betrayed him in the worst way. Why would he come for you?

Jonah could not push back the accusations. After all, satan was the accuser of the brethren. It was his job to torment and torture the saints. Although, the enemy was not all-knowing, he knew what buttons to push. Jonah's buttons were anything involving his twin brother. After seven years, Jonah still underwent a dominating surge of guilt about the betrayal of stabbing his brother in the back. He deserved the finger pointing. Jonah deserved to suffer for what he did to Joel. He had hurt his brother in the worse kind of way. Nevertheless, Jonah still hoped.

Pulling out a tattered letter from Aunt Mae, his Aunt Alice's closest friend, Jonah reread the letter he had received two years ago.

3

Jonah,

Your Aunt Alice passed yesterday in her sleep. She had not been feeling well for over a week, but she would not go to the doctor. You know how stubborn Aunt Alice could be. She wanted me to make sure that I kept in touch with you. She said that you had no one but her and the good Lord. So, I want you to know I intend on keeping that promise to my dearest friend and Sister in Christ Jesus. Your Aunt Alice loved you so much. She said that you were going to show the world that you are good and that you are somebody special. Many times, she said your mother named you Jonah because she knew you were a leader. You ran from your calling, like Jonah in the Bible, but God got your attention—not in a whale, but behind prison doors. Alice was so proud when you shared your faith of giving your heart to Jesus. She said to me that day... 'Well I can go home now and be with the Lord because I know Jonah is going to be alright now.' She died two weeks later. Jonah, you have to stay on the straight-and-narrow way, because your Aunt Alice believed in you. Jesus believes in you, and now I believe in you. Your Aunt Alice made me promise to tell you that she wants you and Joel to bridge the huge gap between the two of you. You two are brothers, twin brothers, connected by birth and connected by God. Do whatever it takes Jonah to make things right between you and Joel. You are blood. God gave you each other because He knew that you would need each other growing up, and as you both became men. Joel loves you, he is just hurt and broken. However, God can heal him, just as He has healed you and will continue to heal you. Finally, Jonah, Aunt Alice did not have much to leave you, but she left you her home. It is not much and it needs work, but when you get out of prison come see me and I will give you the keys. I will write to you as much as possible.

In God's love, Aunt Mae.

Every time Jonah read the letter, he became emotional. Aunt Alice was the greatest earthly gift God had ever given to him. She was his rock. She was his *real* mother. Jonah and Joel lived with Aunt Alice from the age of seven until adulthood, because their mother Patrina, known as Trina, was a *crackhead* and could not stay clean. Trina died from a drug overdose when the twins were nine. Not only had his aunt provided a roof over their heads, but she had also raised the twins in the church, giving Jonah and Joel a firm foundation of faith in God. Jonah had strayed far from his upbringing, but the seed had been planted.

"Well Lord, I got $43 to my name. Maybe I can hitch a ride to Holly Hill. Give me favor, Lord!"

My favor surrounds you like a shield. Be at peace. I am with you.

Sweet peace engulfed Jonah. The same peace which had shielded him during confinement, giving him the sustaining power to endure every moment, every hour, every day, every week, every month, and every year.

As Aunt Alice would say, "You got three choices. Live in the past, stay where you are, or keep it moving!"

Jonah chuckled. "Joel's not coming, so I'm going to keep it moving." He started walking toward the interstate, holding his thumb out. Dressed in faded jeans and a white T-shirt, Jonah had traded his orange prison jumpsuit for something less conspicuous. From outer appearances, Jonah had it going on. He was a nice-looking young black man, with a smooth, honey complexion, a muscular physique, standing tall at six-foot two. Yet, no matter how good he looked, Jonah felt as if the world could still see his prison number on the back of his shirt. The change of clothes did not expunge his incarcerated mindset. It would take time and the healing balm of God's love and forgiveness to remove the stains of captivity.

Lord, I do not know what I am going to do when I make it to Holly Hill. Aunt Alice is gone. Joel has abandoned me. And, well, my old friends...are no good for me. What am I going to do?

Trust Me.

I trust You Lord...but...

Trust Me.

I trust You Lord....but right now Lord, I need some water, before I pass out. Hot and sweaty after only walking a short distance, the ninety-degree temperature was stifling. Thankful to be outside, Jonah forgot just how hot it could get in the South.

Lord, You made water come from a rock. I see some rocks ahead. Jonah laughed. Throughout his life, Jonah's sense of humor had been his saving grace. Instead of crying, Jonah often found a reason to just laugh it out. Taking baby steps, Jonah pressed forward. Now on the interstate, with many cars zooming by, his spirit needed a boost—a pick-me-up. Therefore, Jonah did what he normally did in Manchester in tough times, he prayed the word audibly.

"My soul thirsts for You. My flesh longs for You in a dry and thirsty land where there is no water." Psalms 63 was one of his favorites. "So I have looked for You in the sanctuary, to see Your power and Your glory. Because Your loving kindness is better than life, my—"

A blue truck pulled over ahead of him.

"...lips shall praise You. Glory to God!" Jonah sprinted to the driver's side.

"Where are you headed?"

"Holly Hill."

"Me too," the jolly man smiled. "Hop in."

6

Jonah hurried around to the passenger's side.

"Thanks!" Jonah grinned.

"Name is Wilfred." The man greeted him with a friendly smile.

"I'm Jonah."

"Well, Jonah, it's a pleasure to meet you. Are you the Jonah who is running away from or the Jonah who is running to God?

"Running to God and all that He wants me to do for Him."

"Good! Glad you're not going to be eaten by the whale!"

"Already done that!" Jonah smirked.

Wilfred chuckled. "Some of us just got hard heads."

"With soft *behinds*, as my Aunt Alice used to say." Jonah smiled at the memory.

"Yep! We sure do," Wilfred agreed. "I have some cold water on the floor. You're welcome to it."

I will pour water on the parched ground and cause streams to flow on the dry land.

Thank You God for Your favor and for supplying my need.

I am with you always.

It is good to be truly free, spiritually and physically. Thank God for freedom!

CHAPTER 2

Home Sweet Home

Exhausted, sweaty, and hungry, Jonah walked the familiar Main Street where he used to live. Visibly, nothing much had changed, and yet everything had changed. This was his hometown, where poverty, crime, drug addiction, alcoholism, prostitution, gang activities, and wickedness were prevalent on every street corner. Chaos and immorality went hand-in-hand in Holly Hill. Nothing about the urban area was holly or holy, except the holly trees bordering the community, with red berries, shiny evergreen leaves, and prickly edges. Everything else appeared dried up, dilapidated, or dead.

Albeit, the surroundings were familiar, but everything felt strange. The young people hanging on the streets reminded Jonah of the old days when he and the guys used to hang out, getting into trouble, always up to no good. Life back then was a mixture of pandemonium and excitement. Jonah lived on the edge and enjoyed the feeling of recklessness. There was never a dull moment. Yet, even then, something was always tugging at his heart. Being honest with himself, Jonah never could fully enjoy the foolhardiness because his conscious nagged at him perpetually. Even during all those years of choosing to do wrong, Jonah could not silence his soul's cry.

Shaking his head, Jonah desired nothing more than to just shake off the memories of the past. Unfortunately, life did not work that way. Five years ago, he was doing the same things the new-breeds on the street corner were doing now. Watching one of the young boys, probably twelve or thirteen years of age, run to a drive-by car and hand a small package to the guy in exchange for money, brought back sorrowful remembrances. No sooner had the boy turned to walk away that an undercover cop in the car slapped a handcuff on his wrist. All the other boys broke away, running for their lives, forgetting all about the young boy.

Just like they forgot about me. Not one of my homies visited me while I was in prison. Five long years and not a peep from anyone, except Aunt Alice and Mae. Not once did any of them write me a letter or send me a card...not even Dana, who supposedly loved me back then.

Jonah's heart ached for the nameless child, who was somebody's son, somebody's grandson, somebody's neighbor. *Oh, Lord, help him find his way to You before it is too late.* Witnessing the young boy sitting in the back of the car, waiting to be transported to DJJ, peeled open the scab of an old wound on his soul.

Jonah's footsteps robotically steered him to his childhood home. The rundown two-bedroom home was even more dilapidated than before. The windows and doors were boarded up. There was hardly any white paint visible from all the peeling on the dry-rot boards. The home was so ramshackle looking that if a gust of wind just blew on it, it would surely collapse into rubble.

Holding back his emotions, Jonah became sentimental. This place was not much, but in the past this home was all he knew. It was the only place Jonah received unconditional love. His Aunt Alice nurtured them, and was always there for the twins. Even in his worst days, after being suspended from school, being caught smoking reefer, fighting, gangbanging, or hanging out for days, Jonah still had a place of refuge where he could return. Aunt Alice would take him in, clean him up, feed him and then pray over him, beseeching God to change Jonah's wayward heart. She never, ever gave up on him...not like Joel and so many others.

Even before coming to live permanently with their Aunt Alice, the boys often stayed at their aunt's home because their mother, Trina, could not keep a place for them to live. She would work some, get a place, and then lose it because she needed drugs more than she needed to pay rent. Trina was not a good mother, but she gave Jonah and Joel life. For that, Jonah was grateful...most of the time.

Jonah vaguely remembered his father, Jesse Bates. He had left his mother two years after the twins were born. Being too young to remember, the only story Jonah and Joel knew was what their mother had told them, which was that Jesse came home from fighting in Iraq, packed his clothes, and left them all. Trina said he was a no good, deadbeat dad who wanted nothing to do with the twins. Last he had heard, Jesse Bates had a new family. To date, Jonah still had not forgiven him. God was working on him. Nope, Jonah wasn't where he needed to be. But thank God he wasn't who he used to be. He was a work in progress.

Growing up, Jonah and Joel were extremely close, like bone to the marrow. Before coming to stay permanently with Aunt Alice, many nights the young boys clung to each other when their mother left them all alone. They depended on each other to survive. Twin telepathy was real to them. Jonah and Joel had such a deep connection. The twins could read each other thoughts, feel each other's pain, complete each other's sentences, and find pure joy in just being together. Their love was profound and secure for a long time. Although, Joel was rather frail and weakly, there was nothing Joel would not do for Jonah in their younger years.

Joel, older by eight minutes, was the big brother, always looking out for his twin. Trina had complications resulting from her drug usage, and the twins came early. The story goes that Trina gave birth in a crack house and was not taken to the hospital, but instead was looked after by her friends. When Jesse returned from Iraq, on leave for two weeks, he immediately knew something was not fully right with Joel and took him to the doctor. Joel was just four months old. He was told that Joel's kidneys did not fully develop in the mother's womb and that something happened during birth that should have been corrected then. Most likely, Joel would have health problems throughout what was believed would be a short life.

Outwardly, Joel appeared to be fine. Granted, he was more tired than most kids were, but he never complained. Instead of playing outside, Joel usually buried his nose in a book or played checkers with Jonah. He absorbed books like a sponge, taking pleasure in soaking up knowledge.

After Trina died, something changed in Jonah. The abandonment of his mother and father took root in his tender heart and bitterness sprouted. In his preteen years, Jonah shifted gears and slowly spiraled down a path of desperation. He was desperate to fill the void of love from a father who abandoned him and a mother who chose drugs over her own children. The hole was getting bigger and bigger, and Jonah frantically searched for ways to fill or cover it.

Losing a mother was hard on both boys, because no matter how Trina treated them, at the end of the day, she was still their mother. Jonah and Joel could not understand their mother's lifestyle, but loved her regardless. Although the twins looked so much alike, their personalities were rather different. Joel was quiet and reserved, while Jonah was outspoken and outgoing. Both were very smart, but Jonah chose not to apply himself in academics like his brother. Joel shied away from people, while Jonah craved the attention from his peers; he wanted to fit in. He hated being picked on and picked out, so Jonah started gravitating to those who did the picking. Meanwhile, Joel focused on his studies and making good grades with hopes of getting out of the projects. After high school, the two brothers drifted apart. Joel went to college, while Jonah lived the street life, partying, hanging out with the wrong crowds, going from lady to lady. It was not just the physical distance that separated Jonah and Joel; their spirits were different. Joel gave his heart to the Lord, while Jonah gave his to the streets—the devil's playground. Their separation nearly broke Aunt Alice's heart.

Oh Aunt Alice, I wish I had listened to you back then! I wish....wish you could see me now. God changed my wayward heart. I am a new man now.

Jonah wiped his eyes with his shirtsleeve.

The sight of his former dwelling rattled him. Aunt Alice would never sit on the porch again, reading her Bible and drinking fresh lemonade. She would never be there to give him a hug, to encourage him, to pray with him, or to sing one of the old spirituals that calmed him when nothing else could.

I am all alone!

I will be with you always.

With a longing heart, Jonah headed two doors down, to where Aunt Mae stayed, in order to get the key for his home.

After knocking several times, Jonah was just about to leave when someone finally came to the door.

"Can I help you?" a young lady asked, standing behind the locked screen door.

Stunned and speechless, Jonah blinked several times at the beautiful vision that stood before him. She had on a white lace blouse, black slacks, and jewelry that sparkled. Jonah knew the real thing when he saw it, and this lady's jewelry was the real deal. *Probably cost more than my childhood home.* Beautiful, sandy brown, curly locks cascaded down her shoulders, nearly to her petite waistline. Her transparent hazelnut eyes, lined with amazingly thick, long lashes, made her slanted eyes appear majestic. She was physically flawless, her beauty breathtaking.

Okay, Lord are You for real? You have sent me an angel.

She seemed so out of place in this neighborhood. Her clothes alone suggested that she was an upscale woman in a downscale neighborhood.

"Can I help you?" she asked again.

"Oh…I….I'm looking for Aunt Mae," Jonah stuttered.

"How do you know Aunt Mae?" The young woman seemed suspicious.

"Oh, my Aunt Alice and Aunt Mae were best friends."

"Aunt Mae spoke often about her best friend, Alice…" the young lady still seemed perplexed by the young, handsome stranger standing before her.

"Yes, Aunt Alice passed and, well, your Aunt Mae has been writing me and…"

"Oh…are you Jonah?"

"Yes." He smiled kindly, feeling somewhat dreadful that

perhaps this beautiful young lady knew more about him than he wanted her to know.

"Aunt Mae said that you would perhaps come looking for her."

"Is she home?"

"My Aunt Mae passed away four days ago. I'm just returning from her home-going service," she hesitated, pondering whether to invite him in or not.

Wow! Pain squeezed his chest, making it rather difficult to breathe. Life had sucker-punched him again. Aunt Mae had helped him through a lot of dark days. Since he no longer received letters from Aunt Alice, Aunt Mae's letters had given Jonah the encouragement and hope needed to endure the final two years.

Kayla thought Jonah was going to faint or something. His face took on a sickly pallor. Opening the screen door, she gestured, saying, "Please come in."

"Thank you. I'm so sorry for your loss." He swallowed several times, trying to move the clogging in this throat. The news shattered Jonah more than he could express. So much dying, loss after loss. Flashes of the past flooded Jonah's mind. Many happy memories were derived from Aunt Mae's home. The widows' friendship had been solid as a rock. They often spent time at each other's homes, enjoying their extended families. When all was said and done, Alice and Mae had been closer than any blood relatives could ever be.

The same grayish pleather couch sat in the middle of the room, where the twins had sat many times, watching television while Aunt Mae and Aunt Alice baked, cooked, read the Bible, prayed, or just talked about anything and everything. Jonah and Joel spent many days on either that couch or the wooden floor.

"Nothing has changed," Jonah said aloud.

"No, Aunt Mae liked things just the way they were. She said if it's not broken—"

"Then don't fix it," Jonah finished the truism.

Bashfully, Kayla smiled at the memory of her aunt.

"So, you know I'm Jonah, Jonah Bates…and you?"

"Forgive my rudeness," she stuck out her hand, "I'm Kayla Lovett."

Shaking her hand, Jonah's eyes never left her face. "It's a pleasure meeting you, Kayla Lovett." The simple touch ignited a sensation that jarred Jonah's heart to spasm.

Electricity warmed her entire being as their hands touched, somewhat unnerving Kayla. "Would you like something to drink?"

"Yes."

"There's not much in the refrigerator. I can offer you some bottled water or Diet Sprite. Aunt Mae loved her diet sodas." Kayla's eyes reflected sorrow.

"Water will be fine."

"Please have a seat while I go get it."

Returning shortly, Kayla sat in the old recliner, not trusting sitting next to the stranger, and yet, he did not seem like a stranger at all. *If Aunt Mae loved him, Jonah has to be all right.*

"Aunt Mae enjoyed writing to you. You made her feel alive. She said your words on paper were always like a story."

"I felt the same way," Jonah replied anxiously, still wondering if she knew he was an ex-con. "After Aunt Alice died….I…uh…needed someone to talk to."

"I wish I had…more time in getting to know Aunt Mae." Tears on the corner of her eyes surfaced as Kayla struggled to keep her feelings in check.

Her sadness engulfed Jonah. He wanted to reach out, take her in his arms, and somehow comfort Kayla. Surely, she would think he was crazy if he did such a thing.

"How did she die?"

"In her sleep," she sniffed. "I woke up and, well, I didn't smell breakfast. You know Aunt Mae, she has to cook a big breakfast every morning. I've gained ten or fifteen pounds in the last three month staying here."

"You stayed here three months?"

"Only on the weekends," she answered. "Anyhow, when I didn't smell breakfast, I went straight to her room. And…there she lay…with this wide grin on her face." Kayla wiped her eyes. "There was such a peace in the room. It felt…like I was not in the room alone. I know that sounds crazy, but…"

"No, it doesn't. The Presence of God was always around Aunt Mae and Aunt Alice. You could feel His Presence. There was such a sweet presence wherever they were."

Kayla nodded, so glad that he understood. "She died happy."

"She's in a better place," Jonah said with conviction. "She and Aunt Alice are probably having one big party right about now."

"Do you really believe that?"

"Oh, I do. Believers get to spend eternity with the Lord. It has to be one big celebration when one enters into their Heavenly Home!"

"You sound like Aunt Mae. She really believed that."

"You don't believe?" Jonah held his breath. Surely, this beautiful angel had to know his God.

"I want to believe it, but…" Kayla looked away, not wanting

to see the disappointment in his eyes; the same disappointment she saw in her Aunt Mae's eyes. *God hasn't given up on you* her Aunt Mae said the night before she closed her eyes for good. *And neither will I. The seed has been planted. Someone else will water it and God will give the increase. He will save Your soul. I have no doubt about it.* "My father and mother don't go to church. My father is an atheist," she shrugged. "I'm not sure what mother believes. She just follows whatever father says."

"Hmmm." Bizarrely, his heart ached for her to truly know Christ Jesus. Something about Kayla moved Jonah. There was an instant connection between them, which he could not explain. He wanted to get to know her better. Yet, their lives were so different. Here he was, an ex-con, and Jonah was certain she was an educated, successful woman. Most definitely, Kayla was out of his league. It did not take a lawyer or well-educated man to know that. Her expensive clothes, mannerisms, perfect enunciation of words, and the way she carried herself gave it away. Jonah and Kayla were complete opposites. A jewel contrary to a pebble. A damaged pebble, at that.

"I don't remember Aunt Mae mentioning her niece in any of her letters," he said, changing the subject.

"I only discovered Aunt Mae even existed about six months ago. My father kept her a secret."

"Why would he do that?"

"Because Aunt Mae was different from him. Like I said, my father is an atheist. He could not abide by Aunt Mae's religious views. So, when she married a pastor, he cut off all communication with her."

"Sounds like a cruel man to me." The words rolled off his tongue without thought. "I apologize. I don't mean to be disrespectful."

"It was cruel of him." Kayla agreed. "My father is like that. He was and still is very controlling. If…if you don't do what he says, he'll cut you off."

Since she had been a toddler, Kayla had spent many nights worried that she would do something wrong, something that would cause her father to disown her. Or worse, just ignore her or not speak to her for days, weeks, and even months. Drew Lovett had done that to both mother and daughter. Kayla's fears were deep. Being adopted as a three month-old baby, Kayla never felt secure in her home. The threat of returning her, or giving her to another family, was never spoken, but always implied.

"Wow. So, how does he feel about you being here?"

"He doesn't know."

"You mean he doesn't know that his sister died?"

"He knows," Kayla swallowed, "but he doesn't care."

Heartless man! How could someone like that be the father of someone so sweet and beautiful?

"I told him, showing him the announcement in the paper. I had hoped that he would have a heart and come pay his last respect to his sister, but I was wrong. He burned the newspaper and told me never to ever mention Aunt Mae's name in his house again."

Yep, heartless! "I'm so sorry."

"Don't be. I had a good life. I went to the best schools. Graduated from an Ivy League University with a master's, and now I am working on my doctorate. I have not wanted for anything." *Except unconditional love, which I finally received from Aunt Mae.*

"I'm glad you had a good life," Jonah responded, not believing that any of those things made her happy. Kayla's glossy eyes told another story, revealing a loneliness he understood all too well.

"Anyhow!" Kayla stood, trying to shake off her melancholy. "Aunt Mae said if you ever were to come by, I was supposed to give you something. Let me go get it."

Thank God, she does not seem to know about my past. Oh, God, she needs You, that I am certain of. Help me to help her to discover her need for You. Aunt Mae planted and perhaps I can water. Jonah looked up and smiled.

Silence.

Okay...Lord, do it however and with whomever You choose. Just save Kayla.

"Here it is!" Kayla returned with a box. "There has to be something really special in this box; Aunt Mae acted like it was a million dollars. She made me promise to find you and give it to you if you did not come for it. She must have known you were going to visit soon."

Yes, she knew I was getting out of Manchester within a month. I wanted to surprise her. Just one month earlier and... Jonah felt regret. *Three choices. I choose to keep it moving.* "She did."

"Where were you?" Kayla innocently inquired.

"In...Barnwell."

"That's not too far...about three hours away."

"Yes, about that far," he nodded, feeling uneasy.

Taking the box, Jonah did not want to open it in front of Kayla. This was private, and he needed private time to cherish whatever Aunt Mae kept for him from his Aunt Alice.

"When are you leaving?" Jonah asked.

"Tomorrow."

"Oh," he sighed.

"Or maybe I'll stay a few days. I really need to pack some things before the new family moves here."

"Wow. That is fast. Who is moving in?"

"Aunt Mae left this house to the church. The pastor told me today that there was a single mother who needed a place to stay. I think he said she had two kids, and asked if they could move in soon. I told him they could move in this weekend if they wanted to."

"That's good."

"Yes, I think so."

"I better be going," Jonah headed for the door. "Hopefully, I will see you again before you leave."

"I'd like that," Kayla beamed.

"I'm uh…living down the street, on the corner." Jonah felt like a lovesick teenager.

"I know, Aunt Mae showed me."

"You take care and lock up. This isn't the safest neighborhood." Suddenly, Jonah worried about Kayla sleeping in the home alone. He could take care of himself in this neighborhood, but Kayla did not belong here.

"I'll be fine. Aunt Mae says her home is covered by the blood of Jesus, that's why she had a sound sleep every night."

"My Aunt Alice said the same thing," Jonah said, grinning. "Well, take care."

"You, too." Watching Jonah walk away, Kayla felt utterly alone.

Jonah could not help himself. Getting to the end of the sidewalk, he turned and waved at Kayla as she stood looking out the screen door.

She is beautiful, Lord. You sure made her a masterpiece! Fearfully and wonderfully made!

21

Feeling vulnerable and empty inside, Kayla went to Aunt Mae's room and seized her aunt's Bible. There was a hole in her soul that needed to be filled. Man couldn't fill it. Things couldn't fill it. Only God. Remembering her aunt's last words, *the seed has been planted, someone else will water it...*

Aunt Mae, God sent Jonah to water it...

She cried. "I want the Gift offered...I want Jesus..." Dropping to her knees, Kayla she began to pray, "Dear Father, God, my Aunt Mae said all I had to do was just talk to you, like I'm talking to her. Here it goes." She read the Salvation prayer from the back of her Aunt's Bible. "I am a sinner in need of a savior. Forgive me for all of my sins. I confess with my mouth the Lord Jesus and believe in my heart that God raised Him from the dead. I love You and thank You for accepting me into Your family and making my heart Your home. In Jesus' name, amen." Now she was a part of the Family of Believers – Aunt Mae and Aunt Alice's family – and Jonah's family. She was one of them.

CHAPTER 3

Man Up

Jonah was near his childhood home when he heard a name he had not heard in five years.

"JoJo!"

The familiar voice from his past shouted Jonah's street-name. Two other men simultaneously got out of a black Ranger Rover.

"What's up?" PJ, who had been Jonah's partner in crime back in the day, embraced him. "I heard you were getting out! You look good, man. Prison life didn't mess you up or taint your pretty-boy look!"

Oh, if only you knew…

"Hey, PJ. You look the same." *Still wearing the grill in his mouth. Still big, black, and buff. Still PJ! Still arrogant!*

"Hey man, you know I *got* to keep it right for the ladies! Got to keep them coming back for more!" he laughed.

"I see you *ain't* changed a bit," Jonah stated.

"No need! I got the money and the ladies!"

"What's up, Ed…Corky?" Jonah acknowledged them.

"Good to have you back in the hood," Ed said.

"Yeah, good to have you back," Corky echoed.

"It's good to be out."

"Sorry about Aunt Alice," PJ began, "she used to keep this street clean. I remember her walking up and down, praying for folks and feeding the sick. She was good people. Hate you couldn't attend the funeral. It was packed. Me and the fellows showed our respect in honor of you."

Externally, Jonah kept a straight face. However, internally, the aching of his heart made him feel ill. The one regret that Jonah would have for the rest of his life was the fact that he could not attend Aunt Alice's home-going service. He did not get a chance to say goodbye properly.

"Joel was there, acting all stuck-up. He and his snooty wife had their noses so high in the sky, I'm sure they both left with nosebleeds. I asked him when was the last time he talked to you, JoJo." PJ was all talkative, something that usually was not in his nature.

Jonah's ears perked up, eager to know Joel's response.

"He said, 'JoJo who?'" PJ smirked. "I told him, he could run from his past, but he couldn't hide! And in his past, he had a twin brother, who we call JoJo. His wife looked at me as if I was crazy. You could tell she did not know Joel had a twin brother. That is just sad. How could one just deny he had a brother, a twin brother at that?"

Sorrow and grief seized Jonah like a thick rope, wrapped around his heart, causing him to feel as if he was suffocating. The death of a loved one, who had not even died, ripped his heart apart.

"Joel always thought he was better than us!" PJ was still talking. "But I got more money than he could even think to have!" He sucked his teeth. "So what, he's some big time engineer, living in some fancy home. He still came from the hood! He still doesn't make what I make!"

24

It is always about you, PJ, always!

"I also heard that Joel is some associate pastor at some uppity church. Hypocrite!" Disdain dripped from PJ's lips.

Jonah could picture Joel preaching the gospel. As a child, Joel loved searching the Scriptures and going to Bible study. If the church doors opened, gladly he would go with Aunt Alice, while Jonah mumbled and grumbled about it.

"And one day I'm going to knock that pompous look right off his baby-face – preacher or no preacher!"

Jonah never understood why PJ hated Joel so much. After all, Joel walked away from him, not PJ.

"Just give me two minutes with that pretty wife of his and I bet you I will turn her head, just like you did with…"

"PJ!" Jonah shouted. "Don't go there!"

"Oh, still a sore spot with you, I see." PJ looked Jonah over, from head-to-toe, then wrapped his arm around Jonah's shoulder. "I've got a new crib, man. It is nice. Five bedrooms, three garages, all filled with my toys. Got an in-home theatre. You have to see it man. The sound is off the chart and…"

"I'm tired, PJ." Jonah needed to quickly distance himself from PJ and all that the past represented. Temptation was calling his name and Jonah refused to answer—this time.

"I bet! You should come stay with me *till* you get yourself together."

"Thanks, but I'm going to stay here," Jonah said as he looked at his pitiful home, which seemed like a mansion when compared to where he had slept the previous night.

"You've got to be kidding." PJ and the fellows laughed. "It's a dump, JoJo! It is worse than ever. You can't stay here."

"I'll be fine."

"Man, you *got* no electricity, no water, and it's probably

infested with roaches and who knows what else."

"Doesn't matter," Jonah insisted. "It's my home. In time, I'll fix it up."

"Do you have any money?"

"Some."

"Here," PJ reached in his pocket and took out a wad of bills with one hundred dollar bills on top.

Always the showoff!

"No, thanks," Jonah lightly pushed PJ's hand away.

PJ stepped back. "Don't tell me you're too good to take my money, now?" The sound of wrath vibrated in his tone. "You're not too high and mighty are you, JoJo? This money ain't too dirty for you, is it?"

Ed and Corky drew nearer to PJ, ready to have his back if necessary.

"It's nothing like that, PJ." Jonah was not the type to back down from anybody, including PJ. He might be saved, but he was not one of those doormat Christians. He was not going to let people walk all over him, but he knew when to fight and when to stand still. At present, it was time to stand still. "I'm fine. I have money." *Okay it is only $43, but it is clean, honest money.* "I appreciate the offer, PJ, I really do. Once I get a job, I am going to fix this place up...on my own. It's something I want to do, for Aunt Alice."

PJ eyed him. "I get that. But, you know you always *got* a job with me. You can start tomorrow if you want to. I just got this big deal with..."

"No thanks, PJ. I can't afford to get caught again. I am on probation for two years. Three strikes and then I am in prison for life. That's not the life I want anymore."

"You're not going to get locked up. You've just got to

be smart like me," PJ said, tooting his own horn, as always. "You *got* busted because you let your guard down. I told you something was not right with Junior. I sensed he was a cop. My nose can smell a cop for miles away. You trusted him…first mistake. Your second mistake was that you went alone with him to seal the deal. Thirdly, you let a stupid female cloud your judgment. Dana is only good for one thing and you know it!"

Suppressing his resentment for his ex-friend, Jonah permitted the words to go in one ear and quickly out the other. It was a little too late for PJ to give reprimand, counsel, or show concern. Where was PJ when Jonah needed him the most? Not once did PJ offer or try to help with getting Jonah better legal representation. During the jury trial, PJ did not even show up. Being locked up for five years, not once did PJ visit him at Manchester.

God help me hold my peace!

"That's all water under the bridge," Jonah grinned and bore it. "I'm never going back to prison. I am going to bust my butt working, even if it is cleaning bathrooms, flipping burgers at a fast-food joint, or picking up trash. My life of crime is over." Jonah did not bat an eye as he looked at PJ. "I hope you can understand what I'm saying. I don't have any beef with you, but my past is just that—my past."

"Nobody is going to hire you, JoJo. You are an ex-con. You have no degree. You have no family. You are kidding yourself. I am offering you a chance to redeem yourself, redeem your manhood. But if you don't want it," PJ scoffed, "then your bad! But if you get tired of living like this," he pointed to Aunt Alice's home, "then call me. My number hasn't changed!" PJ climbed in the passenger side of the vehicle while Ed got behind the wheel.

"See you around, JoJo!"

"See you, PJ!"

Jonah watched as the Range Rover drove away.

God, I surely wanted to smack him! He is such a self-righteous punk!

Love your enemies, bless those who curse you, do good to those who hate you, and pray for those who spitefully use you and persecute you, that you may be sons of your Father in heaven, for He makes His sun rise on the evil and on the good, and sends rain on the just and on the unjust. For if you love those who love you, what reward have you? Do not even the tax collectors do the same? And if you greet your brethren only, what do you do more than others? Do not even the tax collectors do so? Therefore, you shall be perfect, just as your Father in heaven is perfect.

I am far from perfect Lord. But I am striving every day to be more like Jesus. Help me walk in love, especially with PJ.

Perfect love covers a multitude of sin.

You are right. It will take love to cover all the sin that PJ has done.

What about you?

Jonah laughed. *You got me there, Lord.*

⟡⟡⟡

It took a while for Jonah to rip the boards off the front door. He had to go to the neighbor's house and ask for a hammer. One by one, he pulled out the rusted nails. Just before sundown, he was able to use the key that was in the box to open the door.

Sluggishly, Jonah entered his childhood home. It was Aunt Alice's, and now it was his. It felt surreal to be back in the one place that gave him comfort and security. Though the home was stifling hot, with a musty odor, tears streamed down Jonah's face as he stood and looked around. His eyes fastened on the painting of Aunt Alice hanging above the worn out couch. It was Aunt Alice's second most prized possession. Her Bible was the first. A member of the church had painted the picture before Jonah was locked up. Aunt Alice cherished the painting, so much. She had said, "God could make any child of His look beautiful."

"I'm home, Aunt Alice! I wish you were here with me."

Years of pain, years of grief, and years of regrets now rested on Jonah's shoulders as he crumpled to the floor and wept like a baby.

"I'm so sorry, Aunt Alice! I am so sorry that I did not get to see you one more time. I was such a fool! Such a hardheaded knucklehead, as you would say. But you loved me anyway. You loved me in spite of my faults, in spite of my wrongdoings. You never turned your back on me—like PJ! Like Momma! Like the sperm-donor! Like Joel!

"Oh, God! I miss Aunt Alice so much! I'm sorry!"

Son, you are forgiven. Now, you must forgive yourself.

"I'm not worthy of forgiveness!"

You are worthy because of the blood of Jesus!

Jonah wept all the more. He wept until there were no more tears to shed. A great cleansing took place in his soul. For five years, Jonah had mastered the art of concealing his pain, for tears were a sure-sign of weakness in prison. He had to show that he was tough and that he did not wear his feelings on his sleeves. Years of holding back caused the dam to break as Jonah came to a familiar place of serenity. Getting up, he felt extremely blessed. "It's not much Lord, but its home. Home sweet home!"

With tender care, Jonah placed the wooden box in the top drawer of the cabinet. He was not ready to go through it just yet. The hidden treasures in the box were too valuable and sacred. Somehow, the box represented closure for Jonah, and he was not ready for closure just yet.

Knowing there was nothing in the kitchen, Jonah checked the cupboards anyway. To his delight, he found two tuna cans, several cans of Pork 'n' Beans, and a can of corn.

"Probably ancient, Lord, but I'm hungry!"

Jonah searched the drawers and found a rusty can opener.

"It's no steak and potatoes, but it sure will fill this hungry stomach of mine!" It was strange hearing his own voice talk aloud. Usually, Jonah kept his thoughts to himself, especially after Wayne had died in prison. He even prayed silently, having a true heart-to-heart with God, where only God could hear him. Now Jonah wanted to talk. He wanted to verbalize his thoughts. Pray openly to God. This was freedom! He was no longer captive behind bars, at least not physically.

After eating and putting his dish away in the sink, Jonah searched for a flashlight or candles. It was beginning to get dark in the home. Remembering that Aunt Alice always kept candles in the hall closet, Jonah ebbed his way to the back, not wanting to trip over anything. And there they were, candles and matches. "Thanks, Aunt Alice! You were always prepared."

"Always be prepared Jonah!" he could hear his aunt saying. "You never know what kind of storm life will throw your way. Storms come and unexpected moments happen, so you must be prepared. Always have candles and matches. Always have canned food and perishable items. You don't want to be caught unaware in a storm like the five foolish maidens when the King came." Aunt Alice could always make the Bible stories come to life. She was spiritual and practical.

With a lighted candle in hand, Jonah peeped into his old bedroom. The same bunk beds were still there in the tiny room. Aunt Alice had made them matching bedspreads. The top bunk belonged to Joel. Seating himself on the bottom bunk, precious memories of him and Joel talking during the nights, when they were supposed to be asleep, popped into his head. They shared secrets, dreams, hopes, and even hurts during those late night conversations.

Oh, how Jonah wished for those days again. Days when he could talk to Joel again about anything and everything, or the times when they would just sit quietly. Oftentimes, neither had to say a word, but each knew what the other was thinking.

I miss Joel, Lord. Help me to keep the promise to Aunt Alice to make things right. I do not even know where to begin, but You do!

All things will work out for your good, Jonah. All things!
I believe, Lord, in You!

Wearily, he got up and sauntered to the next room, Aunt Alice's bedroom. Jonah pushed opened the bedroom door. It was as if nothing had changed. Still the same lavender curtains, the same colorful handmade quilt on the full-size oak bed, the mismatched dressers beside the far wall. Pictures of Joel and Jonah as babies with their mother were on the dresser, and over that hung two separate collages of Joel and Jonah's pictures, detailing their lives from kindergarten to senior graduation.

Jonah peered at the pictures of his brother. They looked so much alike, and yet, they were so different. "I wish I could have been more like Joel!" He picked up the picture of his mother, an image of her younger days. She was so beautiful, so happy and alive back then. *If only she could have stayed clear of drugs. If only my sperm-donor had not left her, left us, things could have turned out differently.*

Jonah had played the blame game for over twenty years. It was time for him to look in the mirror and take ownership of his own mistakes.

"You can only control you," Wayne had counseled in prison. "You can't control another person. Likewise, you cannot blame another person for the choices you have made. Man up and take responsibility for the things you did. I am here in jail because I snapped. My wife cheated on me. I came home and caught her in bed with him. Yes, she was wrong. But I was wrong for taking a gun and blowing her and the guy's head off! I did it! Nobody made me do it! I did it!"

Wayne's wisdom was the key to Jonah dealing with so many past issues. He still had not conquered taking responsibility for his own actions, not fully. Looking in the mirror, Jonah gazed at the face staring back at him. "I am to blame! Not the Sperm-donor! Not momma! Not PJ! I made bad choices! Joel is not to blame! I *gotta* man up and take ownership of my wrongs, Lord!" He spun around and peered at the painting, *The Last Supper*, of Jesus and his disciples, which hung over his aunt's bed. It was not Jesus, for sure, just a representation of Christ. Still, Jonah found peace in the painting. *The Lord sure could have blamed all those disciples for deserting Him, and yet He still died for them...and me.*

"Lord, You bore my sins in your body on a tree. You took my place on the Cross. You died for me, even though You knew I would mess up, time and time again. Yes, I have messed up and done horrible things to people, including my brother, Joel. It's nobody's fault but mine. I cannot blame anyone...only me.

I know that You have forgiven me. Help me to forgive myself and move forward, 'to keep it moving,' as Aunt Alice would say. Help me to make things right." The floodgates opened, and Jonah wept again. Crawling under his Aunt's Alice covers, Jonah wrapped himself up tightly and cried himself to sleep.

Yet he was not alone.

He knew without a shadow of doubt that God was with him, comforting him.

CHAPTER 4

Discouraged

"**We**'re not hiring right now, but we will keep your name on file," the elderly man stood behind his desk and extended his hand to Jonah.

"Thank you, sir. I appreciate it." Jonah forced a smile. He left the cleaners, feeling more dejected than ever.

All week, Jonah had been relentless in his search for a job. This was his fourteenth rejection. Jonah went from place to place, everywhere he saw a "Hiring" sign in the business' windows and in the newspaper ads. He left his home before sunup to catch the bus and returned after dark. Jonah was willing to take any job. He applied for janitorial services, as a cook at fast food restaurants, waiter, car washer, etc. Name it, and Jonah applied for it.

Lord, no one will give me a chance. The minute they discover I have been in prison, they turn their noses up at me.

Persevere!

I am trying Lord, but it is hard, and I only have $15 left after buying the bare minimum of food to get by. Food that does not require cooking, since I have no electricity. Thank God, Aunt Alice had plenty of candles on hand that I can use.

Persevere, son. Be patient.

Frustrated, Jonah did not feel like applying for another job. He just could not handle another rejection. All this negativity was definitely squashing his ego flatter than a pancake. Not wanting to return to a dark home with no water, Jonah wandered to a nearby park and sat at a bench. He was lower than low. Having himself a private pity-party, Jonah allowed the circumstances to steal his joy.

It is so embarrassing, washing up at the gas station around the corner. I have to get up early, wash up there, change my clothes and then catch the bus. What I wouldn't do for a hot shower, a medium-rare steak, and a fully loaded bake potato. I feel so alone. And…and I cannot get Kayla out of my mind. I heard her knocking last night, but I ignored her. I was not going to let her in my dark home and have her pitying me. She is the queen and I am a pauper. I have nothing to offer her. No job! No college degree! No food, really. I cannot even take her out. Besides, when she finds out about my prison record, she will reject me just like everyone else. I have nothing. Shoot! I am nothing! I am a loser. An ex-con with no skills, but the skill to steal and to sell drugs.

If only—if only I could talk to Joel. If only he would forgive me. I miss him so much. I feel as if a part of me has died. We were one. We have always been connected. Now, I am good as dead to him. I messed up big time. I had no right to sleep with his fiancé. She was no-good anyhow, just agreeing to marry him because she knew Joel was going to be successful. If it weren't me, she would have slept with someone else. Shoot, I did Joel a favor! Jonah reasoned with himself, trying to push guilt out of his consciousness. *I was wrong! I was dead wrong, Lord. I need Joel. I need my brother.* His heart weakened. The solitude was depressing. The pity-party was making him even more miserable. *Yes, I did the crime, but I paid the time—five long, awful years. Lord, I need a sign. Show me that you are still with me.*

"Hey Jonah!" Walking toward him was the best sign Jonah could ever receive, an angel. She was the loveliest woman he had ever seen. His heart pounded in his chest. Surely, Kayla could hear it, beating like a drum. Just like that, his gloom was replaced with sweet, pure joy.

"Hi Kayla," Jonah's grin widen, unable to contain his pleasure in seeing her.

"I came by to see you last night, but it was dark, so I figured you weren't home."

No lights! "Sorry, I..."

"Ummm," the female standing next to Kayla cleared her throat.

"Oh, excuse me. Jonah this is my best friend, Lisa Walsh," Kayla introduced.

"Nice to meet you." Formally, Lisa shook his hand, thoroughly looking Jonah over, emphatically unimpressed.

"Jonah, can you take a picture of us with my phone," Kayla asked. "Lisa is moving to Virginia."

"Uh, sure. I'd be happy to."

"Great!"

"On three," Jonah positioned the phone. "1...2...3!"

"Take another one, please, just in case," Kayla beamed. *He is so handsome!*

"Sure." *She is amazing!* Jonah could hardly contain himself. "Ready? 1...2...3!"

"Let me see!" Kayla rushed over, giggling with her friend. "Oh, they are great. Lisa, I'll send them to your phone." Kayla pushed the buttons, sending the photos in no time to her friend.

"Lisa, I am going to miss you so much. This is our last day together!"

"We'll talk all the time and text and email. We'll never stay out of touch."

"I know, but it won't be the same and—oh, I'm sorry." Kayla remembered Jonah standing behind them. "Thanks again for taking our picture." Impulsively, Kayla gave him a hug. Stepping back, Kayla and Jonah were in a trance, eyes fixed on one another.

Jonah could not help but notice sadness clouding her eyes. *Such beautiful eyes like hers should never be so sad.*

"I'm leaving tomorrow. So, would you like to…maybe get together, tonight?" Kayla asked Jonah.

"Umm…" *I cannot afford to take her out.*

"How about I cook for you?" Kayla sensed that Jonah was about to say no. "I can make a *mean* steak, and we can have baked potatoes and salad."

Really, Lord, only You. "I'd like that." Jonah struggled not to just gawk at the woman. She was absolutely breathtaking. Dressed in a sky blue sundress that loosely flowed, pewter wedged sandals, matching teardrop blue earrings, and her hair pulled back from her face, cascading down her back. Kayla looked like a fashion model about to walk the runway.

"Say around," Kayla looked at her watch, "seven, if that's not too late."

"Perfect." Jonah's heart was in overdrive.

"Great! See you then." And off the two women went.

Her beautiful face was etched in his memory. *Man! She is so beautiful. I was almost hypnotized by those large hazelnut eyes and thick eyelashes. She has the most flawless honey skin I have ever seen on a woman. And that shape, man! She looks like a model from head to toe. My Lord, it took everything in my being not to reach out and touch her long, wavy hair. It looked so soft. I wonder if it is real. So many chicks wear fake hair now, it is hard to tell. But it sure looked real. She looks mixed—half white, half black. Stop it! I better get my head out of the clouds. I do not stand a chance with an uptown woman like that! Not a chance!*

⋈⋈⋈

"He's handsome," Kayla beamed, her cheeks flushed.

"He looks...rather poor," Lisa stated flatly.

"Oh shush! Did you see that smile of his? Heavenly. And his perfectly round brown eyes. And his muscular physique. Oh, and that curly hair of his. I just wanted to run my fingers through it."

Lisa rolled her eyes at her friend. "There you go again, trying to help another stray. Only this one is human, not a lost puppy or a hurt cat."

"Did you notice how downtrodden he seemed at first? I just wanted to hug him or something, anything to erase the pain from his face."

"Kayla, he is dirt-poor. Did you see that wrinkled, dirty shirt...and those shoes? Girl please! Your mom would have you committed if you even thought about bringing him home for supper. He is broke, busted, and disgusted. I'm telling you, Kayla, he is trouble, for sure!"

Miffed, Kayla stopped walking. "Stop that! You sound just like mother, so judgmental. Does everything equate to dollar signs with you?"

"No, but money isn't evil, Kayla. It is the love of money that is evil. He is not one of us, Kayla. No matter how you look at it, you and he are cut from different cloths. You're silk and he's polyester."

"I felt my spirit pulling toward him, Lisa. Not just today, but the first time I met him I felt like he…needed someone. He is all alone. He seems hopeless."

"Maybe he is homeless…."

"No, he has a place. His Aunt Alice and my Aunt Mae were best friends, like us. He lives in his aunt's old home."

"Yuck, in the projects! Girl, if your mother knew that you were staying in that rundown place, she would have a heart attack. It is unsafe! It is contemptible! Your father would disown you."

Lisa's words hurt, digging up old insecurities in Kayla.

"My aunt's home feels more like a home than living under the roof of my parents' home filled with beautiful things… but I still felt empty," Kayla sighed. "I only knew her for a short time, but Aunt Mae has impacted my life, far more than anything or anyone. I am going to miss Aunt Mae so much. She was truly a woman of deep faith. She talked about God as if He was right there in the room with her. I've never known a Christian like that before."

"Sounds more like a fanatic to me!"

"Lisa, that's mean. You didn't even know her."

"No, but the way you talk about her…" Lisa stopped her train of thought. "I'm sorry. I know you're going to miss her."

"Aunt Mae talked about Jonah frequently. They had a special connection, obviously, because they wrote letters to each other all the time. She wanted me to meet him. She was worried about him. I owe it to Aunt Mae to help Jonah, if he needs it. I wish you could understand that."

"I don't," Lisa replied honestly. "But, I know I'm not going to change your mind."

"I didn't try to change your mind about Dan," Kayla tossed it out there.

"He's no Dan!" Immediately, Lisa was on the defensive. "My Dan is a proud lieutenant in the air force. He is a distinguished gentleman. Dan is not and never was poor or hopeless. And you would never catch Dan wearing dirty clothes, such as the ones *your* Jonah wore today. I'm offended that you would even compare that stranger with my Dan!"

"I'm just saying, Dan wasn't raised like either of us, and I liked him simply because you loved him. Jonah is good people and, well, there is something about him that I like."

Lisa gazed at her friend for some time. She knew that look in her friend's eyes. "You're smitten with this Jonah and don't even try to deny it. I know you all too well, Kay."

"I feel drawn to him, Lee," Kayla said, shrugging her shoulders slightly. "I don't know why. I just do."

"Just promise me that you will be careful, Kay, and take it really, really slow. I think the guy has some skeletons in his closet and you may not like what you find once the door is opened."

"I promise."

"And promise me you will be honest with me and keep me updated on what's going on between the two of you."

"Hey, I'm just making dinner for him tonight and after that we probably won't see each other again."

"Yeah right, and I'm singing at your wedding!" Lisa laughed, knowing she could not sing a lick. "Let's just drop it for now. We better be heading to the airport before I miss my flight."

"I can't believe you're moving," Kayla swallowed the

pain lodged in her throat. They had been best friends since kindergarten. They grew up as neighbors in a very affluent community. They went to private schools from kindergarten to graduation, and then to college and graduate school. Kayla and Lisa were inseparable. Even after Lisa married and moved from their upscale condominium, the two talked every day. At the insistence of her parents, Kayla moved back home.

"I'm just glad Dan is out of the Air Force. He's a civilian now, and he will be managing one of my dad's real estate offices in Virginia. Of course, dad is going to take him under his wings and teach him everything about real estate. I am just so happy things are coming together for Dan and I. I'm so happy we will finally be together," Lisa happily exclaimed.

"I am so glad you are happy, Lee."

"I want you to be happy, too, Kay. I thought Isaac was that special someone for you," Lisa paused. "His tragic death shocked all of us, especially Dan. They were close, like us. You both seemed to hit it off so well."

Too well. "Yes, it's hard to believe Isaac didn't make it back with Dan from Iraq. Truthfully, Lee, we did not have what you and Dan have. We tried too hard to make a connection. We both knew that it wasn't going to last. Besides, my parents would not have approved of him. His tattoos would have disgusted father."

"You're right about that," Lisa chuckled. "But Isaac was a good man."

"He was."

"Do you remember how mother reacted when I finally told her about Dan?"

"I thought she was going to blow a gasket. She was mortified," Kayla laughed. "She fainted."

"Yes, she's so dramatic."

"Just like my mother," Kayla nodded.

"When he asked me to marry him, and I showed mom the ring. She said, 'You are supposed to marry up, not down.' She would not talk to me for days. Now, she is at least cordial to Dan. Dad likes him."

"Your mom has come a long way."

"And she has a long way to go."

"We will keep praying for our mothers," Kayla added, her thoughts turning to Jonah.

"Be careful Kay," Lisa cautioned. "I know you're lonely and just want somebody to love you for you."

"Am I hopeless, Lee?" Kayla's heart yearned to have what her best friend had. "Am I unlovable?"

"Oh, Kay," Lisa embraced her, "you're the most loveable person I know. One day soon, the man of your dreams is going to walk into your life and sweep you right off your feet."

I think he already has...

CHAPTER 5

Possibilities

"Are you coming in?" Kayla opened the door. For the past fifteen minutes or so, she had watched Jonah pacing back and forth in the front yard.

"Uh, I..." Tongue-tied, Jonah became lost in her beauty. Kayla was so unlike any other woman Jonah had dated, ashamedly more than he'd care to remember. Shoving his hands in his pocket, Jonah felt completely out of his league.

What am I doing here, Lord? Look at her! She is a queen and I am...

A priest, a child of the King!

"Jonah," she called his name sweetly, "please come in."

He stood still.

"Is something wrong?" Kayla detected Jonah's discomfort. "I promise, I won't bite."

He grinned.

"And I promise my cooking won't make you sick."

"Are you certain?"

Jonah's crooked smile sent her heart soaring. "I'm positive. Besides, once we bless the food, it can't help but be alright."

"Hmm," he stepped up on the porch. "I'll have to take your word for it." Their eyes met. Kayla cheeks flushed. Her stomach was doing all sorts of things being near this handsome man. "Dictum Meum Pactum." *Yikes! Why did I throw that at him?*

"My word is my bond," he smirked. "My aunt used to say that."

"So did Aunt Mae. Probably the only Latin words our aunts knew," Kayla smiled kindly. "So are you coming in?"

"Lead the way," Jonah's resolve to keep as much distance between them as possible, weakened.

Kayla opened the door at the same time Jonah reached for it. Their hands brushed. The touch was electrifying, sending Kayla's sensations in high gear.

"Everything is ready, so we can just go in the kitchen." Nervously, she escorted him to the small area. "Have a seat and I'll place the meal on the table."

"Can I help with anything?"

"No, just hope you have a healthy appetite."

Lord, if only she knew. I am so hungry I could eat anything about right now. Thank You, Lord, for providing me a home-cooked meal through this angel of Yours. I know I don't deserve this, or her. Help me not to make a fool out of myself.

"What would you like to drink? I have sweet tea and lemonade and, of course, diet soda."

"Tea." Jonah enjoyed watching her move around the tiny kitchen. She seemed so out of place, and yet at home.

"This is good," Jonah practically gulped the iced tea down.

"Thank you." Kayla sat down after placing the grilled ribeye, baked potatoes, rolls, and bowls of cheese, bacon, sour cream, chives, and a large bowl of tossed salad. "The ribeyes were marinated in Aunt Mae's homemade teriyaki sauce," Kayla said proudly. "She taught me so much in just six months. I even made my first pound cake. We can have it later for dessert."

"First?" Jonah's dark-brownish eyes teased her.

"Yes." Kayla placed the napkin on her lap.

Proper. Should I place the napkin on my lap as well? Nah! I am just going to be myself. No need in pretending to be something I am not.

"I'll be the guinea pig tonight."

"It'll be worth it, I promise." She smiled.

Inwardly, Jonah's heart swelled with utter joy. Feeling discouraged earlier, God had a way of sprinkling sunshine in the midst of darkness. Today, that sunshine was Kayla.

"Will you pray?" Kayla extended her right hand to him. Her hands shook slightly. Although she had not been one to pray before, Aunt Mae had blessed every meal, and Kayla wanted to honor her aunt's tradition of praying at the dinner table.

"Sure," Jonah closed his eyes. "Father God, we thank you for this meal that we are about to partake of. Bless the gentle hands that prepared this special meal, and Lord bless this meal because this is Kayla's first time cooking it." He squeezed her hand and opened one eye. She was staring back with a smirk to match his. "And, well, I don't want it to be my last meal."

Kayla squeezed his hand hard.

"Bless it in Jesus' name, amen."

"Amen." Kayla reluctantly removed her hand from his. "I see you *got* jokes."

"Who's joking?" He laughed.

Jonah brought out something in Kayla that had been stifled for too long: laughter.

"Let's eat."

During the meal, which Jonah thoroughly enjoyed, he most

enjoyed listening to Kayla talk about her aunt. It was evident that she was heartbroken, the wound was still fresh. Kayla was grieving, and he could sense that she was struggling to deal with the grief.

"I hate the fact that my parents robbed me of knowing my aunt at an early age. It makes no sense. Just because she was different, they believed Aunt Mae's religious beliefs would have a negative influence on me. That seems so ludicrous now." Kayla paused, wiping her eyes with a napkin. "I needed her." Her mouth trembled as the words were spoken.

Jonah slid his chair over next to hers and impulsively slid his arm around Kayla, drawing her closer to him. Resting her head on his broad shoulder, Kayla allowed her grief to be released through tears. The two sat in silence for some time before Kayla pulled away.

"Please forgive me for being such a big baby." She felt remorseful. "Here I am crying and carrying on when we're supposed to enjoying our meal."

"I have enjoyed our meal," Jonah tenderly wiped her tears with his fingers, "and your company. It is okay to cry it out. I'm just glad to be here for you." Jonah meant more than his words could openly express.

Staring at him, Kayla could not deny the fact that there was definitely a spark between them, an intense attraction. His tender compassion moved her in ways that she could not explain. "Thank you for saying that. I am glad you are here, as well."

"We both miss our aunts. I understand your pain. My aunt raised me from the age of seven. Aunt Alice was more of a mother to me than my birth mom. She sacrificed so much for me. I wish I could have said goodbye to her properly, but…"

he looked away.

Kayla reached over and turned his head gently to face her. Moisture had welled in his eyes. "Maybe she didn't want to say goodbye, because that's so final. She knew she would see you again. Plus, she is with you now," Kayla put her hand to his chest. "She'll always be with you."

Jonah put his hand over hers and just gazed at this beautiful masterpiece, created only by his Heavenly Father. She seemed so pure, lily white. Kayla was sweetness in its purest form. Jonah wanted nothing more than to just kiss her soft lips. To hold her tight and never let go.

Kayla's pulse accelerated. Somehow, she needed to gather her bearings. Concurrently, her feelings excited and frightened her.

"We were both blessed by God to have strong women in our lives, for however long," Jonah spoke so low, Kayla could barely hear him.

Thunderstruck, Kayla nodded.

A warm, cozy feeling consumed Jonah. Being so near Kayla felt right. They fit perfectly. Something surreal flooded his being. *Could this be real? Could one find such contentment in someone they hardly know? Could this be what I have missed out on and longed for, for so long? For someone to love me, to hold me, to look at me the way Kayla is looking at me now. Oh, God, I am losing the fight to stay away from her. But—*

"Would you like a slice of cake?" Anxiously, Kayla slid her chair back. She could not contain her emotions. This man made her feel alive. Inwardly, she longed for him to kiss her, and yet she was afraid. Afraid of falling so hard and so fast for this guy, who could possibly turn her structured world upside down.

"Sure," Jonah stood, "but let me help you clear away these dishes."

"Oh, no." Kayla fanned him away. "Why don't you go in the living room and watch television. It will not take me long. Then we can enjoy this cake, and I have ice cream if you like."

"Sounds good." Jonah gazed at her one more time before turning away. "Oh, by the way, that was the best ribeye I've ever eaten. And I'm still alive." He winked.

Kayla's heart melted like marshmallows in hot chocolate.

Okay, Lord, I am new at being Your child, but Aunt Mae said I could talk to You at any time and You would listen. If You are who Aunt Mae says you are, You already know my secret. Jonah frightens me and excites my heart all at once. He is going to either love me to life or hurt me to my own demise. I need to guard my heart. Yet, my heart seems to be doing its own thing where Jonah is concerned. Lord, you know my parents will not like Jonah, but I cannot seem to control my feelings for him. If he is not the one, please show me now. Remember my secret, which won't be a secret for long.

Man looks at the outward, but I look at the heart. Don't judge the tree that appears fruitless; the season has not yet come. In due season, it shall bud and produce a mighty harvest for My Kingdom.

Inwardly Kayla heard Him whisper in her heart. It startled and also, soothed her. It was the first time she had really heard Him. *Thank You, Lord. Help me help Jonah. He seems so unhappy and alone.*

After cleaning up the kitchen, Kayla brought cake and ice cream on a tray to Jonah. Watching a basketball game, the first in years, Jonah did not mind the distraction of Kayla. He could watch her all night.

"Are you enjoying the game?" Kayla sat next to him on the loveseat.

"I am," he grinned. "I haven't watched a basketball game in a long time."

"Oh," she eyed him. "Why not?"

"Um, well, I've been too busy," he fibbed.

"Oh," she did not buy it. *Why is he lying?* "So, tell me about yourself, Jonah. What do you do for a living?"

Here it goes, Lord. She is going to discover just how much of a failure I am. "I'm looking for work right now."

"What did you used to do, then?"

"All kinds of jobs," he said, truthfully. "I was a jack of all trades."

"What trade did you like best?" Kayla played his game.

He stared at her, shifting uneasily on the couch. "Can we talk about something else?" Suddenly, everything felt awkward.

"Well, Jonah, what do you like to do for fun?"

"Let's not talk about me," Jonah was really uncomfortable talking about himself. "Tell me about you, Kayla. Why are you here in this unsafe neighborhood? It's obvious that you don't belong in such a place."

"I just wanted to be near my aunt's things. It makes me feel close to her."

"What about your home? Where is that? Why are you defying your father's wishes?"

"I feel like you're interrogating me." She swallowed. "But, I'll answer. First, my home is in Macon City, Georgia. Unfortunately, I live with my parents. Second, my parents do not own me. Yes, my father forbade me not to see my aunt, and when I told him about the funeral, he did not want me to attend, but I came anyway. Right now, they think I'm with Lisa. But, like I said, I'm an adult and I can make my own choices."

"What are you running away from, or should I say, who are you running from?"

"I'm not running. I just needed to find myself, if that makes sense." Kayla leaned back on the couch. "I feel so lost, Jonah. I do not know who I really am anymore. I love my job. I'm a counselor. I have an office at my father's practice. I counsel patients before and after they have plastic surgery. Also, I have patients at local family practices, clinics, and hospitals. Still, something was missing in my life. I came here, hoping to find it."

"So, did you find what you were looking for?"

"Yes," her countenance glowing, "I found Jesus."

Jonah glowed with understanding. "There is no thing and no One better."

"I'm a baby, but it's liberating to know that I have Someone there for me who will never leave me or forsake me, no matter what." Sitting up, Kayla turned and faced Jonah. "Why are you here, Jonah? What are you running from?"

"I'm here because I have no other place to go," he answered truthfully, his eyes revealing deep anguish.

"Do you have any other family?"

"I have a twin, Joel."

"Oh, how great!" she smiled. "Why don't you go to him?"

"I can't." Jonah swallowed, lowering his eyes. "I haven't seen my brother in over seven years. I'm the last person he would want to see."

Curious, Kayla debated whether to pursue this conversation. "You could be wrong, Jonah. You should at least try. Seven years is a long time for healing to take place, and forgiveness."

Jonah did not know why he was letting Kayla in to his innermost secret closet, but he could not help himself from cracking the door slightly. "He hasn't forgiven me. Aunt Alice tried to reach out to him, but Joel refused to give me another chance. I'm not the saint you think I am, Kayla."

"Neither am I," she confessed. "I've made some mistakes, Jonah, that I can't run from even if I tried."

"Neither can I. My past is my present." He shrugged.

Kayla pondered his statement, wondering if she even wanted to know the truth. "It doesn't matter about your past. What really matters is that now you're a different person, right?"

"I am different, Kayla." Jonah reached for her hand. She freely gave it to him. "But, sometimes, the consequences of past sins can haunt a person for the *rest* of his life."

"Aunt Mae says God forgives and forgets," she whispered, gently caressing his cheek with the palm of her hand.

Warmth, resembling the heat of a summer day, sprouted wings in Jonah's heart, ready to fly into the future of great possibilities.

"God forgets, but not man," Jonah amended.

"How did you get this nasty scar?" Kayla traced her finger over the prominent mark on the right side of his face.

"A fight." Jonah answered honestly, thinking he would frighten Kayla away. She was too good for him.

It didn't work. "Jonah, you're a good man. I just know it."

"Don't be so sure," Jonah warned, leaning closer. He had a blemished past and he had the external scars to prove it. Still, the secret scars, the ones that woke him up from a deafening nightmare, ate him up inside. Could he ever erase his past? Would Kayla still want to be this close to him when

53

she discovered his hidden secrets?

"Kiss me," Kayla boldly demanded.

"As you wish," Jonah responded, teasing her with a kiss on her right cheek, then her left, then her chin, then her forehead. Slowly but surely, his lips came down on hers, igniting a fire within him that exploded. Time stood still. Harmony rang in the atmosphere. Flames flashed, leaving a residual aura. And then fear tiptoed in.

"I, uh," abruptly, Jonah leaped up, "I better go."

"Oh!" Clumsily, Kayla stood, feeling as if he had just slapped her. "I guess it is getting late."

"It is. I have to get up early, hit the streets again, and hope to find a job."

"Well, I know some people that..."

"No, thanks," Jonah cut her off, sounding harsh, and then attempting to soften his tone, "but I appreciate it."

What in the world just happened? I thought we were hitting it off. But now he acts like I have leprosy or something. Kayla was confused.

"Thank you so much for the dinner. Everything was great." Heading for the door, Jonah gazed at her for a moment. Kayla appeared so fragile at that moment, shaken by his sudden leaving. Jonah's heart was pulling him in two different directions. To run toward Kayla and wrap her in his arms. Likewise, to run as fast as he could, far away from the woman, who scared the daylights out of him.

"Hope to see you again," Kayla managed to say.

"Me too. God bless you on your travels tomorrow."

"Thank you."

He flashed her a smile and then left.

Watching the door close, Kayla let the silent tears flow. Her lips still tingled from the passionate kiss they shared. Jonah's departure left an aching in her soul. She couldn't understand it, but Jonah had rapidly captured Kayla's heart. Sadly, he didn't even know it. "God, please be with Jonah. He's running not just from me, but seemingly from his past, and yet he is living in it. *Free Jonah! Free me!*

CHAPTER 6

Secrets

"Stupid! Why in the world did I kiss her?" Jonah slammed his door. "There is no way I can have a relationship with her! She does not know my past, my long criminal history. She doesn't know what I did to my brother. She doesn't understand how deep I was into drugs. She can't possibly understand about what happened to me in prison. I am not good enough for her! She's royalty, for *Pete's sake*!" Jonah was his worst critic. He could not see past his own past to look into a future of hope and promise. All he could see was his failures, his wrongdoings, his jobless situation, his indiscretions, and his dishonorable, browbeaten deeds.

"Yuck!" A cry from the pit of his guts came forth. A howling sound of anguish echoed in the dark house. It pierced the Father's ears, as it pierced Jonah's soul. "God, remove these thoughts! Remove these horrible memories! Please, please, please! Yeah, I did the crime, but will I ever really pay the time? Pay the time for something I could not control! I'm not locked up anymore, but I sure feel locked up!" Feelings of self-reproach and penitence saturated Jonah's being, like a bucket of scorching, hot water, pouring from the crown of his head to the soles of his feet. He was inundated with the phantom thoughts, haunted by his days at Manchester. Jonah thought by leaving prison that he could escape those nightmares forever—let bygones be bygones. But he could not. *I just want to be free Lord!*

Opening the prisons for those that are bound.
I am bound, Lord. Bound by my hands and man's hands.
Liberty to those who are captive.
Liberty. When? How? Why?
Whom the Son sets free is free indeed.
I am trying!
Stop trying and be. Be Free!

Jonah spent a restless night reliving his past torture in prison. Nixon's face flooded his dreams. Sweet dreams became nightmares, and joy quickly turned to sorrow. *Why couldn't I be strong enough?*

Jonah woke up in a cold sweat. Shooting straight up, he swung his legs to the side of the bed. He bent over, running his fingers roughly through his curly locks. *These curls caused me nothing but torture in prison. Pretty boy, that is what they called me. Smooth, baby skin, light-skin complexion, not a pimple on my face, caused unwanted attention from the prison population. Especially Nixon.*

He touched the right side of his face. The jagged scar was the remaining, physical evidence of the first fight he had with Nixon. It was a fight for his dear life and for his manhood.

The memory of the bulky, six-foot two black man repulsed Jonah. Nixon ran Manchester. He had connections inside and outside of prison. It was known that several crooked security officers gave him special privileges and turned a blind eye to his illicit deeds. What Nixon wanted, he got. The moment the bars closed behind Jonah and Nixon got a whiff of him, Nixon wanted Jonah. Consequently, the other prisoners knew not to touch Jonah. Jonah belonged to Nixon.

Shaking his head, Jonah wanted to purge himself from the many times he feared being in Nixon's presence. No matter how hard Jonah tried to stay clear of the big beast, seemingly, he found himself alone with the man time and time again. The memory of Jonah's first encounter with Nixon clouded his vision, causing him to break out in a sweat. In the prison's kitchen, clearing dishes, suddenly Jonah found himself all by himself with Nixon.

"Oh, God!" Jonah cried aloud. "Please take the memory away! Please!"

Jonah had struggled with the man, but Jonah was no match.

"You know what I want! We can do this the easy way or the hard way!" he could hear Nixon's cynical voice even now.

That first day was the beginning of hell in prison for Jonah. No matter how he stonewalled Nixon, the big bully took what he wanted and kept coming back for more.

It was not until Wayne entered his cell that Jonah found a reprieve from his torturer. Wayne was bigger and taller than Nixon, and was not afraid of anybody, including Nixon. But, Wayne did not fight with his fists; he fought with his words of faith. It was a spiritual fight for him, and Wayne believed wholeheartedly that he could not lose with God on his side. In time, Wayne shared his faith with Jonah. Slowly, Jonah accepted Christ Jesus into his heart. The foundation had already been laid by his Aunt Alice, so it seemed almost natural for Jonah to accept the lifeline given to him by his friend, Wayne.

Although Nixon did not touch Jonah while Wayne was at Manchester, the threats from him hung over Jonah's head constantly. When Wayne died of prostate cancer in prison,

Nixon assaulted Jonah again. Jonah resisted with all his might and prayed that God would remove this huge mountain in his life. Jonah had to learn to stand on his own faith. And then, he got the word that his parole hearing had been set.

For three days Jonah fasted and prayed for God to give him favor with the parole board and that he would speak through him, guiding his tongue to only say what was needed. God heard.

God answered.

Jonah was granted parole. God did not move the mountain, Nixon. Rather, He moved Jonah—right out of Manchester. But the past would not release him.

Jonah felt trapped. Nothing could erase the afflicting torment stored in his brain. It was perpetual, day in and day out. "God I need relief!" Jonah wept in the early hour of the morning. The sun was just awakening. But God, who neither slumbers nor sleeps, heard the cry of His precious child.

"How long, Lord? Will You forget me forever? How long will You hide Your face from me? How long shall I take counsel in my soul, having sorrow in my heart daily? How long will my enemy be exalted over me?" Jonah quoted Psalms 13 once again. "But I have trusted in Your mercy; My heart shall rejoice in Your salvation. I will sing to the Lord because He has dealt bountifully with me. I may not understand it, Lord, but I trust You."

Blessed is the man who Trusts in Me!

❃❂❃

Arriving at her parents' home around noon, Kayla was surprised to find her mother sitting in the dining room. Typically, on a Sunday, she would be out shopping or having lunch with her socialites.

"Hello, mother," Kayla pecked her on the cheek.

"Hello, Kayla," her mother said, putting down her coffee. "Lucky you showed up today. You saved me the task of hiring a private investigator to find out your whereabouts."

"What?" Kayla gasped. "Why on earth would you do such a thing?"

"Your father doesn't like being lied to," Kathryn bluntly replied. "After he found out from Lisa's parents that Lisa was in Virginia and you weren't. Drew is furious, obviously."

"I was with Lisa. She just left before I did," she twisted the truth, slightly.

"According to Lisa's parents, you went to your aunt's funeral and she went with you, but then left. You were gone a full week before Lisa came down and then she left you in that godforsaken place!" Kathryn Lovett snubbed her nose.

"Well, you actually owned up to there being a God." Kayla could not help herself.

"Don't you get sassy with me, young lady!" Kathryn raised her voice. "Drew is mad and you disobeyed him. You know how he is. Why would you do that, Kayla? Why?"

"Because, Aunt Mae is family and, well, someone from the family should have been there. Dad should have been there. That was his only sister! How could he be so heartless?"

"Now, you just stop right there, Kayla. Your dad is a good man. A good provider. He has taken care of us and makes sure that we have the best of everything."

Here it goes...

"Why, don't forget, he adopted you. He picked you out of several other cute little babies and gave you the Lovett name. If it were not for him, you would be in an orphanage, or worse yet, with some poor people who could not afford to send you to the best schools and to the best university. You would not have a BMW, or wear the finest name-brand clothes, or enjoy any of these luxuries in life. You should be thanking your lucky stars for Drew, instead of being so selfish!"

"Selfish!" Kayla shrieked. "I do everything you and father ask of me. I wanted to go to public schools; you forced me to go to private. I wanted to go to Duke; you forced me to go to an Ivy League university. I did not want a BMW, but father insisted. I say and do exactly what is asked of me because I don't want to disappoint either of you." Tears swelled up in her eyes. "It's hard living up to your expectations. I have always feared that if I do not do something, you both would take your name away from me and everything that goes with it! Like divorce me. I'm twenty-four, and I still fear that you will take me back to the orphanage and leave me there because I'm not perfect!" Kayla pushed her chair back. "It's exhausting being the perfect daughter."

"How dare you turn this on us!" Kathryn stood up. "Don't try to make this about us, when you're the one who disobeyed your father's orders."

"I'm not a kid anymore, Mother. I can make my own choices."

"Yes you can, and you certainly can learn to make it on your own, as well. Remember, your father is paying your bills, not you!"

Kayla stared at her mother in disbelief. Finally, the threat was spoken aloud.

"Fine!" Kayla walked away.

"Come back here!" Kathryn insisted. "Now! I am still your mother," her voice softened.

Kayla pivoted around.

"We were worried about you, Kayla. Your father and I love you very much. If something ever happened to you," Kathryn's eyes misted, "it would crush us. You are our only child, and we want nothing but the best for you."

"I know," Kayla drew nearer.

"Oh, Kayla," Kathryn embraced her daughter. "I am glad you are home. I will have the cook to prepare your favorite, Chicken Parmigiana, red garlic potatoes, and triple-layered chocolate cake."

Kayla examined her mother. She knew deep down that her mother really cared for her and wanted Kayla to be happy. Right now, being in her mother's arms felt so good. However, Kayla loathed facing her father. She knew he would not be so easily persuaded to forgive and forget her disobedience.

"What about father?"

"He may fuss at first, but then he'll be all right, in time," Kathryn hoped. Kayla had pushed him too far this time, and she had spent many nights trying to convince him not to disown Kayla.

"Okay. I am tired. I think I'll just go take a nap."

"I didn't want to mention it," Kathryn began her faultfinding. "But you look rather pale, and your midsection is rather puffy. You probably need to see our personal trainer soon. He will get you back in shape. And your hair! Kayla, it is too long. Surely, you need a new style. All that thick, long hair is not becoming. You need a haircut. No decent man is going to look at you if you do not start taking care of yourself.

"Oh, and we have a new neighbor. He is a plastic surgeon, like your father. I think Drew said he was thirty-three. That is a good age for you. And…"

"Mother, please! I am not interested in dating a doctor, someone who is never home and hardly has time for a family. Dad is enough doctor for me!"

"A doctor can provide for you like this, especially a sought after surgeon like your father. You shouldn't snub your nose at the hands that feed you," Kathryn added. "Besides, Leon is coming over for dinner tonight."

"Mother!"

"Drew invited him over before we even knew you'd be here today. I'd say this is fate."

"More like matchmaking to me," Kayla sighed. "I'm going to take a nap."

"Yes, you do that, and when you get up maybe I can have my hairstylist come over and do something to your hair before dinner."

"No, mother! I like my hair."

"I'm afraid you're the only one who does, Kayla," her mother shouted after her.

Closing the door, Kayla plopped herself on her king-size bed. *I should have stayed away! Oh, but an investigator would have found me! I cannot believe they were going to hire an investigator! Lisa!* Needing to vent, Kayla dialed her friend's cellphone. "Lisa, how could you do it?"

"Kayla," Lisa was stunned by her best friend yelling at her over the phone. "What are you talking about?"

"You told my parents I went to the Aunt Mae's funeral and that I stayed for over a week."

"I didn't tell them anything," Lisa denied. "I was talking to Dan and had no idea my nosey mother was eavesdropping at my door."

"Oh," Kayla calmed down. "Can you believe my parents

were going to hire a private investigator to find me? It is crazy. They rule my life, Lisa! I have no life! My life is their life! I have to follow their strict rules. Don't do this. Don't say that. Don't go there. Don't wear this. Oh, and don't keep your hair so long, it's unbecoming!" Kayla was angry. "Why can't they just love me for me, Lisa? Why can't they allow me to make my own decisions and be my own person? They adopted me, so they think they own me." The emotional pangs reopened wounds for Kayla. "Why am I not good enough just the way I am? Why can't they just love me?"

"They do love you," Lisa replied as always. "They just don't know how to show it sometimes. I think it is something in rich people's genes, like my parents. They want what's best for us, but they think their viewpoints are the rulebooks, which we must live by."

"That's controlling, Lisa. I am tired of being controlled by them! I'm tired," she vented.

"I know," Lisa sighed. "So, how did your date go with Jonah?" Lisa wisely changed the subject, hopefully to cheer up her best friend.

"It was great at first," Kayla began to tell her everything. "But after the kiss, he acted like I had some kind of disease. He couldn't wait to get away from me."

"Wow! You kissed him on the first date!" Lisa joshed. "That's moving really fast."

"Hush! It wasn't like that. It was magnetic, like some electric force drawing our lips together."

"You are reading way too many romance novels," Lisa laughed. "So corny."

"It is," Kayla chuckled, "but I really like him. I know that sounds stupid to you, but I can't help what my heart is doing?"

"Maybe it's rebounding after Isaac."

"Isaac and I dated for three months before he left for Iraq, and I never felt anything like this with him."

"Are you sure?" Lisa was not convinced. "He was your first, remember?"

"It only happened once. When Isaac returned home for his father's funeral last month, I had planned to break up with him, but he was so pitiful and I was so lonely. I had just had that huge blowup with father. He said just because Lisa's parents let her downgrade to marrying someone in the military did not mean he would stoop so low. He warned me not to see Isaac. So, I rebelled and only ended up hurting myself."

"No one knows about it but me, Kayla. Your secret is safe with me."

"I missed my monthly," Kayla finally admitted.

"What?" Lisa squalled. "Oh my goodness, Kay. You don't think you're the p-word do you?"

"I'm nauseous and, well, mother said I'm pudgy around the midsection."

"She always says you're fat," Lisa dismissed. "What are you going to do?"

"I guess I'll get a pregnancy test and go from there."

"OMG," Lisa said. "Why don't you come here and stay with us for a while. I know Dan won't mind, and we can get the test here. You know you don't want your mother snooping around."

"I wish I would have kept our condominium. I do not think I can stay here if I am. Father will definitely disown me. Finally, his precious, perfect little protégé would have done the most dishonorable thing."

"You don't know that for sure, Kay."

"I think I do, Lee. I'm ninety-nine percent sure that one stupid night of pain, not pleasure, is going to change my life forever."

"You'll always have me, Kay. I will be there for you and the baby. I like the thought of being an auntie," Lisa optimistically chimed.

"I'll call you tomorrow," Kayla could not find any joy in anything right now. "I need to take a nap. Mom is playing matchmaker with the new neighbor, who happens to be a doctor."

"Yikes!"

"Yikes is right!"

CHAPTER 7

Another Lifeline

Hurrying to catch the bus, a twinge of sadness consumed Jonah as he ran past Aunt Mae's empty home. Kayla had been gone for over a week, and he could not forget her. She was etched in his mind and carved in his heart.

He missed her.

In such a short time, Kayla had opened Jonah's heart with hope that something good could happen to him and that perhaps things were going to get better. However, crossing boundaries with someone like Kayla could be far more painful than his already bruised past. He could lose his heart to a woman who had everything, while he had nothing. Jonah was too vulnerable for that. He could not risk it. *Or could he?*

"Hey JoJo!"

Contempt covered Jonah's countenance as he beheld the ghost from his past. Dana Maple leaped out of a white Lexus.

"You're not going to speak, JoJo?" Dana stood in front of him, so close he could smell her Forever perfume. The kind he used to buy her all the time.

Jonah remained silent.

"Come on, JoJo," she reached up to trace her finger on his cheek.

Jonah snatched it away.

"Ah, JoJo, don't be like that. I missed you," she purred like a cat. "I'm so glad you're back."

"Really?" he smirked. "Sure had a funny way of showing it. Not one letter, not one visit and you accepted not one of my collect calls," he scoffed. "For five long years I have not heard a peep from you and now you say you miss me! Girl, tell that to somebody who believes you, and it *sho' ain't* me!"

Before being locked up, Jonah believed Dana would be there for him, always. After all, she confessed her love for him over and over again. However, in the end, Dana abandoned him, just like everyone else.

"Oh, JoJo, you know I can't stand prisons. I would not even visit my brother."

"You could have written."

"JoJo, you know I'm not much of a writer."

"That's all you got, Dana? Please, don't waste my time." He saw the bus approaching. "We have nothing to say to each other."

"Oh, but JoJo, I want to make things right. Please, don't walk away. I missed you, JoJo. You were my only true love."

"Street talk says that PJ is your only love now."

"I work for PJ, that's it."

"Doesn't matter," he shrugged. "Five years ago I was locked up and the life I had before then disappeared. Disappear, Dana, just like you did then." Jonah got on the bus.

Sitting on the bus, Jonah let out a pent-up sigh. Seeing Dana brought back too many reminders of his past. Actually, the reminders seemed to be popping up everywhere. PJ and his boys had paid him a visit, trying to sway him to do a job for him. Knowing that Jonah was jobless, he preyed on

Jonah's weaknesses: finding employment and lacking money. Everywhere Jonah had gone, people were bringing up his old days, when he used to do all kinds of illegal things. Jonah could not escape his past living in his aunt's home. His surroundings were closing in on him.

'You cannot take fire to your bosom and expect not to be burned. Nor can you walk on hot coals and your feet not be seared.' The verses from Proverbs launched like a rocket through his being. *I need to get out of Holly Hill. It is dangerous. The temptation is strong, Lord. If I do not find a job soon—but....*

Yet, Jonah had nowhere else to go. Still, he had not opened the wooden box that Aunt Alice had left him. It was all he had left. To discover its contents would be like putting closure to his life with Aunt Alice. Jonah still wasn't ready to let go.

Getting off the bus, Jonah prayed that one of the three leads he had for employment would come through for him today. Jonah needed a breakthrough. With no more money and barely any food left, Jonah did not know what he was going to do if something did not happen for him soon.

❋❋❋

"We're not hiring," the first manager said at the café, after reviewing Jonah's application.

"But the sign on the window"

"Forgot to take it down," the man interrupted.

"You're not qualified," the woman at the gas station replied.

Really? A gas station attendant. How hard can that be? "I learn quickly, Ma'am. All I need is a chance to prove myself. I'll work for minimum wage, even lower if you just give me the chance."

The woman glanced at his application again, her eyes fixated on the checked felony box. "I'm sorry, but—but we're looking for someone who has already worked in this line of work before. But, we'll keep your name on file, and if something comes up, we'll give you a call."

Fat chance of that ever happening. "Have a good day, Ma'am." Jonah forced a smile.

Finally, someone spoke the truth. "We don't hire ex-cons," blurted the man at the bar, with the cigar in his mouth. "We run a respectable joint here, and we can't go ruining it with people who have been locked up."

"I've paid my time."

"Maybe so, but not here you haven't," the man spoke. "I'm tired of my taxes paying for lowlifes like you. You think you can just get out and take a job from someone else who lives by the Golden Rule. Do unto others as you would have them do unto you. People who do not kill, steal, or sell drugs or do those things you people do…"

You people! Jonah's nostrils flared, and his jaw clenched.

"Go! Get out of here and don't come back again!" The man yelled. Suddenly, two other men stood by him.

Jonah glared at the man.

"Get, now!"

He talked to Jonah as if he were a dog.

"God bless you, sir," Jonah replied as kindly as he could muster.

"Get out! I don't need your God blessing me!"

Jonah left the bar, feeling lower than an ant buried way under the ground. The owner's offensive words cut deeply. Although the others didn't say it, Jonah knew they were thinking it. Either way, it left Jonah with the *stinking* feeling of rejection.

Not wanting to go home, Jonah just started walking. He kept walking away from Holly Hill. The more he walked, the more Jonah was convinced that he could not go back. *Lord, help me!*

"The Lord is my refuge and my strength and ever present help in the time of need," Jonah quoted aloud. "Well, if ever I am in need of Your help, Lord, surely its now."

"Hey, you need a ride?"

Jonah had not noticed the silver Lincoln MKX that had pulled over on the side of the rode.

"Uh," Jonah looked back. He did not even realize he had walked so far that he was in the city part of Holly Hill. "Um, yes."

"Hop in," the man smiled.

Feeling cautious, Jonah scrutinized the guy. Back in the day, Jonah was good at judging someone's character. He had to in his former line of work. The guy didn't appear loco or homicidal.

"Are you coming or not?"

"I'm coming," Jonah said, and climbed in the passenger side.

The man pulled off. "Name is Steven Hutto."

"Jonah Bates."

"Pleasure to meet you, Jonah."

"Likewise."

They had only driven a few blocks away, when Steven shocked Jonah by his straightforward question. "So, what were you in for?"

"Huh?'

"You served time in prison, right?"

"How did you know?"

The man chuckled. "You have the same look that my brother Shane had fifteen years ago. The look of freedom! He was locked up for burglary in 1998. He was just turning twenty. Shane was a good young man, but he was restless and reckless. He was hanging around the wrong crowd. He and some guys robbed a liquor store. He served two of a five year sentence." Steven paused, suddenly caught up in the remembrance. "Shane was never the same after he got out. Prison changed him."

Speechless, Jonah looked the man over. Dressed in a navy suit, crisp white shirt, with a light blue tie, Steven appeared to be a man of good fortune, a well-to-do businessman. His eyes, matching the color of his tie, sparkled. His smile was wide and welcoming. There was nothing hard about this man. He seemed like the soft, lily-white type.

"Prison will do that," Jonah's tongue finally loosened.

"What were you in for?"

"Distribution," Jonah answered. "Served five years of an eight year sentence."

"Hard time that is. Hard, long time." Steven shook his head, shaking off the sadness he felt when talking about Shane. "It will get easier. The memories will fade with time. Can't say they will go away for good, but they will fade."

Jonah eyed the man. How could he understand the horrors of prison life? Looking away, Jonah fought to keep his composure. Prison was atrocious. Death seemed better for a man who was considered good-looking, thin-framed, and unprepared for hard criminals. Locked up at the age of twenty-four, Jonah never knew the true meaning of bullies until being locked up with grown men who embraced bullying the newcomers, as well as those who appeared *soft* or were *pretty boys*.

"God will help you."

Jonah looked to him again. "I believe that."

"Do you have family?"

"A twin brother, his name is Joel," Jonah answered. Every time Jonah thought of Joel, which was frequently, an ache in his heart emerged. Painful recollections materialized in his subconscious. Jonah had been in and out of county jail so many times, he couldn't count. However, he had been locked up two times, which required being locked up and sentenced for the crime. After his first arrest of drug possession, Joel borrowed money to get him out of jail. The second time he was arrested, Joel did not come to his aid. Jonah could vividly remember their last conversation five years ago.

"Hey El, I need you to come get me out jail." The twins had their own private names for each other. Jo for Jonah and El for Joel, the first two letters of Jonah and last two letters of Joel.

"No!"

"What? Come on, brother. I promise I will go straight from now on if you get me out. I will even go to night classes. Please do not leave me here. I cannot stay, El! I cannot. Please! You promised you'd always have my back!"

"And I have!" he shouted through the phone. "And what did you do the minute my back was turned? You stole my money. You stole my car. You even stole my fiancé! I told you the last time when I bailed you out that it would be your last and I meant it! You have done nothing but make promises that you never keep and never will! I wash my hands of you, Jo!

I do not have a brother anymore! Stay away from me! Do not call me from prison and do not write me! You have disgraced our family's name! You are a disgrace! Bye!"

For five years, Jonah had written his brother, never receiving a letter in return. He wondered if his brother would see him now.

"Do you want me to drop you off at your twin's home?"

"No," he sighed. "He doesn't want to see me." Jonah noticed the Welcome sign of Greenville. He was no longer in Holly Hill. *Lord, I'm not sure where this stranger is taking me, but it's away from Holly Hill. I don't want to go back to Holly Hill. Protect me, Lord. Provide for me. Show me what to do.*

"Do you need a place to stay?"

"Uh, yes."

"You can stay in the back apartment. It's nothing fancy, but it'll do until you can get on your feet."

"Really?" *Why is this strange, white man being so nice to me, a black ex-con?*

"You can work at the store," Steven stated, not asked.

"Huh?"

"You need a job, don't you?" Steven turned into Hutto's Department Store. It was a well-known department store, one of the biggest stores in the city. He drove the SUV toward the back of the store.

Jonah's mouth dropped as he beheld one of the most popular department stores. *Steven Hutto as in Hutto Department Store. My goodness! Lord, You sure know what You are doing. This has to be the favor of God!*

"Yes, I need job!"

"My family has twelve stores in the South, all managed by family members. I run two, the one in Holly Hill, and this one here in Greenville," Steven stated matter-of-factly. "This is where you can stay." Steven turned the truck off, parking in front of what appeared to be a small duplex of some kind.

"My family had this built in honor of Shane." Steven opened the door to one of the duplexes. Jonah followed him inside.

"Where is Shane now?"

"He died a year after he was released," Steven swallowed. "The prison memories haunted him. He couldn't overcome it, so he committed suicide."

"Oh. I'm sorry."

"Me too," Steven put his hand on Jonah's shoulder. "Shane was a great brother. He just lost his way. So, my family, we do whatever we can to help those who were once incarcerated to find their way back to living. It is not going to be easy, Jonah. People will not let you forget your past, but God not only forgives, He forgets. He remembers our sins no more. He will heal every hurt that you have. It is up to you to allow the process to begin. Today. It's a new day, a new beginning. Do not waste it. In honor of my brother's memory, take this chance and prove to all the other Shane's that God restores."

Jonah felt overwhelmed.

"Now, I have seven simple rules that you must abide by. If you cannot, say so. Let's not waste each other's time." Steven's tone turned serious. "There will be no drinking, no drugs, no partying, no stealing, and no lying, and you must go to church. I don't care what church you go to, but you must go to church."

Jonah had kept a mental count. "That's six."

"The final is you must pay it forward. Since God is giving you another chance, you must help someone else. I do not care if it is volunteering at a shelter, feeding the poor, giving a coat or food to the homeless, just do something. You have to pay-it-forward. If you do not hold up to your end of the rules, then you are out. Do I make myself clear?"

"Perfectly," Jonah replied.

"God instructed me to pullover and give you a ride. Not just a ride, but, also a chance to start over again. I have my family. And well, since you have no one right now God wants me to help you. I am throwing you a lifeline, Jonah. It's up to you what you do with it."

"Thank you, Steven," Jonah extended his hand, sealing the agreement with a firm handshake. "I won't let you down."

"Don't let God down!" Steven shook on it. "He's the One giving you another chance. I am just the vessel He's using. In addition, honor my brother's memory."

"I won't let God or you down." Jonah felt a weight lifted from his shoulders. He had just about given up, but God made a way out of no way. God had ordered his steps to Steven Hutto, the owner of a popular department store chain.

Won't He do it?!

CHAPTER 8

Hutto's

"A hot shower!" Jonah relished the water running down his body. "I've waited over five years to feel the sting of hot running water. No more cold showers!" This was a luxury of which so many took for granted. Surely, Jonah was just like that before being locked up in Manchester. The prison did not have hot showers for the inmates, only cold showers. Of course, the security people swore they had hot water, but the warm water must have all turned cold by the time Jonah got his chance to take a shower. This was a heaven-on-earth experience, for sure.

Walking through the duplex, with a clean-fluffy towel wrapped around his mid-section, Jonah looked in the closet. Steven told him there should be some clothes that would fit him. "My Lord!" Jonah exclaimed, enthusiastic about the amazing wardrobe at his disposal. Nice dress shirts, in various colors—including pastels, diverse slacks, several pairs of jeans, khakis, polo shirts, t-shirts, and suit jackets.

"Thank You, Lord, for Your bountiful provision." Jonah's eyes misted. It was hard to believe that all of this was for someone like him. "Bless Steven Hutto and his family, Lord. Never let them lack anything in their lives. Help me to pay-it-forward. I want to give back to those like me." His emotions got the best of him. Jonah dropped to his knees and began to silently praise God through his tears. He felt so unworthy, undeserving of such kindness. The Lord had truly been good to him, even when he hadn't been good at all. "Through the Lord's mercies we are not consumed, because His compassions fail not. They are new every morning. Great is Your faithfulness."

Following, Jonah went to the kitchen, his appetite ready to be satisfied. The day had been long, and Jonah had not eaten since breakfast, a bowl of dried cereal.

"Praise You, Jesus!" Jonah beheld a refrigerator filled with all kinds of things, such as bologna, ham slices, franks, fresh fruits and vegetables, soda pop, apple and orange juice, and so much more! The freezer was filled with a variety frozen dinners. Jonah took out a frozen pizza, made himself a bologna sandwich, and then plopped himself on the couch to watch a basketball game. Tonight, Jonah would go to bed with his belly full, his needs met, his heart content, and hopefully, he would sleep like a baby.

Jonah's sleep was sweet, initially. He found himself in the arms of Kayla, dancing the night away. Just the two of them, sashaying in what appeared to be a park, surrounded by too many flowers to be counted. Another one of those heaven-on-earth experiences, only it was a dream. The sunny dream soon turned to darkness. The dance was interrupted by a big, black bear of a man, Nixon. He snatched Kayla away and dragged Jonah around, making him dance with him. Jonah struggled to free himself, but he could not. Once again, he was no match for the man. Then, Nixon...

"No!" Jonah screamed, rousing himself from the nightmare. "I hate Nixon! I hate what he did to me! I hate what he continues to do to me!" Jonah cried aloud. "I hate…"

Love him.

The two words pierced Jonah deeply. "I *can't*."

Love him.

But he…he—Jonah could not even think the heart wrenching word.

Love him. You must love him. How can you love Me, who you do not see, and not love your brother, who you do see?

The command seemed too hard for Jonah to carry out. His flesh struggled to give in, to release and relinquish his heart to someone so undeserving. How could God expect such a thing?

Hope does not disappoint, because the love of God has been poured out in our hearts by the Holy Spirit who was given to us. Holy Spirit has poured perfect love into your heart. Through Him, you can love your enemy. Alone, you cannot. But with Him, you can do all things.

Silent tears trickled down Jonah's face. He felt defeated, so he began to pray in the spirit. He needed supernatural strength to do what God expected him to do. After all, God did not ask him to do something He had not already done.

Hanging on the cross, Jesus beheld his enemies and cried out, "Father forgive them, for they know not what they do." Love poured through the precious lips of Jesus Christ even when His enemies were unlovable people.

Jonah spent a few hours reading the Bible and praying, being renewed in his spirit, so that he could be ready for his first day at Hutto's Department Store. Dressed in black slacks, a pale yellow shirt, and a fashionable tie, Jonah admired the man in the mirror staring back at him. He looked like a new man. Overlooking, the wretched scar on his face, Jonah looked unflawed. "I'm a new creation. Old things have passed away, behold all things have become new."

Wanting to arrive on time, Jonah rushed out the door. What a satisfying feeling to know that he was going to work. He wasn't going to a gas station to clean toilets, pump gas, nor was he going to a restaurant to serve and wait tables, which were all reputable jobs. God saw fit to take him to a renowned store, to work, perhaps, as a janitor. It didn't matter. All that mattered was that God had opened a door that could lead to more opportunities.

Won't He do it? Jonah could hear Aunt Alice's declarative praise.

Here we go, Lord. Not sure what I am going to be doing. I may be overdressed for janitorial duties. I should have asked Mr. Hutto what job he was hiring me for. Well, I can go back and change. I do not care if I have to start at the bottom, I am just thankful for a job.

Entering the large department store, Jonah was impressed. He had never shopped at Hutto's before. It was consider a *blue-blooded* store, for uppity people.

He stopped at the jewelry counter. "Hello, I'm looking for Mr. Hutto."

"Which one?" Nicole, the saleswoman, asked, batting her long, fake eyelashes.

Jonah grinned. Being away from women for five years, he reveled in any female's attention. "Steven Hutto."

"Go all the way in the back and take the escalator to the third floor. All the big executive offices are on the third floor."

"Thank you," Jonah smiled.

"My pleasure," she said, smacking her lips.

Get behind me, satan! Jonah hurried away. Being out in the real world offered too many temptations.

Reaching the third floor, Jonah recognized Steven talking to the receptionist.

"Hi, Jonah!" Steven rested his hand on Jonah's shoulder. "You're early."

"Yes, sir."

"No need for the sir stuff around here. We're all on a first name basis." Steven was pleased with the way Jonah looked. Amazing what new clothes and a good shave could do for a person.

"Ready for work?"

"Yes, s—" Jonah caught himself, "I am."

"The sales associate in the men's department is on sick leave, so let's try you out there." Steven led Jonah to the escalator to go down to the second floor. "Patrick will train you today. I am sure you will catch on with no problems. If you have any questions, do not be afraid to ask. Patrick will help you. I've already told him to take you under his wings and show you everything you need to know."

"I appreciate it."

"Patrick and you have a lot in common," Steven mentioned.

Jonah grinned. "So he's an ex-con, too?"

Steven nodded. "Been out for three years. He is married and has a baby on the way. God gives us all second chances."

"Some of us, second chances over and over again." Jonah added.

"You got that right!"

⋇⋇⋇⋇

Jonah liked Patrick immediately. Patrick was white, standing a little shorter than Jonah, with a lean frame. Patrick shared his work ethic and how he started out as a sales associate, worked his way up to assistant supervisor, and was now a supervisor on the second floor. Patrick was a cool guy. He worked hard and made each customer feel special. In the few moments when the store wasn't busy, the two talked as if they had known each other forever. Besides being locked up, Patrick and Jonah had several other things in common. Both liked playing tennis. Also, in high school, they were both state track and field medalists. Most importantly, prison life brought them to their Redeemer. They both wanted to give back in life, pay-it-forward, and not just because Steven expected that them to. They wanted to stop young people from ending up in prison by the making the wrong choices. The young didn't have to learn the hard way, like they did. Besides, learning the hard way wasn't the best way. Learning the best way, without making all the crazy mistakes, sure could save a person a lot of time, and a lot of heartaches.

Patrick invited Jonah to his church and invited him over for dinner. The two even made plans to play tennis afterwards. Jonah had a good feeling about Patrick. He was going to be more than just a co-worker, or supervisor, but a friend.

God always has a plan.

A man's heart devises his way, but the Lord directs his steps.

During Jonah's lunch break, the saleswoman he met earlier came to the break room shortly after Jonah had entered.

"Hi there, handsome," she flirted. "You don't mind me sitting with you, do you?"

Jonah shook his head as he bit into an apple. Steven had given him a brown bag lunch, saying his wife Paula had sent an extra lunch in case someone needed it. Jonah was glad. He had rushed out of the apartment, not giving a second thought about lunch. He would have gone back to the apartment for his thirty-minute break, but Steven showed him the break room.

"I'm Nicole." She extended her hand.

"Jonah," he wiped his hand on a napkin before shaking hers.

Nicole didn't want to let go. He practically had to snatch it away. *She's dangerous!*

"I like you, Jonah." Straightforward and to the point, Nicole toyed with her hair, giving him a provocative look. Seemingly, she wasn't there to eat food, but to entice him.

Swiftly, Jonah put down the apple. It reminded him of Adam and Eve. Similarly, Jonah wondered if he was sitting with a snake.

"You don't even know me," he countered.

"But I'd like to get to know you," she moved closer. "You can come over to my apartment after work."

"No, thank you."

"Why not, Jonah?" Nicole reached for him.

Quickly, Jonah leaped up. "I have to go."

"I won't bite, Jonah," she followed him out the room. "But I sure know how to give—"

"Nicole," he barked her name out, "I'm not interested."

"Surely an ex-con could use some loving," she purred.

"How did you know?"

"Steven's always hiring ex-cons, trying to honor his brother's memory." Nicole rested her hand on his shoulder. "Speaking of memories, we can make some good memories together. I can show you a good time, Jonah."

"Nicole, do you know Jesus?" he asked boldly.

"Oh, no, not another religious nut!" Nicole stepped away.

"No, I'm not a religious man."

"Good," she perked up.

"I'm a Christian. There is a difference."

"Whatever!" she turned away. "I thought you were a cool guy. I guess I was wrong."

"I guess so," Jonah smiled and went to clock back in.

He volunteered to work a double-shift when the evening sales associate called in sick. Even though he was tired, it was a good tired. Jonah liked working at Hutto's. From assisting customers, to making sure the area was neat, even working at the cash register, Jonah felt respected. He didn't feel like an ex-con, just another employee.

By the time he got home that night, Jonah felt really good about himself.

"Aunt Alice, if you're looking down, I know you are pleased. For the first time in my life, I had an honest-day of work, and it felt good, really good!"

I wonder what Kayla is doing? I wish I had her number. I sure would like to tell her about my new job. The vivacious beauty was always on his mind. The passionate kiss they shared often invaded his thoughts, leaving Jonah wanting more. More of Kayla. *Lord, if it's Your will for us to be friends, or even more, let me see her again. If not, please help me to forget her.*

There's a time to love and a time to hate. Now is the time to love.

CHAPTER 9

Two Are Better than One

It had been two weeks since Jonah had left Holly Hill. Detaching himself from his old life and the temptations of the past was the right thing to do. Just as a recovering alcoholic should not go to a bar, if he did not have the strength to resist, Jonah didn't want to put himself in a position to be tempted by the evil one. Besides, PJ was not going to just let him go like that. He knew his old friend all too well. He would keep showing up until he had worn Jonah down. Jonah had learned a long time ago, never say never. Even the Apostle, Paul, declared, "For the good that I will to do, I do not do, but the evil I will not to do, that I practice."

Saturday afternoon Jonah caught the bus to his childhood home so that he could check on the place and retrieve a few mementos to put in his duplex and make it feel more like home. Mainly, the picture of his Aunt Alice, he just had to have it. It would make him feel somehow close to her. The pictures of him and Joel, for sure. Additionally, he wanted to bring the wooden box, with hidden treasures Jonah felt he was now ready to unearth.

I wish...Kayla... Get her out of your mind! She is long gone and never to return!

❧❧❧

"I could fly in to see you tomorrow and perhaps stay over and we both can fly back on Monday," Leon called early Saturday morning, waking Kayla up around 9:00 a.m. Money meant nothing to Leon. He could just fly anywhere at any time, because he knew people and had the money to do it. Nevertheless, Kayla had a restless night after standing up to her father about going away for the weekend. She didn't feel like dealing with Leon. Even after she had promised she would be in the office on Monday, her father was still annoyed and said she was *behaving* like a child; when, in fact, he was the one *treating* her like a child. Kayla could not take one more day of her parents practically pushing their neighbor, Dr. Leon White, to the marriage altar. It was too much.

"Leon," Kayla sat up in the bed. She had returned to Holly Hill on Thursday, trying to escape her parents and Leon. Ever since her parents invited him over for dinner, he seemed overly enamored by her. Maybe at any other time in her life, Kayla would have been flattered. However, right now she had too many things going on in her life and what she needed more than anything was space. Time to adjust to her new situation.

"Don't say no, Kayla," he interrupted. "I know we've only known each other for a few weeks, but I feel something deeply for you. I am not trying to scare you off, but I just want to put all my cards on the table. I was hoping we could go out for dinner and discuss it. Then, after that, if you don't want to see me, I will respect your wishes."

Kayla felt trapped. "How are you going to get a flight out

at this late notice?"

"My friend has a private plane, he's on standby for me," Leon replied. "Please say yes, Kayla."

She hesitated. Leon was truly a nice man. Her parents liked him, which usually meant he was a bore, but Leon was rather interesting. He wasn't a stuffy surgeon like her father. Leon was quite the opposite. He listened to Kayla, which was a plus. There just wasn't any chemistry between them. It was more like a brotherly connection, which was fine with Kayla. However, Leon wanted more. Kayla had nothing else to offer him. Moreover, Leon did not make Kayla's heart go pitter-patter like Jonah. *Lisa is right. I'm reading way too many romance novels.*

Jonah! I wish. Taking in a long breath, Kayla finally responded. "Fine, Leon."

"Great! I should be there by five, tomorrow. I can pick you up shortly after that, and like I said earlier, we can fly back together."

He was being a bit too pushy. "Leon, pick me up at six." Kayla deliberately did not respond to his other invitation.

"Text me the address."

"I will. But where I'm staying is not what you would consider a good neighborhood."

"No problem, Kayla. Wherever you are is where I want to be."

"Goodbye, Leon."

"See you soon, Kayla."

Kayla hung up the phone, feeling anxious about going out with Leon. "I should have just said no and been done with it."

Around lunchtime, Kayla decided to walk around the corner to the neighborhood burger joint. There wasn't any food in the home for her since she had cleaned it out, thinking the single woman and her kids would have moved in, but that didn't happen. She didn't feel like using her rental car to go anywhere, figuring it would be safe since it was so early in the day and just around the corner.

Kayla had walked no more than a few feet, when she realized she was not walking alone.

"Hey, beautiful," the man hailed, whistling at her.

Kayla kept walking, refusing to pay him any mind.

"Beautiful!" He called her again.

Kayla kept her eyes on the ground and kept walking, ignoring him as best she could.

"Oh, you think you're too good for me," the invader was up on her now.

"Please leave me alone," Kayla said with pursed lips.

"I'll leave you alone, alright." He grabbed her arm a swung her around.

A shiver moved up and down her arms.

"You uppity chick! I'll show you how to act when you're with me." The tall, bulky man harshly forced his lips upon hers. Kayla struggled to free herself, reaching up and raking her long fingernails on the side of his face.

"You…"

"Hey! I think the lady doesn't want to be bothered." Jonah's stern voice got the man's attention, as she attempted to get away.

"JoJo, this *ain't* your fight." PJ glared at him, still holding Kayla.

"Kayla," Jonah's heart dropped. He had no idea the victim

90

was her. His heart pounded like drums. Anger welled up inside of him.

"Let her go, PJ!" Jonah squared his broad shoulders, clenched his fist to his sides and looked the enemy right smack in the eyes, ready for a fight.

"And if I don't?" PJ did not like anybody ordering him around. He was the boss! The king of Holly Hill East Side.

"Come on PJ, she's my friend."

"So! Your friend disrespected me, and no one does that and gets away." PJ took a rigid stance.

"PJ, I'm asking you to let her go."

"And I'm telling you…"

All at once a few of PJ's boys appeared on the scene. "Hey PJ, you want me to handle JoJo?"

"Oh, it's like that?" Jonah's nostril flared as he struggled to keep his temper in check.

"Yeah, it's like that," Corky said.

It was only the sight of the neighborhood patrol car that spoiled PJ's plans.

"You can have her for now!" PJ shoved Kayla toward Jonah, his speech seethed with fury. He scowled at Jonah and stormed away. This wasn't over.

Kayla clung to him, burying her head in his chest. Her knees trembled, her pulse raced out of control and her arms shook, but she felt safe.

"Are you okay?" Jonah's voice was deep with concern.

"I…I…uh," she stammered trying to find words.

"It's okay." He tenderly ran his fingers through her long tresses, something Jonah wanted to do the very first day he had met her. "I'm here."

"You saved my life," she gazed at him, starry-eyed. *Way*

too many novels!

Jonah's heart quickened, beholding how vulnerable she was. "I was only helping you get away from an overbearing admirer."

"Admirer! He was going to assault me, I'm sure and..." Kayla sucked in air, finding it difficult to breathe. The thought of her attacker frightened her all over again. "How do you know him?"

"I told you before that I'm not a saint." He swallowed past the painful reminder of who he used to be. "I used to hang out with PJ."

"Oh," Kayla lowered her head, trying to absorb the information that Jonah could even be associated with such a man. She thought Jonah was different.

"I should not have been walking by myself." Kayla pulled away, uncertain about her jumbled feelings.

"What are you doing here?"

"I just needed to get away and, well," she shrugged, "the only place that felt like home was Aunt Mae's. I still have the key. The single mom that was supposed to move in instead moved away with a sister in another state."

"Seriously, Kayla," Jonah pulled Kayla's chin upward to face him, "you shouldn't ever walk the streets alone. This *ain't* a place for good girls like you." His eyes twinkled.

"I know," she flashed a pleasant smile, "Aunt Mae warned me."

Though she was still visibly shaken, Jonah could not help but gawk at the beauty that stood before him. Kayla was breathtaking, standing there wearing a burnt orange blouse and jeans.

"Where were you going?"

"I was hungry, and there is nothing in the house, so I remembered Andy's Wings around the block."

"I haven't been there in a long, long time. They have the best chili-dogs."

"Sounds good."

Jonah took her hand in his. Kayla did not pull away.

"Do you think that guy will mess with us?"

"Nah, not now anyway. PJ is probably riding around, blowing off some steam."

"I'm glad you were here." Kayla looked at him finally, her cheeks flushed. She seemed almost afraid of him after Jonah revealed that he used to hang out with PJ.

"Me too." His heart melted.

Later, after returning to Aunt Mae's home with the chili-dogs and fries, Kayla and Jonah shared their meal at the table. Kayla seemed shy around him. So unlike the last time they were here sharing a meal together.

"This chili-dog is really good." Kayla cut into her chili-dog with a knife.

Jonah practically gulped down his two chili-dogs. "They are the best."

"How are things going, Jonah?"

"I found a job," he blurted happily. "I'm a sales associate at Hutto's."

"Jonah, that's great. I love that store. They have the cutest purses. And the jewelry is really exquisite."

Exquisite! Lord, we are too different. And I cannot remember having a conversation with a lady that uses the word exquisite. Why not just say expensive? I mean, who cuts a chili-dog with a knife? Who does that? Rich people!

"I even have this neat place to stay," Jonah continued. "The owner, Steven, let me stay there until I can get on my feet."

"What about your home that Aunt Alice left you?" Kayla took a sip of water.

"As you experienced firsthand, this place isn't safe. I do not need to be around my past. It's my old world."

"I'm glad you're not like that anymore." She lowered her eyes. It somewhat unsettled her to be drawn to a man with a bad-boy past, who had hung around a man like PJ.

"Kayla," Jonah softly called her name, "look at me, please." She complied.

"I can't change my past, who I was then, but, with God's help, I can certainly change my future. I can be who God wants me to be. I'm far from perfect, but I do serve a Perfect Father, who loves me just the way I am." Laced in his words was an imploring cry for Kayla to see him for who he was now.

His words touched her. "I, I…" she dashed out the kitchen, making it to the bathroom just in time.

Jonah followed her. There was an alarm ringing in his ears, and a tightness in his chest. Kayla was sick, and for some reason it scared him. Leaning over the commode, Jonah grabbed a towel and ran cold water on it. As she emptied her stomach, Jonah dabbed the cold rag on her forehead and behind her neck.

"Thank you," Kayla replied, kneeling. Finally, the heaving stopped.

"No problem." Jonah knelt next to her, tenderly pushing back the loose strands of hair form her face. "Are you feeling better?"

She nodded.

"Must be those chili-dogs," he smiled. "You're not used to greasy food."

Kayla did not respond. Jonah's compassion moved her.

She could not imagine another man caring for her like Jonah, and then looking at her with those alluring eyes after being sick like that.

"I must look a mess." Kayla felt self-conscious.

"You're gorgeous." He traced his fingers down the side of her face. *Do not kiss her!*

"You're blind."

"I have twenty-twenty vision." His gazed fixed on her lips. *Don't do it. She just vomited, man!*

Sensing his dilemma, Kayla pushed herself up. "I am going to brush my teeth and freshen up a little, if you don't mind."

"I don't." He stood. "Are you sure you're okay?"

"Much better."

"I'll go clean up our mess in the kitchen." Jonah closed the bathroom door. *Lord, I'm a goner! That woman has taken my heart and there ain't a thing I can do about it!*

When a man finds a wife, he finds a good thing and obtains the favor of the Lord.

A wife! I'm talking about the possibility of a girlfriend, not a wife! It's way too soon for that!

Two are better than one, because they have a good reward for their labor. For if they fall, the one will lift up his fellow. But woe to him that is alone when he falls, for he has not another to help him up. Again, if two lie together, then they have heat, but how can one be warm alone? And if one prevails against him, two shall withstand him, and a threefold cord is not quickly broken.

Lord, I'm an ex-con! She started acting funny the minute I told her I used to be like PJ. Now, imagine how she's going to respond when she finds out I was locked up for five years!

Tell her.

I can't.

After cleaning the kitchen, Jonah sat on the couch and turned on the television. Feeling dazed by his spiritual heart-to-heart, Jonah silently prayed.

"What are you watching?" Joining him, Kayla plopped on the couch next to him.

"I'm not really sure." Jonah looked at her. "You okay?"

"I am," she said, and smiled.

"Kayla, where are you staying tonight?"

"Here."

"You can't. I'm sure PJ knows where you are. This is a small town, people talk. PJ may have walked away, but trust me, he doesn't forget. He's going to come for you, and probably for me."

"Aunt Mae says this home is covered by the blood of Jesus. Don't you believe God is covering me?"

"Yes, and…"

"Okay then," she turned her attention to the television.

"Aunt Alice used to quote this Scripture all the time and I thought about it the day I left here, not sure where I was going. All I knew is that I had to leave this environment. It is found in Proverbs, and it says, 'You can't take fire to your bosom and not be burned. Nor can you walk on hot coals and your feet not be seared.' In other words, you can't play with fire and not expect to get burn. PJ is fire and if you play with him, you're going to get burned. This is his territory, and for now, we should stay away from him."

"You mean run!" Kayla stood up, crossing her arms.

"No." Jonah stood beside her. "But you can't stay here alone. It's not safe, Kayla."

She could never tire of hearing her name rolling off his

lips. "You can stay with me."

"Huh?" he was floored by the proposition.

"I mean sleep on the couch," she quickly added.

His mind was running a mile a minute. He didn't feel right about staying because it gave the appearance of something evil; but he wasn't about to let her stay by herself.

"Are you definitely leaving tomorrow?"

Abruptly, Leon popped in her head. "No. I am flying out Monday morning."

"I can stay tonight, but I'm not sure I can stay Sunday."

"Don't worry. A friend is coming tomorrow." She looked away.

"A friend." He was suspicious. "Who?"

"You don't know him."

Him! "A male!" Jonah stepped back. "What kind of game are you playing, Kayla?"

"I don't play games, Jonah," she answered. "He lives next door to my parents and he'll be here tomorrow on a private plane and I'm riding back with him on Monday."

"I see," Jonah walked away, jealousy riding his back.

"You don't see," Kayla scooted in front of him. "Leon is just a friend, nothing more."

"Does he know that?" Jonah swallowed hard. He had no legitimate reason to be jealous of anyone Kayla was seeing. He did not own her. She was not even his girlfriend. Yet, his heart ached to think of her being with another man.

"We're going to have a serious talk tomorrow," she admitted. "But Jonah, what do you care? We are practically strangers." She said aloud, but her heart did not concur.

"I care," he replied. Unable to contain his emotions, Jonah leaned over and his lips caressed hers. Kayla wrapped her arms around his neck, surrendering to the passion burning within. The kiss intensified. They were both playing dangerously with fire now. Somewhat losing himself, Jonah pulled away. "Whew! We can't be kissing like that," he said. "I am a Christian, but I'm still a man."

"You kissed me first," Kayla was breathless.

"I like kissing you," his eyes mimicked his feeling. "It is just hard pulling away. Sex is for marriage and I tell you, Kayla, thoughts of taking you in the back room…well, let's just say I got a lot of repenting to do."

"So, you're not going to kiss me anymore?" She felt slighted.

"Not like that," he replied. "It's dangerous."

She playfully pouted.

"Kayla, you're doing something strange to my heart."

"You're doing the same to mine." Kayla affectionately caressed his face with the palm of her hand.

"It will never work," he spoke his mind. "You eat hotdogs with a knife."

"Haven't you heard that opposites attract, Jonah?"

"I'm serious, Kayla. I have nothing to offer you."

"I'm not asking you to marry me, Jonah." *Although I would love to be your wife.* "I like you, Jonah, a lot."

I love you Kayla. "But what about Leon?"

"After tomorrow, Leon will no longer contact me."

"You can't be so sure."

After he finds out I am pregnant with another man's child, he will run away gladly. And so will you. This second thought pierced her heart.

"I'm sure. We'll just take it slow, Jonah, if you want to."

"I want to."

She embraced him. *How in the world am I going to tell him I am pregnant?*

Lord, how am I going to tell her about my past? Jonah fretted.

CHAPTER 10

Saved by Grace

"Stop! Stop!" Jonah woke up to the loud cries. Unclear whether or not he was hearing his own shouts from a dream, Jonah scooted up on the couch.

"No! Please don't," Kayla cried from the bedroom.

Moving like a madman, Jonah barged through the bedroom door.

Kayla was tossing and turning in her sleep. Her long locks were all over the place.

"Kayla!" Jonah called her name, shaking her slightly. "Wake up, Kayla."

"Stop!" She bolted upward, trying to free herself.

"It's me, Kayla. Jonah."

"Jonah," she blubbered, recognizing his face.

Wrapping her in his arms, Jonah held onto Kayla, making her to feel safe and secure.

"What a horrible nightmare," she sobbed. "It was so real."

"I know what you mean," Jonah's thoughts reflected on his own nightmare. The one he had been dreaming when he heard Kayla's cries. Same old dream about Nixon.

"Your friend, PJ." She rested her head on his shoulder.

"PJ is not my friend anymore," Jonah corrected.

"I'm sorry."

"Don't be. I just want you to understand that PJ is my past life. I am a new person, Kayla. I am a new creation." His eyes pleaded for Kayla to believe him. Even with her sandy brown hair all tangled up, no makeup on, her eyes reddened with fresh tears, and dressed in a pink gown, Kayla was the most beautiful woman he had ever seen. And even at this moment, the most desirable.

"I know," she mumbled. "The dream frightened me, that's all."

"I will never let PJ hurt you, Kayla. I promise you that."

"Thank you."

"But right now, I'm going to get out of this bed." He unraveled himself from Kayla's tight embrace. "It's not…"

She frowned. "So you can't even be near me, Jonah?"

"Not with you in that prissy pink gown and me bare-chested.

She could not help but notice his rippled mid-section and buff chest. Jonah was so appealing, so handsome in every aspect. *Be still, my heart!*

"Please stop looking at me like that," Jonah warned. "Or you and I both are going to regret it."

She lowered her eyes and reclined back on the bed. "Would you think badly of me, Jonah, if I told you how badly I want you?"

"No," he grinned. "I'm glad you feel the same way I do. But, we've got to do the right thing."

"I know. I am not that kind of girl, Jonah. I usually have control over my feelings and I want to live right, I do."

"That's why I have to be strong for the both of us," he sighed. "God sent me to you, Kayla, yesterday. That was His way of protecting you. I had planned to catch a later bus, but my spirit kept urging me to go earlier. You have to believe God is watching out for you. He made sure I was in the right place at the right time for you. Think about that, Kayla," Jonah stood in the doorway. "I've been attending this church by the store. I really would like for you to go with me this morning. The service starts at ten o'clock."

"I'll go." Tears sprung forth in her eyes. Jonah's words moved her inwardly. To think that a Big God would care so much about her, pregnant Kayla, was like a burst of fresh air, giving her hope that truly God was ever so near. "Thanks, Jonah."

"Welcome," he winked. "Are you hungry?"

"No."

"Me either. I am going to go to my home and get a shirt to change into. I'll be right back."

"I'll shower and change for church while you're gone."

"Kayla."

"Yes."

"You're special to God, and to me."

"You're special to me, Jonah, very special."

❃❃❃

Jonah and Kayla entered the church just as the choir began to sing.

Kayla looked up at him with uncertainty in her eyes. Grasping her hand, Jonah smiled at her, quickly silencing her fears. Even though she had accepted Jesus into her heart, this was her first time attending church since Aunt Mae's funeral.

The worship music moved Kayla. She clapped her hands and sung along with the words on the screen. Joy flooded her soul. Looking around, the congregation seemed so...so free to praise God. Kayla glanced over at Jonah, who was fully absorbed in the music. With his hands raised, he seemed to be in a place of his own. Suddenly, the music changed from a fast-paced tempo, to a soothing, unhurried tune. The familiar song flooded Jonah's soul with peace as the two stood near the front of the church. *Aunt Alice loved this song.* Jonah could almost hear her soprano tone singing it in his ears. What sweet peace!

> *It was God's amazing grace*
> *That saved me,*
> *Kept me*
> *And never left me*
> *I was oppressed, but now I have joy*
> *I was blind, but now I see*
> *I was brokenhearted, but now I am healed*
> *I was captive, but now I am free*
> *It was God's amazing grace*
> *That saved me,*
> *Kept me*
> *And never left me.*

Unable to stop the flow of tears, Jonah wept. He did not understand it back when his aunt used to sang it. The meaning of the song became real, alive in his soul. Kayla pressed her hand in the middle of his back, wanting him to know she was near, not caring about anyone else around him. His emotions were raw and real, so real that she could feel it.

You are free Jonah! His spirit whispered. Softly, the music played, without the choir singing.

"Whom the Son sets free, is free indeed," Pastor Reggie Goodwin shouted from the pulpit. "Whom the Son sets free, not whom man sets free, because man can't free you. Man cannot make you whole. Man cannot erase your past. Man cannot heal the brokenhearted. Man cannot make the captive free. Oh, but God can!" The pastor shouted himself happy. "Oh, but God can set you free by His grace! By His loving, amazing grace! My brothers and sisters don't let the devil keep you in bondage today. Do not let him bind you in the chains of the past. Do not let him throw accusations at you and make you feel you are unworthy of God's grace. Listen, you cannot earn God's grace. You cannot make God love you anymore or any less than He already does. The devil is a liar! To be free is to live in God's grace. We are under grace, not under the law. The law could not save us. We are saved by grace. The law could not heal us. The law could not set us free. Jesus Christ our Lord and Savior has freed us through His shedding of blood. Do not go back. Do not look back. Do not stay back. No! Keep moving forward. Keep pressing forward. Keep looking upward to the hills from whence comes our help. Our help comes from the Lord.

"He wants to help you, but some of you are holding onto the past. You are still broken, when He wants to heal you. You are still captive, even though He has freed you. It is up to you. You have to choose to accept His gift of freedom. By His grace, God is offering you freedom. Freedom from sin. Freedom from guilt and shame. Freedom from your past. Freedom from sickness and disease. Freedom from eternal death. Freedom! If you want to be free, I mean really free, please come to the altar. Step out on faith and believe that God will totally free you! Believe that He will save you! Believe that He will do whatever it is that you need for Him to do for you. Do not let another day go by, allowing the enemy to keep you in bondage. Not another day!"

Jonah got up from his seat. He wanted this gift of freedom

more than anything. He wanted to be free from the past. Free from the dreams and nightmares about Manchester Institution. Free from Nixon. Free from his guilt.

"Do you want me to go with you?" Kayla asked.

He shook his head. Jonah needed to do this alone.

The altar was filled with men, women, young boys and girls, all wanting to be free of something. Some were crying, some were silently praying, some had their heads hung down, and some were carrying the same weight on their shoulders as Jonah carried. Jonah most definitely was not alone. One by one, the pastor and the ministers prayed for each individual.

"God has forgiven you, son," Pastor Goodwin whispered for Jonah's ears only. "Now you must forgive yourself." He spoke and then laid hands on Jonah. Something gentle yet powerful came over Jonah. The Presence of God consumed him. Unable to stand, Jonah slowly fell back, slain in the spirit. Nothing like this had ever happened to him before. He looked as if he was sleeping, and yet the Holy Spirit was working a work that only He could work. He was being calmed, soothed, encouraged, and strengthened. God was dealing with Jonah, surgically removing the stains of the past. Even if he wanted to, and he did not, Jonah could not get up. God had him right where He wanted him, safe in His arms. Even after the altar cleared, Jonah remained there on the floor.

"Don't worry about him," the pastor said to the ushers as they came to assist the young man up. "God is not through with him yet. Church, those that remain here, I want you all to stretch your hands toward this young man and pray for him. Pray in the spirit. God has a work for this young man to do, a mighty work, and the gates of Hell shall not prevail against him. Pray, church. This is God's anointed vessel, called to do great works. He has been through a lot, and He needs God's grace and strength. I declare and decree this young man is free! Free in Jesus' name."

In her seat, Kayla overwhelming felt the need to drop to her knees. She needed to be free herself. She needed God's peace. She was tired of running, tired of hiding, tired of walking on eggshells—tired of being afraid.

"God, I surrender," she sniffed. "Aunt Mae said You were waiting on me to surrender my heart to you. Here it is…my heart, Lord I give to you, not for Aunt Mae or for Jonah, but for me. My very life I give to You. I want You, Lord more than I want anything or anyone. Forgive me, for my wrongs. Forgive me for my selfishness and my secret sins." She cried even more. "I want to be free, Lord. Please free me, now."

"You're free," the First Lady, Evangelist Lauren Goodwin touched Kayla's shoulder gently. "You're free."

Kayla looked at her. The beautiful lady was glowing with the same peace Kayla had witnessed in Aunt Mae. "How do you know?"

"Because you asked Him to free you. God loves you, daughter. He loves you and your husband very much."

"He's not my husband," Kayla corrected.

"He is," the pastor's wife spoke with conviction. "He is." She touched her again and walked away.

Kayla stayed on her knees, praising and praying, while Jonah rested in the sweet arms of holiness. About thirty minutes after the church service was over, Jonah slowly pushed himself off the floor with the help of an usher.

"How are you feeling, young man?" Pastor Reggie Goodwin asked, beaming. He and his wife waited patiently by the young man's side, praying quietly.

"I, I feel…drunk," Jonah laughed. "I mean…high."

"Nothing like getting high for Jesus," the pastor understood.

"Jonah," Kayla came and sat by him. "Are you okay?"

He nodded, not taking his eyes off of her. She was glowing like the pastor and his wife. Something had happened to her. "You're shining like a star, Kayla."

"I feel so good, Jonah," she smiled.

"Me too," he reached for her hand, "but I don't know how I'm going to walk out of here."

"Young man," Pastor Reggie Goodwin beckoned him.

"Jonah," he introduced himself.

"Jonah," the pastor laughed. "God truly has a sense of humor. God showed me you the other night. You and your wife."

"We're not married."

"You will be." With assurance, the pastor replied, glancing over at his wife, who nodded in agreement. "He showed me that you were to teach young men and women, the younger generation, about Him. I have been praying for a youth pastor, since my youth pastor and his family moved. I believe you're it."

"Me?" Jonah gasped. "Not me. You do not know my past. You don't know my story."

"No, but God knows your past, present, and your future. He knows your entire history, and He knows how to use it for His glory. God has plans for you, big plans. Only He knows those plans, Jonah. Seek Him and He will reveal them to you."

Jonah had never heard anyone speak with such authority and conviction about God, other than his Aunt Alice.

"Let Him use you, Jonah. God has work for you to do for His Kingdom."

CHAPTER 11

Coming Clean

"Kayla, we need to talk," Jonah said at the restaurant. He and Kayla went to a small diner not far from the church after service.

"I know," she sighed.

"I have to come clean about my past, Kayla and it's not a pretty sight."

"Neither is mine."

"Kayla, I don't want to lose you," Jonah reached across the table for her hands.

"You won't."

"After I come clean, you may not say that, and I wouldn't fault you."

"Jonah, God freed us both today," she smiled. "Now I know I'm a Christian, like you."

"I'm so happy about that, Kayla. That is why I have to be honest. I don't want anything to come between us if we stand a chance at making this relationship work."

"We have a relationship?" she perked up.

"We'll see…"

"Oh, Jonah, no matter what you tell me, I am going to still love you." Kayla released her heart, making her more vulnerable than ever.

"You love me!" Jonah repeated the three words that meant more to him than Kayla could ever imagine.

"I do."

"Oh, Kayla, I could just kiss you right now," he looked around, "but it wouldn't be proper."

"Who cares about proper," she dared him.

"I do. I would never do anything to tarnish your reputation, Kayla. I will always put you above my wants and needs," he spoke seriously. "Do you understand that?"

She nodded. "Jonah, can we leave? I can't eat another bite, and I want to talk privately."

"Sure, there is a park nearby." Jonah signaled for the waitress. After paying the lady and leaving a generous tip, Jonah assisted Kayla out of her chair and escorted her to her rental car.

"Are you feeling well?

"I'm fine."

"Do you mind if I drive?" Jonah inquired.

"Of course not," Kayla handed him the keys to her rental. Looking at her watch, Kayla frowned.

Jonah noticed. Driving away, he asked, "What time is Leon coming to get you?"

"At six."

"It's two o'clock, so we have some time."

"I'm sorry, Jonah. I had no idea I would see you." Kayla felt bad. She did not want to leave Jonah. Not now, not ever!

"I'll forgive you this time," he winked, "but Leon better not come around again, or I can't promise I will behave like a gentleman."

Kayla chucked. "I only have eyes for you, Jonah."

"Good!"

Arriving at the park, Jonah laced his fingers around hers as the two walked through the park.

"You're sure you don't want to rest?" Jonah looked at Kayla. "You look a little pale."

A wave of nausea washed over her. *Lord, please don't let me get sick, not now.*

"Stop fussing over me. I'm fine." His concern made her feel special.

Walking in silence, both Kayla and Jonah struggled to find the right words to unleash their hidden secrets.

"I was a hothead growing up," Jonah began. "I wouldn't listen to anybody. My twin, Joel, desperately tried to reason with me, begging me not to hang out with the street boys, not to sneak out of the house, not to drink, not to smoke weed, not to play with girls' feeling, but I wouldn't listen. Joel was a weakling in my eyes, physically and emotionally. He was always too tired to do this and too tired to do that. Joel was sickly, you see. I guess I just wanted him to hang with me and since he couldn't, I found people to hang out with—not good people, mind you. Aunt Alice prayed and prayed that I would do the right thing, but I was so angry, Kayla. I was mad at the world."

"Why?"

"I guess because my father left us. My mom was a crackhead and she left us and then she had the nerve to die on us," Jonah exhaled. "I hated my parents! The only people I loved were Joel and Aunt Alice. The same two people who I hurt the most. I did some bad things, Kayla. Are you sure you're ready for this?"

Kayla squeezed his hand. "I'm sure."

111

"I was in prison for five years," he admitted, not looking at her. Kayla's hand went limp in his, but she did not let go of it.

"I was arrested for drug distribution. I served five of an eight-year sentence. I'm on probation for two years."

Kayla was speechless. She had not expected this.

"Behind bars…" Jonah gulped for air. Just thinking about Manchester sickened him.

"You don't have to talk about it," Kayla was not sure she could handle more.

"Let's just say that behind bars, I, uh—" he paused, finding it difficult to breakthrough his pain. "I'm not sure how to say this without sounding like a punk, but I uh, endured some horrible things. Inhuman things."

Kayla's mind battled to find the meaning of his exposure. However, she was naïve to Jonah's world. Her parents sheltered her from such a world.

"I was tortured by this guy in Manchester, Nixon. He ran the prison. He was a big bully and he…" The tremor in his voice nearly did Kayla in. He was in so much pain, and there was nothing she could do to make the pain stop. Jonah could say no more. The pain engulfed him.

"Oh, Jonah!" Kayla reached for him. "We'll get through this together!"

Jonah held onto her, fighting back his own demons as his lips trembled and agony resurfaced. The two clung to each other, in silence. No words were needed. Just the comforting touch of the other. The two began to walk again. "There is something else I want to tell you, Kayla."

Oh, God, I am not sure if I can handle another blow. First, he served five years in prison for selling drugs. Then something dreadful happened to him in prison. Now what else, Lord?

"The reason why Joel doesn't speak to me or want me in his life," he hesitated. "I slept with his fiancé."

She gasped, loudly. "Jonah, how could you do that?' This hurt her more so. "That's your flesh and blood. How could you betray him like that?"

The disappointed look in her eyes wounded Jonah severely. "I could blame it on drugs and being high, Kayla, but it would be a lie. That is the lie I told Joel. However, I was selfish. I hated the woman who came between us. She was not good enough for Joel, either. Truthfully, Joel did not need me anymore. He did not respect me anymore. He left me for her." The truth hurt.

"Oh, Jonah, Joel didn't leave you, I'm sure. You said so yourself that you were living a different life from his. Joel couldn't accept your lifestyle, but he still loved you."

"I know that now," his voice was wobbly, his eyes watered. "I told you, I was a hothead."

"Yes, you were." Kayla reach up and wiped his tears away as best she could.

"Am I going to lose you?" His heart faltered.

"No, Jonah. That is all in the past. I love you for who you are now."

He pulled her into his arms and held her delicately. "I love you more now than I did a moment ago, and I didn't think that was possible." It boggled his mind how someone so sweet, pure, and lovely could be interested even the slightest bit in someone like him.

"There aren't any more secrets, are there?" she asked.

"No."

"Good, because I don't think I could handle anymore right now," she smiled.

"You still love me?" He just wanted to hear her say the

words.

"I still love you."

He kissed her passionately.

Gathering his wits, Jonah stepped back, trying to maintain some form of self-control. "What do you have to tell me?"

Kayla lowered her head, shamefaced. Tenderly, Jonah cupped her chin with the palms of his hands. "Don't do that. You can face me, Kayla. You can always count on me to stand by you. Just tell me."

"I'm pregnant."

Jonah felt a sucker punch right to the gut. The fact that she had been with someone else surprised him. She did not seem the type. "Wow!" His eyes immediately went to her midsection. To him, Kayla was washboard flat.

"Wow is right."

"How far along?"

"About six weeks." Kayla bravely stood, swallowing her pain and holding back her tears.

Jonah was blown away. The realization that she was carrying another man's baby did not lessen his opinion of the beauty in his arms.

"Wow!" he repeated. "And the father?"

"He died in Iraq. He did not know anything about me being pregnant. We were together only once."

"Did you love him?"

"No. It was a mistake. I was lonely," she admitted.

He understood. "How do your parents feel about it?"

"They don't know. They will probably disown me for sure."

"That's crazy."

"My father has high expectations for me, Jonah. It is hard

living up to his expectations. He expects me to be perfect and to live a perfect life. All my life, I felt that if I did not walk a straight and narrow line, they would get rid of me. I was always under so much pressure, to be the perfect little girl for fear they'd take me back to the orphanage."

"That's too much pressure for any kid." He held her tighter, feeling her pain. "Well, you don't have to worry about that anymore. You got me and I'll help you with the baby."

"Jonah, I don't want to hurt my parents," she sniffed. "They gave me a home. They adopted me, picking me out of so many other babies. I just want them to love me for me, even if I made a mistake."

"Marry me, Kayla?" He proposed without thinking.

"What? You can't be serious."

"I'm very serious. I believe God brought us together. So, why wait? I may not be able to give you the lifestyle you are accustomed to, but I promise to take care of you, Kayla—you and the baby. If you can look beyond my past, I can promise you that we will have a happy future together. It may not be all good, but the good will definitely outweigh the bad."

Kayla's heart was reeling faster than racecars on a track. She smiled at him as if he had hung the moon in the sky just for her benefit. "You're not just asking me because of my parents, are you, or the baby?"

"I'm asking you because I love you and I want this baby to have my name. I want us to be a family."

"Yes!"

"Whew!" He picked her up and swung her around. "Oh, I'm sorry. I'm not hurting you or the baby?" Jonah gently put her down.

"No, I'm fine," she laughed. "I'm so happy, Jonah."

"Me too!" Jonah captured her in his arms again and sealed his proposal with a kiss, which held promises of a loving marriage.

"I'm not going out with Leon tonight," Kayla said after coming up for air. "I can't. It wouldn't be right."

"It's up to you, Kayla. I'm okay with you breaking the man's heart," he said and winked.

"When he comes and gets me, I'm just going to tell him I'm engaged."

"But you don't have a ring," Jonah pulled away. "Oh, but wait…" He thought about his aunt's box. He remembered seeing jewelry at the bottom. "Can we go now? I want to go to Aunt Alice's." Jonah could never think of the home as his anymore.

"Sure, but I don't need a ring, Jonah." She snuggled close to him as they walked to the car. "All I need is you."

Irresistibly, he claimed her lips again. "See, that's why we got to hurry up and marry or I'm going to burn for sure," he teased. "You're dangerous, Kayla. Very dangerous."

On the way to their aunt's neighborhood, the two rode in silence. Kayla feared that Jonah was having second thoughts. "Jonah, if you want to change your mind, I understand. Everything is happening so quickly."

"Never! Are you having second thoughts?"

"Never!"

Jonah dropped Kayla off at Aunt Mae's home before going to Aunt Alice's home alone. He needed some private time to uncover the contents of the box.

In his Aunt's room, Jonah sat on her bed and unearthed the secret treasures that his Aunt Alice had left behind. First, he pulled out her treasured Bible. Running his fingers over the cover, he pulled the Bible to his chest, cherishing his aunt's most precious gift. It was more than sentimental value, it was holy. "Aunt Alice," he swallowed hard, "I promise to read this daily, and to seek God's wisdom and counsel through His Written Word." Putting the Bible aside, Jonah pulled out a scrapbook. Opening it, he sighed, beholding Joel's wedding picture. Looking at a near image of himself, Jonah allowed the tears to fall freely. His chest felt constricted. Trembling with fear, he turned the pages. Joel appeared so happy, but much thinner than Jonah had ever seen him. *I wonder if he's healthy. He was always so sickly.* His bride was beautiful. The way they looked at each other revealed a true love story. In the back of the book was an index card with Joel's address and phone number. *I wish I could have been there. I wish Joel would have wanted me to be there.* Not having a relationship with his brother left an emptiness inside of Jonah that he could not conceal. Raw hurt ate as his soul. Closing the scrapbook, Jonah laid eyes on Aunt Alice's ring, it was a family heirloom. He remembered her saying it was the only thing she had of value. The ring was an antique sterling silver ring, adorned with Tahitian pearls, white sapphire, blue topaz, and pink tourmaline accents. *I hope this is not too old-fashioned for Kayla. She probably wants something more modern. Later, I will buy her the diamond of her choice.* Jonah admired the exquisite ring. It was unique, and more valuable than any monetary amount. Unfortunately, Jonah wouldn't be able to give Kayla the ring tonight. Aunt's Alice's fingers were rather chubby and larger than Kayla's. He would have to have the ring resized to fit Kayla's petite fingers.

Lastly, Jonah opened the sealed brown envelope. To his surprise, it contained five one-hundred-dollar bills. "Aunt Alice was holding back!" Jonah chuckled, wiping his eyes.

Often she said, 'Money don't grow on trees, boy. I don't have any money to give you.' She probably knew I would buy drugs with it or do something stupid with it." There were two letters, one addressed to Joel, and the other addressed to Jonah. As he began to read the letter with his name on it, tears flowed like a river down the sides of his face.

Jonah,

I have said all that I really need to say to you. I have no regrets. I have no unspoken nuggets of wisdom to give you. I have lived my life. I have raised you and Joel to know Christ Jesus and now that He is your Lord and Savior, I am at peace. My soul is happy and truly, I am ready to see Jesus. Oh, what a time it is going to be. My heart rejoices that I will see both you and Joel again. My only prayer that has not been answered yet, but I have no doubt will be answered, is that you and Joel reunite and love one another as you once did when you first came to live with me. Nothing could tear you two apart then and I believe in the future, the bond will be even stronger. When the time is right, and you will know it, give Joel the letter. Joel needs you, Jonah, more than you could ever know. He really needs you.

Jonah, I left you the house because I knew you needed a place to stay when you got out. But, I do not want you to stay in it because this neighborhood is not fit for you anymore. It is worse than ever. Sell it if you can or donate it to the church. Use the $500 to start over. Find a good, godly woman and marry her. Love her, have children, and raise them to know our Savior. Oh, Jonah, you have a good heart. And just like Joel is preaching the Gospel, I do believe you are supposed to do the same. Do not let your past, keep you from being all that God has called you to be...a Minister of the Gospel. Walk in the shoes He has designed for you and not the shoes of the past. I know you have been wounded in the prison. I know you feel shamed by it. But do not be, Jonah. You could not control what happened to you. Yes, I know things. God spoke to me often about you and told me to pray. Well, Jonah prayer brought you through then and prayer will bring you through now and again and again.

118

Never rely on yourself, but always rely on God. Be happy Jonah! Be free! It is nothing like freedom! Nope, nothing like it. I love you, Jonah. You lit up my world from the moment you and Joel came to live with me. My light is still shining.

With all my love, Aunt Alice.

Such priceless words of wisdom and guidance by the woman who had guided his footsteps from a young age. She had left a legacy to Jonah, which could not be contained in a box, but in his heart to share with the generations yet to come.

CHAPTER 12

Joel

Meanwhile, three hundred miles way, God was stirring the pot in Joel's life as well. Joel Bates ministered to a large congregation of over a thousand members, not counting visitors or regular attendees. Now in his third year of pastoring the flock, membership had doubled. Joel was on fire for God. He was a mouthpiece used to teach God's people how to live godly lives and to walk in their God-ordained purpose.

On the surface, all appeared perfect in Joel's life. He had a good wife, a good job, was now a full-time pastor, and would soon be a first-time dad. He had a good home, and seemed to have a good life. However, in the past year, Joel had been experiencing inner turmoil. He struggled with hiding his past. For years, Joel attempted to cover his wounded heart by staying busy, preaching God's Word, doing good unto others, and living as best he could as an epistle, known and read by all men—written not with ink, but by the Spirit of the living God, not on tablets of stone but on tablets of flesh, that is, of the heart. Yet, it didn't keep the dreams of Jonah from interrupting his sleep. It could not heal his broken heart, which was constantly raw with both painful and pleasurable memories of the twins' younger years.

Furthermore, Joel's health wasn't up to par. After graduating from college, Joel's health took a nosedive. His kidneys were failing and he had to undergo dialysis. For five years, he had been going through dialysis, two to three times a week. Now, the dialysis wasn't really helping him, just sustaining him. Joel's only hope was a kidney transplant or a divine intervention of the Master's Hand—a miracle healing by the Healer. There was a probable kidney match, his twin, Jonah. However, Joel wanted nothing from Jonah, even knowing that Jonah could save his life. Jonah was, for all practical purposes, dead. He could never rely on Jonah, but he could always rely on his faith in God. Thus, today's message was hard for Pastor Joel. Feeling rather weak early Sunday morning, Joel called his associate pastor, Jerry Mack, to deliver the message. The Spirit was swaying the message right into Pastor's Joel's bruised heart.

"When the Son of Man comes in His glory, and all the holy angels with Him, then He will sit on the throne of His glory. All the nations will be gathered before Him, and He will separate them one from another, as a shepherd divides his sheep from the goats," Minister Mack began quoting the familiar passage of Scripture from Mathew 25. "And He will set the sheep on His right hand, but the goats on the left. Then the King will say to those on His right hand, 'Come, you blessed of My Father, inherit the kingdom prepared for you from the foundation of the world: for I was hungry and you gave Me food; I was thirsty and you gave Me drink; I was a stranger and you took Me in; I was naked and you clothed Me; I was sick and you visited Me; I was in prison and you came to Me.'

"Now, we know in reading further that the righteous people were slightly confused. They said, 'Lord, we didn't see you hungry, thirsty, homeless, naked, or sick or in prison. We didn't do anything of those things for you.' And Jesus simply said, 'When you did it for the least of these, my people, my children, you did it to Me.'

"In other words, what Jesus is simply saying is that we are His church, Christ being the Head, and we, being the Body of Christ, are one. What affects my children, affects Me. When you take care of My people, I will take care of you. Sisters and brothers, every day we have the availability to show kindness to our fellow man. When we show kindness to others, we are showing kindness to Christ Jesus."

Joel squirmed in his seat on the pulpit, looking at his wife. She knew that this message was hitting home. It was sucker punching him right in the depths of his soul. Wiping his face with the cloth, Joel couldn't stifle his own inner struggles. The Word was convicting him.

"Which are you today? Are you the sheep, or the goat? Are you helping others out or sending them on their merry way? Now I know this world is unsafe and you cannot just be taking in a stranger or a homeless person. However, there is a way you can help them. You can show compassion, instead of turning your nose up at them. You can feed them. You can try to find them some help. Now it may inconvenience you some, but imagine your Heavenly Father looking down on you and just smiling, saying, 'That's my son, that's my daughter! They are not just talking the talk, but they are walking the walk— that I have already walked! That's my sheep!'"

Did you visit me in prison?

Joel cringed. He couldn't push back the inner voice. God wanted to change Joel today. He wanted him to practice what he preached. Sure, Joel was a righteous man, but in the flesh dwells no good thing. Joel's flesh kept him from releasing his brother. He was imprisoned by un-forgiveness.

Today if you hear my voice, harden not your heart. Forgive, Joel. Forgive and you will be forgiven.

But...

"In closing, I ask that you truly remember the Words found in Isaiah 58. We are supposed to be the Repairer of the Breech - the Restorer of the Streets. We are supposed to feed the hungry, help the homeless, clothed the naked, share our food with those that are starving, visit those that are locked up and are bound. Jesus came to set the captive free." He paused, giving the congregation time to let the Truth soak into their spirits. "Are you a sheep or a goat?" Pastor Mack asked the questions again, jarring Joel to search his own heart. Pastor Mack looked over to Pastor Joel to signify that he was finished. Rising from his seat, after he embraced his friend Jerry, Joel went to the pulpit.

The congregation watched as Pastor Joel stood silently at the podium. Words wouldn't come. Everything became cloudy. The color drained from his light-skinned complexion. Joel was paler than a ghost.

Then suddenly....

Darkness hazed over Joel. The lights went out. Joel crumpled to the floor.

"Joel!" his pregnant wife, Yasha rushed to the pulpit.

"Pray, congregation!" Minister Jerry Mack admonished.

"Call for an ambulance," Yasha whispered to one of the deacons. She knew her husband was in serious trouble. Silently and fervently, Yasha prayed for God's mercy and healing balm to once again cure Joel's heart and his body.

Yasha waited anxiously in the emergency room with Minister Mack and several other members of the church. Like Joel, Yasha had no other family. After her parents were killed in a plane crash, she had been alone since the age of eighteen. Her aunts and uncles, on both sides, were still living in Liberia. Those that surrounded her in the waiting room, the church folks, were Joel and Yasha's family.

"It's going to be alright," Doris, Minister Mack's wife, whispered while rubbing Yasha's hands. "Doctor Jesus is with him."

"I know," Yasha sniffed. "I just wish someone would tell us what's going on. It's been over an hour. I just need to see my Joel."

"You will in time," Doris encouraged. "You just can't be worrying. You've got your baby to think about and you know what Pastor Joel would say. Why worry if you are going to pray, and why pray if you going to worry?"

"I can't tell you how many times he's said that," Yasha smiled. "Joel needs a kidney transplant, Doris. That's the only thing that is going to save him."

"God created the kidneys. He surely can give him a new one." Doris firmly believed this. "Now whether He does it surgically by man, or miraculously by His mighty power, is up to God. We're just going to have to trust Him to do it His way and in His perfect timing."

"But Joel doesn't have much time." The floodgates opened, Yasha couldn't contain her fears or her tears. "He may...not... see our baby."

"Hush that," Doris gently chided. "You've got to have faith, Yasha. Whatever reason you and Joel are going through this, you both have to keep the faith even in the most trying times. God will see you through. God will bring Pastor Joel out. I believe God is trying to take Pastor Joel to another level, but there is something Pastor Joel has to do or learn from this."

Yasha immediately stood when she recognized the doctor coming toward them.

"How is he?" she impatiently asked.

"He's conscious now," the doctor replied. "Can I speak with you in private?"

"It's okay." Yasha looked around at those standing by her side. Her church family filled the space. Counted in the number were: Doris and Jerry Mack, Vanessa, the choir director and dear friend, Duran the Minister of Music, Sharon and Philana (ushers), Sherry, the Sunday School leader, Alanna, the youth director, Deacon Harvey and Deaconess Erica, and the church mother, Patricia Grant. Mother Grant was a praying woman, no doubt she was sending up umpteen prayers to God on Joel's behalf. "We are family."

"Mr. Bates needs a kidney transplant, immediately," Dr. Thomasina Benson instructed. The committed doctor had been overseeing Joel's medical care for the past five years. She had become an extended member of the family to the Bates'. Recently, her family had started attending the church, whenever her schedule permitted. "There is not a match on the waiting list, as you know. Are you sure he doesn't have any living relatives, a sister or brother, or perhaps an uncle?"

"He has a twin brother," Yasha hesitated. "But I'm not sure he can. He's in prison, I think."

"We need to find out for sure," the doctor advised. "He may be our only chance."

"God is our only chance," Minister Jerry interjected. "God is able to miraculously heal Pastor Joel. When all else fails, faith prevails."

"I, too, believe," Dr. Benson acknowledged. "But God also uses man in the healing process. I suggest Mrs. Bates that you try to find your husband's twin brother and continue to pray for a miracle."

"Can I see him now?"

"Sure, but only for a short while, and I'm afraid no other visitors will be allowed right now. We're going to admit him."

Saying goodbye to her extended family, Yasha rushed away to be with her husband. *Lord, please let Joel live to raise this baby! Please!*

Joel's eyes opened the minute he sensed his wife's presence. "Don't cry," his voice was low and trembling.

"Oh Joel! I am so worried," she admitted. "I trust God, but..."

"Help your unbelief," he understood.

"Dr. Benson confirmed that you need a kidney transplant immediately," Yasha said aloud. "We've got to try to find Jonah."

"No!" his voice was stronger.

"But Joel, he's your only chance."

"God will heal me."

"Didn't you hear the message today? Didn't it do anything to you? Convict you or..."

"Yes," he nodded. "I'm a goat."

"Huh?"

"When it comes to Jonah, I'm a goat." His eyes watered, tears sliding down his thin cheeks. "I didn't visit him in prison."

"God will forgive you, Joel," she caressed his face. "And so will Jonah."

"Jonah hurt me." Still Joel ached inside. Just as his body

needed healing, so did his heart. The message today had opened and peeled back the scab over his heart, causing fresh soreness. "I can't seem to forget."

"But you can forgive, Joel. You have to. You need Jonah."

What his wife said was truth. The realization paralyzed him, leaving Joel disabled in several ways.

"Can't you remember the good times with Jonah? I know that you shared a lot together in your younger years." Yasha was grasping at straws, anything to awaken her husband from the cruelness of Jonah's betrayal. "For all we know, Jonah could have changed. Can't you give him another chance?"

"I forgive him, Yasha, I do," Joel breathed in and out, trying to push the wind through his lungs, so he could breathe easier. "But I don't want him in my life. He can't be trusted. Every time I threw out the…rope…for him to…grab on….he ended…up….hanging…me."

"Please, Joel," Yasha was desperate, "please for our baby's sake, let me find Jonah. We all need him," she cried.

"I…don't want," he swallowed trying to muster strength to go on. "I don't want to see him out…of…need. I need time… to deal with this…and time to heal…my heart."

"Joel, Honey, we don't have time," Yasha spoke the truth. "Don't harden your heart. Live out what you preach every day, Honey. Jonah is your twin and…well, he owes you that much."

"I'm tired," Joel closed his eyes. "I'm really tired."

❈❈❈

In the interim, while Joel was in the hospital, fighting for his life, Jonah was pacing the living room floor, waiting for Kayla to return from her date with Leon, three hours ago. All kinds of thoughts invaded his mind.

Maybe she's changed her mind about marrying me.

Leon is a doctor, not an ex-con. He has more to offer her than me.

I wonder if they are having an intimate moment.

Will she come back?

Maybe Leon wants to marry her.

I'm not good enough for Kayla. Maybe it's good that she is with Leon and not me.

Pray for Joel. He needs you!

The sudden groaning in his spirit startled Jonah.

"Where did that come from?"

Joel needs you.

"Joel doesn't need me!"

Pray! Joel needs you!

Twin's intuition made Jonah drop to his knees in the middle of the floor and pray for his brother. Fear of Kayla leaving him took a backseat to the pain in his soul. This wasn't the first time Jonah's intuition kicked in, signaling that his brother was going through something. Usually, he physically felt Joel's pain without even knowing what was going on. He sensed within that his brother was hurting. While locked up on prison, time and time again, Jonah knew that his brother was going through something, but tried to overlook it, brush it aside. He even asked his Aunt Alice about it, but she kept tight-lipped, making him believe all the more that something wasn't right with Joel. Jonah stifled those intuitions since Joel wanted nothing to do with him.

"Joel is in trouble! Lord, help him. Whatever it is, help him!" Physical pain avalanched upon his chest, nearly suffocating him. Jonah felt weak and ill. Unknown to Jonah, he was feeling the symptoms of what his twin Joel was undergoing at that very moment. "Lord, Joel doesn't need me or want me, but he surely needs You! Whatever is going on, wherever he may be, save my brother! Please save Joel!"

CHAPTER 13

Wedding Plans

"I'm back!" Kayla entered the home.

"Where were you?" Jonah snapped.

"What do you mean? You know I was with Leon."

"It's been over three hours," he looked at his watch. "Three hours and twenty minutes to be exact."

She noticed his red eyes. *Was he that worried over me?* "Jonah, please calm down. We just had dinner. I explained to him that I couldn't see him anymore and, well, we just talked. After all, he flew here to see me, I couldn't just eat and run, that would be impolite."

"Impolite!" Jonah repeated, sarcasm oozing from his lips.

"Jonah, what is wrong with you?" She reached up and rested her hand on the side of his cheek. It was obvious that he was mad, but why? "There is nothing between Leon and I. You know that."

"Do I?" he snatched her hand away. "Perhaps you have changed your mind about us. After being with Leon, the doctor, you probably don't see a need to wed an ex-con! He can provide you with the life you are accustomed to. The baby will have a father who you won't be ashamed of. I knew that this wouldn't work!" Jonah spewed off indictments, wanting to

131

break up with her before she rejected him. "You're a princess and I'm a pauper! It's okay that you woke up from the fantasy. I understand that I was your project—something you could fix. But, Kayla I'm not broken! I am who I am!"

His words cut her deeply. The corner of her eyes welled with tears. She studied his face, and then attempted to walk away.

Witnessing her hurt, Jonah reached for Kayla, capturing her shoulders, he turned her around to face him.

"I'm not like that," Kayla sniffed. "You've judged me harshly, and wrongly. Maybe you're right...we shouldn't wed."

"I didn't say that," Jonah wiped her tears.

"You insinuated it," Kayla ached, uncertainty displayed in her eyes. "What happened in our past doesn't determine who we are now or who we will become."

"I was jealous and afraid you'd changed your mind about marrying me." It squashed Jonah's macho ego to admit such a thing.

"There was no need for you to be jealous. Leon and I were never a couple. And the minute I told him I was pregnant, his feelings for me turned off like a light switch. He just wanted to be friends. So we talked, mostly about my parents."

"Oh," he drew closer. "I apologize, Kayla. I just don't want to lose you."

"You won't lose me, Jonah."

Reaching to the back of Kayla's head, Jonah attempted to unpin the tight bun. He preferred her long tresses to hang loosely. Kayla helped him. Running his fingers through her hair, Jonah leaned over and kissed her forehead, touching her softly as if to see if she was real or not. Their eyes locked.

Their hearts beat in sync. Doubt drifted away like clouds, slow and soft.

Brushing his lips hungrily upon hers, Kayla's toes curled, her knees went feeble, her pulse raced. Encircling her hands around his neck for support, surely Kayla felt she would swoon in his arms. The kiss intensified, sealing their commitment to one another in a way that words could not. Seemingly, time stood still for the couple yet again. Finding strength to resist temptation and stay chaste before God, Jonah stepped back, looking deep into her eyes. "I love you."

"I love you, Jonah." Kayla's eyes danced with the truth. Unsure if she should tread on unfamiliar territory, especially since the two had made up. "Were you crying before I came home?"

He looked away. His thoughts returned to Joel.

"No secrets, remember, Jonah?"

With agony, he faced Kayla. "Joel."

She waited for him to say more.

"Something is not right," he swallowed. "I feel it here," Jonah positioned his hand over his heart.

"Let's find him, Jonah. It's the right thing to do."

"Joel doesn't want to be found, at least not by me. He said he never wanted to see me again. And when Aunt Alice died, he didn't even tell me." The memory still hurt. "He didn't even tell me, Kayla. That proves he wants nothing to do with me."

"It's been a long time, Jonah. Things could have changed by now."

"I doubt it. It's best to let bygones be bygones."

"If you say so," Kayla said with her mouth. However, her heart didn't agree.

Taking her hand, Jonah led Kayla to the couch. "Now,

we've got some plans to make. First things first. You still want to marry in two weeks?"

"Of course."

"Do you want to go to courthouse?"

"No. I want Pastor Goodwin to marry us," Kayla answered. "The first lady said we were going to marry, so I think they both will be in agreement with our marriage."

"We'll talk to them next Sunday, after church service."

"Sounds good."

"Kayla, where are we going to live?"

She pondered his question some time before responding. "We could stay here, after I make arrangements to leave my job. I can't just up and leave," she went on to explain. "I have several patients that depend on me. The hospital is depending on my extended services. Plus, my father is depending on me."

"So, what you're saying is that we get married, but live in separate cities?" Jonah frowned.

"Only for a little while," she timidly replied. "I will come here on the weekends."

"How long will this arrangement be for, Kayla?"

"I know the wife is supposed to live wherever her husband is, but Jonah, are you willing to move to Macon City? My job is so important to me. I have made connections with people and they depend on my care."

"I'm willing to move, Kayla, but not right away. Steven Hutto has been so good to me. I want to stay a little while, save money, and then hopefully transfer. I believe there is a Hutto's Department Store in Macon City."

"There is!" Kayla clapped her hands like a happy schoolgirl.

"Okay, I'll talk to Steven tomorrow. In the meantime, I guess we will see each other on the weekends. It's going to be a long five days for sure."

"But we'll make up for lost time." Her eyes twinkled.

"Making up can be a whole lot of fun." He squeezed her, playfully smooching her face. Then he became serious. "I don't want us to stay here," Jonah stated firmly. "This neighborhood isn't safe. I'm sure Steven will let us stay in the apartment until we can afford to move. I can't afford much right now, but if you stick with me, Kayla, I promise to take care of you and our baby."

"Our baby." Her smile widened. "I like that, Jonah. We are going to be happy together. I'm already happy."

"It may not be the penthouse, Kayla, but it sure won't be the poorhouse."

"As long as I'm with you, Jonah, it is the penthouse." Kayla boldly kissed him, reassuring him of her unconditional love for him.

"Stop that!" Jonah teased. "Unless you want to skip the wedding and go straight to the honeymoon."

"Nah!" She laughed. "I'll wait."

"Well, we better separate and call it a night. You in the bedroom and me on the couch."

"There is another bedroom, Jonah."

"Too close! No need to sleep right next door to temptation. I need all the space I can get right about now. As a matter of fact, I think I'll go take me a cold shower." *Something I thought I would never say again.*

"What time are you leaving in the morning?"

"Since I am not flying now, I need to be on the road by five o'clock so I can be in Macon around eight, turn in the rental and get my car."

"I'm *gonna* miss you," Jonah turned to her.

"Not more than I'll miss you."

Tempting to run back into her arms, Jonah shook his head. "Cold shower! Goodnight, my love."

"Goodnight, Love!"

✕✕✕

Jonah had a lot on his mind Monday morning while working at Hutto's. After another restless night, waking up several times from unpleasant dreams, Jonah was physically tired. Only these dreams weren't about his past at Manchester, or Nixon, they were about his brother, Joel. Joel was falling down a hole, then a pit, then a tunnel. Joel was screaming for help and no matter how hard Jonah tried to get to him, he could not. He could not save him. Such a nightmare was worse than dreaming about Nixon. Jonah woke up in a sweat, his heart pounding, his lungs deflating and his spirit nearly crushed. Something was wrong and Jonah felt decapitated. There was nothing he could really do. Joel made it perfectly clear that he wanted nothing to do with him and he never wanted to see him again.

Although Jonah was torn, he owed Joel that much—to respect his wishes.

Maybe it is just a dream! Maybe it is my guilt that is eating me up! Maybe Joel is going through something right now, but God will bring him through. God does not need me to intervene, surely.

Joel needs you!

Jonah pushed back the beseeching unction. *There is nothing I can do!*

Jonah had to deal with the fact that Kayla had left. Knowing that he would not see his fiancé until Friday night was discomfiting. Finally, he had someone in his life who loved him for who he was without expecting him to be perfect. Kayla didn't expect him to buy her things or do things to prove he loved her. That is how it was with Dana. As long as he lived the fast life, taking her to the clubs, partying, buying her things, being the king of the street with PJ, all was well. He had to sells drugs and do illegal things to keep Dana interested. There were many other females like Dana, who loved the street life and all that went along with it. That was all Jonah knew before prison. Now he had Kayla. Sweet, loving, compassionate, beautiful Kayla. Truly, God had smiled on him when He caused their paths not just to cross, but also to connect.

Why You blessed me so God, I will never know! I thank You for the gift of love and for my bride-to-be!

He, who finds a wife, finds a good thing and obtains favor from the Lord.

Thank you, God!

"Hey Jonah," Steven Hutto was making his rounds on Monday. "How is it going?"

"Good, sir."

"I'm hearing good things about you, Jonah. You are doing a great job. Keep working like you are and before you know it you'll be supervisor material."

"Oh, thank you," Jonah grinned.

"No, thank you. We need strong men like you working at Hutto's," Steven commended. "Everything at the duplex alright?"

"Yes, but I needed to ask your permission about having someone else staying with me." Jonah timidly approached his boss.

Steven was instantly against it. "Well that's not a part of

the deal, Jonah."

"I know, but I'm getting married."

"Married?"

"Yes, I was hoping to speak with you on my lunch break about it." Jonah paused, looking around. Surprisingly he did not have any customers to attend to.

"Let's talk now," Steven was more than curious. He was concerned that somehow Jonah was making wrong choices that could end him back where he started. "This seems a little fast to me. One minute you did not have a decent place to live or a job and now, you are thinking on taking the responsibility of another person."

"Kayla is a great woman," Jonah was ready to defend his decision.

"Then wait until you get yourself more established."

"She's pregnant."

"I see…but still…" Steven automatically assumed Jonah was the father.

"I want to do the right thing, Steven. It's important and I love her."

"Love or lust?" Steven did not hold back.

"I know it seems crazy to you and if I were in your shoes, I'd think the same, but it's love. I love Kayla more than I love myself. I'll put my life on the line for her, just like Jesus did for me. I want to be with Kayla for the rest of my life. She's a diamond, Steven." The more Jonah talked the more excited he became. "She makes me smile. She makes me feel complete, humanly speaking. She is incredible, Steven. Absolutely incredible, and I thank God for such a gift. I want to marry her. I have to marry her—I need to marry her!"

Steven watched Jonah, seeing something he understood

and had experienced firsthand. "You're whipped! You've got it bad," Steven chuckled. "And my family thought I was whipped. I'm a late bloomer, I married my wife two years ago and I'm still whipped!"

Jonah chuckled. "Then you understand."

He nodded. "So, you want to live in the duplex."

"Yes, but just on the weekends after we are married. Kayla will keep her job and travel here on Fridays. And I was hoping that maybe in a couple of months, or however long you see fit, maybe I can transfer to the store in Macon City. Kayla's job is there. She's a counselor."

"Wow!" Steven ran his fingers through his beard. "My brother, Lamad, manages the store in Macon City. I am sure he will be glad to have you. Although, I will be sad to lose you. You are already a key player here. But I understand. You have to do what works for you and your wife. It's all about compromise."

"I need change," Jonah acknowledged. "I'm not living in my old neighborhood, but I'm still too close to it. Besides, I really feel God in all of this—the marriage and the move."

"We sure don't want to get in the way of God's plans," Steven smiled, noticing a customer headed their way. "Go ahead and take care of the customer and we'll talk later. In the meantime, I will talk to Lamad."

"Thanks, Steven, for understanding."

"No problem," he started to walk away. "I think Shane will be proud. Just keep paying-it- forward."

"Oh, I will! That's a promise!"

CHAPTER 14

Drew and Kathryn Lovett

"I've missed you so much," Kayla reclined in the velvet, bronze-finished chaise lounge positioned by her bedroom window, which had a beautiful view of the backyard. The scenic view was a live portrait of a garden, arrayed with various flowers, a manicured plush green yard, an extended pool, and a screened-in gazebo. "I'll be there tomorrow."

"Thank God! I don't think I could take another day," Jonah chuckled. "How in the world did we ever survive without each other?"

"We didn't know that such love existed," Kayla stated. "At least not for me."

"Absolutely. Kayla, I spent all these years trying to find love in other people. Trying to fill the void in my heart for my mother, father, and even Joel. Though I wanted love, I feared love so much, I only allowed myself to experience an imitation of love. I gave what I got, which wasn't much," he paused at the truth seeping through his open heart. "I dated women who were just like me—selfish, broken, lost, bitter, and willing to do anything to satisfy the emptiness. But it never did. The more I tried, the more I kept coming up short. Thus, the cycle kept repeating itself. You keep doing the same thing over and over again, expecting different results."

"My father calls it insanity," Kayla replied.

"Your father is right about that. Kayla, I was really a *bad* person. I am not just saying it to being saying it. I did some bad things to the women I dated," Jonah confessed.

"It doesn't matter to me. It's all in the past."

"I did horrible things to men as well. I know that God has forgiven me, and truly I am working on forgiving myself, but I don't want you to think that the man you see or hear," he chuckled, "is some sort of saint. I have a lot of issues to work through."

"Jonah, so do I. We will work through them together with God."

"You're right. Just be patient with my, Kayla. That's all I ask."

"I promise, Jonah."

"How are your parents feeling about you leaving today?"

"I have to go see my father in a few. He summoned me to his office."

"Stand strong. You're a grown woman and you have a right to be happy."

"Yes, I do."

."Oh by the way, Pastor Reggie Goodwin called me back and said for us to meet him at the church around noon Saturday."

"Good! So, is he going to marry us?"

"He says he needs to speak with us first, in person," Jonah answered. "He seemed open. I think he may have to do marriage counseling first."

"But that could push the marriage back for a month or more," Kayla sighed. "If so, then we'll just go to courthouse."

"Let's just see what he says. You deserve a church wedding. It may not be fancy, and only the two of us…"

"Lisa is coming!" Kayla exclaimed happily. "She is going to be my matron of honor." Kayla had stayed up late convincing Lisa that she had not lost her mind by marrying a stranger. Lisa agreed to fly out to support her best friend's wedding ceremony, even if she didn't totally agree with it.

"I'm surprised she wants to be a part of the beauty marrying the beast."

"She's not like that, Jonah. She just thinks it's too fast."

"So, she doesn't know you're pregnant?"

"Yes. I can trust her. She'll never tell a soul, not even her husband."

"I guess it doesn't matter. No one will stop me from being a real dad to our baby."

Kayla loved him even more for that.

"Jonah, I don't want our baby to feel like a stepchild," she paused thinking about her own life. "Don't get me wrong, I know my parents love me but I always felt like an adopted child. Never just Kayla Lovett, daughter of Drew and Kathryn Lovett. I do not want that for our child. He or she should feel loved, accepted, wanted, and needed. Not coming into the world with something hanging over his or her head. I know that all adopted people don't feel like that, and many have wonderful experiences, but I just want our child to know that we are parents that love him or her—period."

"I promise you, our child will know that I am the father by my actions. We have the same blood; the blood of Jesus will always connect us deeper than fleshly blood. I'm looking forward to being a daddy."

Kayla's heart swelled with pride and joy. "Because of you,

I'm looking forward to being a mom."

"I have a big surprise for you when you get here tomorrow night."

"I love surprises!" Kayla followed his lead in the conversation. "Give me a hint!"

"Nope!"

"Come on Jonah!"

"Let's just say that it's ancient."

"Ancient," she frowned. "What does that mean?"

"The quicker you get here, the quicker you'll find out," Jonah teased.

"Not fair!"

"Who says life is fair?"

⚘⚘⚘

While finishing some paperwork for her clients, Kathryn Lovett entered Kayla's office. "Drew is ready to see you." Kathryn was the office manager, for all practical purposes. Making up her own schedule, Kathryn handle the operations of the Lovett's Restoration Plastic Surgery Center.

Kayla looked up at her mom. She was a beautiful woman, but her appearance had changed so much over the past few years. Trying to preserve her youthful look, Kathryn had undergone several surgeries. Just turning fifty-four, Kathryn looked to be in her mid-thirties. People often thought of Kayla and Kathryn as sisters. Previously, she had undergone blepharoplasty to correct her droopy eyelids and remove excess skin on her eyes; rhytidectomy to eradicate wrinkles under the eyes, between the nose and lips and the fatty, droopy skin under the jaw; lip enhancement, injecting collagen into her lips making them much fuller; rhinoplasty, reshaping what Kathryn saw as crooked nose; liposuction from her mid-section and thighs; and breast implants, taking her from a B to D. Now her mother was considering having a brow lift, to revive her facial features. Kathryn declared she saw new wrinkles, and she did not like looking tired.

Everything about Kathryn seemed so superficial to Kayla as she looked at her mother. Kathryn was a tall woman with long legs and a waistline to die for. No doubt, she was very attractive and wanted to stay that way, but at what cost? Her mother seemed addicted to surgery. On the other hand, maybe she was trying to keep up with her younger husband.

"I'm almost ready," Kayla replied. "Mom, I wish you would reconsider having the brow lift. You do not need it. You're beautiful."

"Thank you, Honey," Kathryn sat down, "but I have to do this for me. I am starting to look old and I do not like it. It's perfectly safe. After all, I'm married to the best plastic surgeon in the South."

"You have had way too many surgeries, Mother. Maybe you're addicted to surgery and should see somebody."

"That's insane," Kathryn rejected her daughter's feelings. "As office manager and part owner of Lovett's Restoration Plastic Surgery Center, I simply have to look my best. It's important that I look the part and feel the part."

"But you're looking different." Carefully, Kayla confronted the issue that had been bothering her for some time. "You are changing who you are. Just look back at your earlier pictures and you'll see that it's not that you are looking younger, but you're looking like a totally different person."

"And what's wrong with that? Your father says I'm more beautiful now than when we married."

That says a lot! "Just pray about it first."

"Pray!" her mother frowned. "I don't need to pray about this. I'm having the surgery." Kathryn stood. "And what's all this about praying. You don't even go to church."

"It's not about church, mother. It's about accepting Jesus Christ into my heart," Kayla hesitated to say more after seeing the look of astonishment upon her mother's face. "I am a Christian, and for the record, I do go to church every Sunday, near Holly Hill."

"Holly Hill!" Kathryn repeated with disgust. "That place is for heathens, and that's why your father wants to talk to you. He will not abide by you going back and forth to that forsaken place. It makes no sense! Church people are lazy people. Looking for some God to help them when they should help themselves!"

"Church can't save a person, Mother. Only Jesus can save. People go to church in search of finding something to fill the void in their lives—a void that only Jesus can fill. The sick need a Healer. The sinner needs a Savior, just as the lost sheep needs a Shepherd."

"You sound like one of those holy fanatics! We didn't raise you that way," Kathryn stood at the door. "You better hurry. Drew hates to be kept waiting."

Drew hates a lot of things!

With dread, Kayla strolled to her father's massive office. Every time she visited his office, Kayla felt like a small fish in a big ocean. The same way she felt standing before him now.

Drew was used to being in charge. Dictatorship was his mantra. He ordered, others followed, including Kayla. She had never defied him before. In her younger years, Kayla revered him and feared him. Now, she just feared him.

At forty-eight, Drew Lovett, did not look his age one bit.

146

Unlike his wife, he had undergone only one surgery, around his eyes. He had inherited youthful genes from his parents and did not need surgery to enhance his natural looks. Being biracial, Drew had the perfect, flawless complexion. His masculine, broad shoulders and tall body frame turned heads and commanded attention. Right now, he commanded Kayla's attention.

"What's this I hear about you going back to Holly Hill, when I forbade you never to go again?" Drew did not look up from his notebook, but he spoke with such authority that Kayla felt like he was piercing her very soul.

"I...haven't found tenants yet, and I promised Aunt Mae I would make sure the church puts the right family in the home," Kayla stammered pitifully.

"That is no concern of yours. Mae had no business leaving that hellhole to you! I do not want you to have any part in it. That place is unsafe and unlivable. No wonder you cannot find anyone to live it in! It's not fit for a human!"

"Aunt Mae lived there and she loved it." Kayla had found her voice.

"Mae was foolish! She did not have any common sense, let alone intelligence, getting herself hooked up with all that religious gibberish! We did not raise you that way, and we do not expect you to follow in her path. Do I make myself clear?"

"Father, I am a Christian," Kayla confessed boldly.

That arrested Drew, causing him to look up from his notebook at Kayla. His eyes were reddening with an anger she had never witnessed before. "No child of mine believes such nonsense! You are not a Christian!"

For whoever is ashamed of Me and My words in this adulterous and sinful generation, of him the Son of Man also

will be ashamed when He comes in the glory of His Father with the holy angels.

Kayla swallowed the mammoth lump in her throat. "I accepted Jesus Christ into my heart. I am a Christian."

"Well, then, you are no longer my child!" Drew lowered his head, ignoring the pain he glimpsed in Kayla's eyes. "Get your things out of the house! Do not contact me or Kathryn again until you come to your senses!"

She stood still, unable to move, unable to grasp the magnitude of what her father had just said.

He disowned me!

He said I am no longer his child.

I am no longer his adopted daughter.

He is abandoning me!

He is giving me back…to who?

To God!

The sweet whispering in her heart eased the heavy burden.

"The thing that I feared all my life," Kayla spoke through her pain, "has happened. I did something that displeased you, so you do not want me anymore. I'm sorry I cannot be the perfect daughter. No one can. There was only one perfect person who walked the earth and that was Jesus Christ and they killed him. Just like you are doing now. You are killing something in me. Just like you did to Aunt Mae. She died loving you, praying and hoping that you would come to her. She died praying for you to know her God so that she could see you in heaven."

Kayla pivoted toward the door and then turned again to face him. "I will forever pray for you, father. And I will forever love you." Kayla left with her heart broken. She was once again an orphan.

"How did it…" Kathryn halted as she saw her daughter's

puffy, red eyes. "What happened?" She entered Kayla's office.

"Drew," she called him by his name, since he was no longer her father, "said I am no longer his daughter because I am a Christian. I am not to contact either of you ever again."

"What!" Kathryn gasped for air. Her perfect world was falling apart before her very eyes. "Let me go talk to him!"

"No!" Kayla called after her. "You and I both know there is no need. He would not even go to his own sister's funeral and she was flesh and blood. I'm adopted."

"Oh, Kayla, he loves you," Kathryn took her daughter into her arms. "He's just stubborn."

"Stubborn or not, I'm leaving. I will move my clothes when I come back Monday and my patients can come to my hospital office. I guess I will be fulltime over there now. And, well, I'm not sure where I will live, but I will find a place." Kayla was rattling out her plans, unsure of any of them. She was still in a state of shock. "Maybe I will stay in Holly Hill or Greenville, and find me a job there."

"No, Kayla. Please do not move there. I will miss you too much." Fresh tears poured down Kathryn's cheeks. "No matter what Drew says, you are my daughter and I love you."

Kayla fell into her arms and cried. She needed so much to hear that her mother still loved her. "I love you, too."

"Now dry your eyes," Kathryn reached for some Kleenex and dabbed her daughter's eyes, along with her own. "If you believe in prayer, then you pray about this and let your God handle it."

Kayla was surprised. "Mother..."

"Oh, I'm not saying I believe in your God or anything like that, but if there is a chance that your God could soften Drew's heart, then that will make me a believer. I am not going to lose my only child, especially when I wanted you so badly. We'll just have to talk to each other and see each other in private for now."

Kathryn Lovett's attitude had surprised Kayla. She expected her to side with Drew. For the first time, Kayla felt her mother's love. She understood the risk her mother was taking in disobeying Drew. This could cost Kathryn her marriage.

"Thank you, Mother."

"Any mother would do what I'm doing," Kathryn made light of it.

"No, they wouldn't." She thought of Jonah. "When I come back, I need to tell you something, something very important."

"Kayla I don't know if I can handle anything else right now. Is it bad news?"

"Not to me, but I want to be honest with you," Kayla held her hands. "I need to be honest."

"Then go ahead and tell me now. I cannot wait. It'll drive me crazy."

"I'm pregnant."

"What?!" she screeched, fanning her hands over her face. "I think I'm going to faint."

"Sit down." Kayla drew the chair under her mother.

"Kayla, what in the world? I thought Christians don't do that sort of thing—sleep around?"

"I wasn't a Christian then," Kayla admitted. "There's more."

"More. Kayla, you're going to give me a heart attack." Kathryn was known to be dramatic.

"I'm getting married. His name is Jonah Bates and he is going to be an excellent father to my baby."

"My baby," Kathryn sat upward. "Is he not the father? Last

I knew you were dating Isaac, but he died in Iraq. All of this is so confusing."

"Isaac is the father of my baby, but as you know, he's not alive. Anyhow, Jonah loves me and he loves this unborn child."

"Kayla, you're moving too fast for me. This is too much for me to take in all at once."

"I know, and I apologize," Kayla said. "But, I need you. I do not want there to be anything between us. You are my mother and well, I need a mother's support. Please say you will be there for me, even if it is private."

Kathryn studied her daughter's face some time before finally responding. "I may not agree with all of this right now, but I do support you. I want to meet this Jonah Bates soon."

"You will!" Kayla hugged her mother. "You'll love him, mother. He's wonderful."

"He better be!"

"Oh, mother, I love you so much!"

"Kayla Lovett, I love you more."

CHAPTER 15

The Calm Before the Fire

Kayla cried during most of her drive to Holly Hill. Drew dismissing her from the family unit was her greatest fear come true. Unexplainable grief pierced her soul. She suffered severely. Only God could help her. She sought him fervently. Praying earnestly with childlike faith, Kayla sought God to alleviate her deep-seeded pain, not wanting it to take root in her heart, incubating seeds of bitterness. She couldn't risk such ugliness in her heart for her baby nor for her sake. By the time Kayla pulled into the driveway of Aunt Mae's home, she felt a little better.

Opening the door to meet his future bride, Jonah saw her hurt through her eyes. "Oh Baby, what's wrong?"

Again, the dam burst as he held Kayla closely. Tenderly, he rocked her in his arms. "It's alright, whatever it is. God, touch Kayla and help her now. You know what it is. She needs You," Jonah prayed aloud. Hovering, he led her inside. "Sit down, Baby." Jonah still held onto her.

"My father wanted me to denounce Christ," she sniffled. "I couldn't. I wouldn't, Jonah."

"Of course not," Jonah was blown away. *What kind of man would want his child to do such a thing? An atheist.* Jonah remembered Kayla saying that about him.

"He said I am no longer his daughter," she cried more. "I always knew he would disown me. No matter how hard I tried to be the perfect daughter."

"There is no such thing, Kayla. He should love and accept you for who you are," Jonah consoled. "He's just mad, but he'll come around."

"He won't. It's either his way or the highway."

"His loss. He'll regret it, Kayla," he squeezed her tighter. "What about your mother?"

"He told me never to call or contact either one of them. However, mom did not agree with him. She wants to see me privately, until she can convince Drew otherwise, which will never happen. She told me that she loved me, Jonah," Kayla looked up into his supportive eyes. "It was risky for her to take my side against my father, but she did. And I told her about the pregnancy, and about you."

"You did?" Jonah felt proud.

"Yes, and that we were going to marry soon."

"Wow! You laid it all out there. I am proud of you, Kayla. I know it wasn't easy."

"She is going to support me, which is nothing short of a miracle. I am so thankful for that. She wants to meet you soon."

"She may not like me, Kayla. I'm not like you."

"I'm glad you're not like me." Kayla touched his chin and smiled. "We would be such a boring couple. I love you for you, Jonah."

"And I love you," he kissed her forehead. "Are you hungry?"

"Starving!"

"Good. I picked up some Chinese food on the way here." Jonah helped Kayla up.

"Sounds good. I'm craving pickles and butter pecan ice cream," Kayla blurted.

"Pickles and ice cream," Jonah mimicked. "I bought butter pecan ice cream, but I'll have to go out and get pickles. Do you want me to go now or wait after we eat?"

"I can wait," she embraced him.

"So, this is what I have to look forward to," he loved holding her in his arms. It just felt so right. "Weird cravings. You'll probably wake me up in the middle of the night, craving cottage cheese and pistachios, something bizarre like that."

"Yuck. I hate cottage cheese."

"Me too," he pecked her cheek. "We'll get through this together. We have each other and most importantly, we have God."

"I'm a little frightened, Jonah," Kayla admitted. "I don't know the first thing about being a mother and well, I didn't have the best example growing up. Even though my mother loves…"

Jonah silenced her with a kiss upon her salty mouth. Kayla instinctively slipped her arms around his neck, forgetting about her worries. Everything seemed better being around Jonah. She may not have her earthly father's love, but she had Her heavenly Father's unconditional love, and she had Jonah's love.

That was more than enough!

"What about my surprise?" she remembered.

"After dinner."

"You're going to make me wait?" Kayla pouted.

"Yes. Don't you know that good things come to those who wait?"

"I guess you're right," Kayla's eyes lit up. "I waited for you."

"Don't even try to win me over by batting those beautiful eyes of yours and with flattery words."

"Come on, Jonah. I've had a rough day."

"The quicker we eat, the quicker you get your gift. So let's go eat, my love," Jonah guided her into the kitchen.

"I thought that you're supposed to spoil me and give me what I want."

"I am. A pregnant woman needs food. I'm giving you what you need, which is food, and what you want, which is me." He winked. "Anything extra is a bonus."

"You think you're slick, don't you?"

"Am I?"

"Yes." She sat next to him at the table. "You're really slick."

Following their Chinese meal, the two sat cozily in the family room. Combining the long day at work and the three-hour drive, Kayla was deadbeat tired. She leaned against Jonah on the couch.

"Before you fall asleep, I better give you your gift."

"Yes!" Kayla perked up.

Dropping to his knee, Jonah pulled the ring from his pocket. "Kayla Lovett, I love you with all my heart. Besides Jesus, you are the greatest gift the Father has given me. Your smile lights up my world. Your kindness softens me. Your gentle spirit humbles me. Your intelligence makes me want to be a better man. Your tender heart completes me. I know I have asked you this before, but I want to do it right." His eyes locked with hers. "Kayla Lovett, I love you with all my heart. I promise to be a good, loving husband to you and our child. I will always be there for you, in the good and bad times. Please make me the happiest man alive by agreeing to be my wife. Kayla, will you marry me?"

"Yes, I will Jonah," her eyes moistened. Kayla felt a sense of peace. This was right. It was all a part of God's master plan and she felt that God was more than pleased.

"This ring belonged to Aunt Alice. It is a family heirloom. It was the only thing that Aunt Alice owned that was priceless to her, excluding her Bible." Jonah choked up. "So it means a lot to me, and I hope you feel the same way," Jonah slid the ring on her finger, which fit perfectly.

"It's amazing, Jonah!" Her face glowed.

"Do you really like it, Kayla?"

"I love it Jonah!"

"I can buy you another ring later, but…"

"Shush! This ring is perfect! I love it and I do not want another ring. We will pass it to our daughter and her daughter's daughter. We will keep it in the family."

Jonah drew Kayla closer, kissing her soundly and wholly. She responded easily.

"Do you still want pickles to go with ice cream?" Jonah remembered.

"Nah! I'm bloated."

"Well, I guess we better go to bed," Jonah helplessly withdrew. "We've got to meet with Pastor Goodwin tomorrow morning. Are you nervous about it?"

"No, especially not after the last Sunday service. I think he will agree to marry us."

"Me too," he walked her to the bedroom.

"I'm going to take a quick shower first. But I know as soon

as my head hits the pillow I will fall asleep. I'm tired."

"You should be," Jonah embraced her. "Sweet dreams, Kayla."

"Sweet dreams to you, as well."

"I pray so," Jonah wanted nothing more than to get a nights' sleep with no nightmares of Nixon, Manchester or Joel."

✳✳✳

The meeting with Pastor Reggie Goodwin went better than Jonah and Kayla expected. After hearing the details of their upcoming marriage, and feeling the peace of God to proceed, Pastor Goodwin agreed to marry them, but only after the couple partook in intense counseling sessions for the next two Saturdays, then he would marry them the following Saturday. Pastor Goodwin suggested strongly for them to date each other and to get to know each other by asking hard questions about their past and their futures and to give honest answers, even if it hurt.

"In three Saturdays you'll be Kayla Bates," Jonah said, holding her hand at the restaurant.

"I can't wait. I should be about three months pregnant by then. I hope I am not showing. People will know that I had sex before marriage."

"Who cares what people think? All that matters is that we are a family."

"I know," she lowered her head. "I just wish my parents could be at our wedding."

"Maybe your mom will come."

"I don't think she can. It'll be too risky."

"At least Lisa is coming, and I'm going to ask Steven to stand by me."

"Jonah," she hesitated before asking the hard questions Pastor Goodwin talked about, "are you certain you want to take on this responsibility? Do you think you will see my baby as another man's baby, or will you truly see him or her as yours?"

"Kayla, this is our baby. Get 'my baby' out of your vocabulary. I am going to give our baby all the love he or she deserves. With the Holy Spirit's guidance, I am going to rear our child to know God and to serve Him. I am going to be a better father than my father. Our baby will carry my name and be my son or daughter. There is no hesitation. I love you, Kayla, and I love our baby."

"Speaking of father, don't you want to find yours? It's been a long time and perhaps…"

"No!" Jonah abruptly interrupted, frown lines on his forehead. "If he wants to find me, fine. But I will not look for him. I didn't leave him. He left me and Joel."

"There may be a reason, Jonah."

"Mom said he left us for another family. He has his own family and forgot about us."

"Not to speak ill of the dead," Kayla began, "but your mother had her own issues. Perhaps she did not tell the whole truth. There are two sides to every story, Jonah. Maybe you should try to find out. If not for you, then for our baby."

"I'll pray about, Kayla," he squeezed her hand. "That's all I can promise you now." Jonah wanted nothing more than to please Kayla. She had such a good effect on him. Unexpectedly, she had captured his heart without even trying. Love took root in Jonah's heart, budding fruits of kindness and goodness to others. Most definitely, Jonah was a changed man.

"That's all I ask," Kayla smiled.

Afterward, the happy couple went to the movies. It had

been over five years since Jonah had enjoyed one of his favorite pastimes. Before being locked up, Jonah would go to the movies late Friday night and stay until the theatre closed if he and his gang didn't go to a club or got into criminal activities. If an action movie or thriller was showing, Jonah was there. But today, it was special. He was sitting in the theatre next to the love of his life, watching a romance movie. *Now this is a first!*

It did not matter that the movie was corny. All that mattered was that he was sharing popcorn and soda with the love of his life. Everything seemed so right.

❃❃❃

After such a great day, Kayla and Jonah slept in different rooms, but their hearts were very much connected. Space could not separate them. God had orchestrated their paths to connect and in a few weeks, it would be consummated in marriage, soul and body. Like a baby, Kayla slept, dreaming of her Prince Charming. Meanwhile, Jonah tossed and turned with consecutive hollowing dreams about Manchester and Joel.

"Jonah!" Awakened by his loud groaning, Kayla shoved Jonah to wake him up. "Jonah!"

"What!" He bolted upward. He was drenched in sweat, heart beating rapidly and slightly disoriented.

"Another bad dream," she coddled him close to her.

He nodded, still too shaken to speak.

"Father God, help Jonah to sleep without these horrible nightmares," Kayla prayed. "Do you want some water or anything?

"No, thank you."

"Was it about Manchester?"

"Yes, and Joel," he confessed. "I keep having bad vibes about him. And, well, he's been the reason I haven't been sleeping mostly." His expression became grim. Jonah did not want to keep anything from his fiancé. "I just wish I could find out if he's doing okay."

"Why don't you call him, Jonah?" Kayla squeezed him, giving him all the love and support she could physically give. She felt encouraged by Jonah's willingness to talk about Joel. Usually, Jonah was closemouthed about his twin.

"Let's not go there again," Jonah's tone was sullen and his face long with sadness.

"Jonah, please call him."

"No."

Kayla released her arms from around him and stood. "I'm going back to bed. I'll pray for you." She marched off.

The warmth that he felt by her nearness was now gone, replaced with coldness and loneliness. He reclined back on the sofa and let the silent tears fall. Jonah was tired. Thankfully, the dreams about Manchester tonight were not so detailed. However, his dreams about Joel were deathly. Jonah even dreamed Joel was in a coffin, with him standing over him. It took Jonah awhile before he finally found sleep again, only to be awakened by shouting.

"Fire!" Kayla yelled.

"Huh!" Jonah thought he was dreaming.

"Fire. Don't you smell the smoke?" She panicked, dressed in her baby-blue gown and matching robe.

Jonah bolted toward the door, bare-chested, with grey sweatpants on. "Call 9-1-1!"

Taking the phone out of her purse, Kayla's hands shook as she dialed the three numbers.

The doorknob was hot as he attempted to turn it. Smoke seeped through the bottom of the door. "We've got to get out of here!"

"The back rooms are filled with fire!"

Jonah snatched her hand and ran toward the backdoor. "I got to get the box!" He ran in the kitchen and took the wooden box Aunt Alice gave him off the counter.

"God help us!" Kayla screamed, as Jonah opened the back door and she saw the blazing fire raging.

"We've got to jump, Kayla!"

"I can't!" she clutched her purse tightly to her side.

Without waiting, Jonah scooped her up and leapt through the burning door. The whole house was in flames. Landing on his back, trying to cushion the fall for Kayla and the baby, Jonah released Kayla and began rolling on his back, trying to stifle the flames.

"You're on fire!" She yelled. "Oh God, help us!"

"I'm alright," Jonah murmured. "Are you alright?"

"Yes," she cried. "Oh, Jonah!" she collapsed in his arms. "The house is gone. Aunt's Mae's home is gone."

Moving fast, Jonah hurried Kayla to the front of the house. They watched the entire house go up in flames.

"Thank You, Lord, for saving our lives," Jonah extolled, securely holding Kayla in his arms.

"Yes, thank You, Lord," Kayla echoed.

Shortly after, the fire truck was on the scene.

"Are you sure you're okay?" the firefighter asked Jonah and Kayla again.

"We are," Jonah answered.

"There was nothing we could do to save the house or any of the contents inside."

"All that matters is that we're alive." Jonah felt overwhelmed. He brushed a light kiss on Kayla's forehead as he continued to hold her in his arms.

"What caused the fire, sir?" Kayla asked.

"This was arson," the firefighter stated. "Someone set fire to the home. We found a lighter under the front porch and two gasoline cans out back. Someone wanted to destroy everything and everyone in this house," the firefighter ventured.

"What?" Kayla went numb.

"It's okay, Baby." Indignation seeped through Jonah's tight-lips.

"Who would have done such a thing?"

"That's what we intend on finding out," the firefighter said. "Do you two have a place to stay tonight?"

"Yes," Jonah replied.

"Well, here's my card. Call me tomorrow so we can investigate this further."

Jonah nodded. *Lord, who would have done such a thing?*

Suddenly, he caught a glimpse of PJ's black Ranger Rover slowly riding by the home.

Jonah's eyes locked with the driver, Corky.

PJ! His body instinctively lurched forward.

"You alright?" Kayla looked up at him. His eyes were steely and hardened.

"I'm fine," he forced a smile. "I'm fine," he repeated, but Jonah was in a fog, anger clouding his judgment. *Lord, help me, because right now the old Jonah wants to rise up and go after PJ and the boys! He could have killed Kayla and my baby! Payback, Lord! I want payback!*

Vengeance belongs to me! Forgive him.

Lord...

Forgive him. I forgave you.

163

CHAPTER 16

Between a Rock and a Hard Place

After such a crazy morning, Jonah and Kayla went to church Sunday. They needed to be in the House of the Lord to give thanks for how God had kept them safe in the midst of the fire. Only He could have spared their lives.

After service, Jonah informed Pastor Goodwin about what had happened.

"Praise God for protecting you both. God is faithful."

"That He is."

After they talked a little more about what happened, Pastor Goodwin changed the subject. "I was wondering, Jonah, have you been praying about where God is leading you, as far as ministering the Gospel?"

"Truthfully, Pastor Goodwin, I believe God is calling me into the ministry, although I feel so unqualified."

"God qualifies the unqualified," Pastor Goodwin rested his hand on Jonah's shoulder. "None of the disciples were qualified. By trade, there was a fisherman, tentmaker, tax collector and so forth. They were all ordinary men, who God called to do extraordinary things. I believe God wants me to train you for a season."

"But we'll be moving to Macon City."

"Son, if you are willing, we can work out the training schedule. We can do it twice a month, on Saturdays, possibly. Also, I trained Pastor Mack, who is an associate pastor in Macon City. I'm sure he'll work with you and teach you what he knows."

"Thanks, Pastor Goodwin. I appreciate all your help, and your believing in me."

"God believes in you, Jonah. It's my honor to pour into one of God's chosen vessels."

❈❈❈

Later, after Kayla left to go back to Macon City, Jonah called the firefighter.

"Glad you called me, Mr. Bates. Like I mentioned last night, we found a lighter on the scene and several gasoline cans. Only an amateur would leave this kind of evidence."

"Were any fingerprints found?" Jonah thought that would be too easy.

"We got lucky," the firefighter chuckled. "We got good prints. In fact, we have identified the guy. His name is Carlos Fenton, a.k.a. Corky. Do you know him?"

"I knew him in my former life," Jonah replied, relieved that someone would pay for almost taking the life of his future wife and child. If only PJ's fingerprints were found. He may not have physically lit the lighter, but he was the mastermind behind the crime. Getting PJ off the streets would be great for everyone. Yet, someone else would step into his gangster shoes. The name may change, but the crime role would be the same.

"Corky was arrested this morning, and he's singing like a bird," the firefighter stated.

"Really?" Jonah felt hopeful.

"He ratted on PJ, a.k.a. Paul Jefferson. Apparently, the police have been after this guy for a long time. We got him now."

Thank You Lord for taking care of this so fast. Vengeance belongs to You!

⚜⚜⚜

It had been a long week for Kayla. Living at the Marriott, in one of the largest suites, Kayla was lonely for Jonah. Being practically estranged from her family, Kayla felt emotional, sadness tugged at her heart. On her first night there, Kayla's curiosity got the best of her. She needed something to connect her to Jonah. Retrieving his wooden box from the walk-in closet, Kayla let her hand run over the hand-carved box. It was so beautiful. Jonah had entrusted her to keep it for him until they found a place to live.

Opening it, Kayla found a bundle of hope and love in the box. She touched the envelope with Jonah's name on it. It had been opened, but she would not read his personal letter. She also put the letter addressed to Joel aside. Then Kayla opened the scrapbook. *They look so much alike! Only Jonah is more muscular frame. Joel was rather thin. But, wow! The likeness is incredible. She made such a beautiful bride. They look so happy.* Turning to the last page, Kayla saw the index card with Joel's address and phone number on it. Kayla keyed the information in her smartphone. *He is not far from here! Wow! Maybe I will....* The final picture on the back of the scrapbook was Kayla's undoing. Noticing the picture of a large family, apparently the bride's family, produced fresh tears to spill over. *I will not have any family at my wedding!* Kayla had a private-pity-party. Loneliness engulfed her. At work, her parents avoided her. Drew had allowed her to maintain her office for the benefit of their loyal clients. Counseling prospective clients before and after surgery was vital. The other coworkers, could sense the tension between the family; therefore, they stayed to themselves. Kayla was an outsider in the workplace and with her family. Sure, Kathryn smiled at her several times during the workday, whenever she was around, but Kayla couldn't overlook the sadness in her mother's eyes. She, too, was suffering.

The highlight of Kayla's week was shopping for a wedding dress with her mother. Kayla did not want anything elaborate for their simple wedding ceremony. However, she wanted to knock Jonah off his feet. Kathryn wanted to spare no expense for her only child. It mattered not that her socialite friends would not attend, nor that she could not attend her daughter's wedding. All that mattered was that Kayla was dazzling from head to toe. No other bride would be as exquisite as Kayla Lovett, wearing a luxurious gown fit for royalty. After several hours gown shopping, Kayla finally consented to her mother's favorite gown. It was a white lace gown with a sweetheart neckline and a detachable princess ball gown skirt. The skirt had layers of silk chiffon, tulle, and lace trim details all over the skirt. The royal train was ten feet long, and trimmed in lace as well.

"You're lovely, Kayla!" her mother's eyes misted with delight. "Oh, I wish I could be there."

"Can you please try, Mother?" Kayla pleaded.

"You know I cannot, Kayla. Your father would renounce

the both of us. For now, we just have to play it safe." Kathryn hated to disappoint her daughter. "Besides, I'll be with you in spirit."

It is not the same. "I know, Mother."

"At least we had this special time together. In addition, I will have a first rate photographer and videographer to take countless pictures so that I will not miss one moment of it. Only the best for my daughter."

Kayla slowly spun around in her dress, eying her image through the glass mirrors. She loved the dress. Even though it seemed over the top for the simple wedding, Kayla was sure to make a lasting impression on Jonah.

"Jonah is going to love it!"

Kathryn searched Kayla's face. "You really love him, don't you?"

"More than I can express!" Kayla beamed.

"Jonah is a lucky man, to have the honor to marry my beautiful, intelligent, kindhearted, compassionate daughter." The adjectives generously rolled off her lips.

Kayla was stunned by her accolades. This was so unlike Kathryn. Something was definitely changing about her mother.

"Thank you, Mother," Kayla stepped down from the stage.

"You're welcome. My goodness! What a lovely ring!" Kathryn finally noticed the engagement ring. "It's so exquisite, and rare." Kathryn admired the antique.

"It's an heirloom. Aunt Alice left it for Jonah to give to his future bride," Kayla said proudly.

"I bet it is costly now."

"Everything is not about money. This is priceless to me. One day, I'll pass it on to my daughter or son."

"That's good."

"I have my doctor's appointment tomorrow. I am having an ultrasound. I might even find out the sex of the baby."

"So soon?"

"Well, I'll be about eleven weeks," Kayla shrugged. "I'm excited and scared at the same time. I wish you could go with me."

"What time is it at?"

"Two o'clock."

Kathryn took out her phone and checked her calendar. "I can make it. Are you working tomorrow?"

"Yes, just taking a late lunch."

"How about we meet at the library around the corner and ride together?"

Kayla was doubly stunned. "Are you sure?"

"I wouldn't want to miss my grandchild's first picture, now would I?"

"Oh, Momma!" Kayla embraced her. It was the first time that she had dropped the formal mother title.

Kayla's simple endearment did not go undetected. Kathryn never felt closer to her daughter than at that moment. She was stuck between a rock and a hard place. On one hand, she feared losing her husband, and yet, on the other hand, she feared losing her daughter.

✖✖✖

The following day, while Kayla waited for her mother in the library parking lot, Kathryn had a time getting away from the Center. No doubt, Drew sensed that his wife was going behind his back to see Kayla.

"Where is Kayla?" Drew asked, standing in his wife's office door, observing her with her pocketbook in hand, ready to leave.

"How should I know?" Kathryn replied, taking out her keys.

"Her car is not in the parking lot."

Looking at her watch, Kathryn replied, "It's lunch time. She is probably having lunch somewhere. Don't tell me you are concerned about our daughter, Drew? Not now, after you've practically disowned her."

"She made the choice. If she wants to be a religious fanatic like Mae, then she can go ahead! But I will not have it in my house. She knows how we feel about it. Religion is a cult and I won't have any family member participating in such ridiculous beliefs."

"Drew, you're a racist!" Kathryn boldly stated, standing face to face with him.

"I think you've had too many cocktails already," he snubbed. "To think that I, a rich black man, am a racist, you must be intoxicated."

"You're not racist against color, only religion."

"You're crossing the line, Kathryn," Drew eyed her with scorn. "And I wouldn't do that if I were you. You are either with me or against me."

"Sounds like the Words of Christ Jesus." She did not flinch. "I remember my mother reading them directly out of the Bible."

"Kathryn, I am warning you!"

"What are you going to do, Drew?" She brushed passed him. "Disown me, as well? Remember, Drew, I own fifty percent of the business." Kathryn headed for the door, intent on getting the last word.

"Kathryn, you're sadly mistaken there," he haughtily called after her.

Stunned, Kathryn pivoted around to face her arrogant husband. "What have you done Drew? Did you forge my name on something that I don't know about?"

"I didn't have to," his crooked smile was wide. "After the Christmas party, you signed your portion over to me. You might not remember, since you were highly intoxicated."

"You took advantage of me, Drew!" Her heart dropped. "Who are you? You are a monster! Any man who could disown their own child, his own sister, not even go to her funeral and now...this! You are worse than a monster! You're pure evil!"

"You can call me whatever you want, but if you are meeting up with Kayla behind my back, then you can...."

"Can what, Drew?" She took the bait.

"You can move in with her, because the document you signed says I get the house and everything in it."

"I hate you!" She marched out of the office.

Appearing cool, calm and collected on the outside, Drew felt like a heel on the inside. Despite his brusque demeanor, Drew was not raised this way. His mother was a loving, God-fearing woman who had raised Drew in the church. His father was the pastor of a large congregation. Differing from his mother, his father was a fire and brimstone kind of preacher. Relentless, Drew grew up thinking he was going to hell for his every wrong thought or deed. He could never please his father. Yet, his hatred for religion did not happen because of his father's preaching tactics, it happened when Drew caught his father leaving a motel with a Hispanic woman. He could still visualize the woman. Much younger than his father, the woman was slender, very tan and had a long, single braid that reached her midriff. He had just turned seventeen years old. He and some church friends were hanging out at the theater across the street. Drew was forbidden to ever step foot in a movie theatre. So, the following week, Drew followed his dad. Sure enough, he and his lady friend met at the motel around six o'clock, and he left at nine. After digging deeper, Drew had found out that this had been going on for a year. His mother never suspected a thing

His father's perceived infidelity changed Drew! From that point on, Drew hated everything to do with religion. He even hated how his mother was so gullible, believing every word that flowed out of the mouth of such a hypocrite. Drew had vowed to never be like either one of them. It broke his sister, Maybelle's heart when he told her he was an atheist. Being only two years a part, the siblings were so close growing up. Maybelle, known as Mae, doted over her younger brother. She was his world. When Drew left home, he never went back. Not to visit his parents, nor his sister. He did not attend the funeral of either of his parents. To him, they were already dead!

Just like he was treating Kayla.

And now, possibly, Kathryn.

You are all alone…

The inward whisper startled Drew as he sat in his office, staring out the window. In darkness he sat, with the lights turned out. The atmosphere represented his mood. There was a lovely weeping willow outside his window, which had drawn his attention.

I feel like that tree! Weeping!

❈❈❈

Meanwhile, Kayla waited in the parking lot for her mother to show for over forty minutes. After dialing her cell phone several times, Kayla decided to leave. She was already going to be late for her appointment.

Lord, please let her be alright.

Kayla's heart was heavy by the time she entered the obstetrician's office. While she waited, her cell phone rang.

"Mom!" Kayla perked up.

"No, I hope I don't sound like a woman," Jonah laughed.

"Oh, Jonah. I was expecting mother. She was supposed to ride with me to the doctor's office, but she didn't show up."

He could hear the hurt in her voice, which made him mad. "Kayla, you know your parents. Why would you think that she would defy your father?"

"Because she said she would come. I told you last night how we had such a good time shopping for my wedding gown."

"I know." Jonah tried not to be judgmental, but it was hard. "Maybe something came up at the office."

"That's what I'm thinking," Kayla held out hope. "I'm surprise you're calling."

"I wouldn't miss my fiancé appointment. I cannot be there physically, but as long as you got this phone, I want to hear everything that is going on. It will be like being there."

"Ahhhh," Kayla felt much better. "Thank you, Jonah. I was feeling all alone and sorry for myself."

"Kayla, Baby, you are never alone. I've got your back, and of course, The Big Guy up in the sky has your back!"

"I love you, Jonah!"

"Love you, too!"

CHAPTER 17

Philemon

Before heading back to Greenville, Kayla used her navigator to locate Joel Bates' home address. It was unbelievable that he lived outside her city in a small rural area known as Graces Way. The navigator led her to an area with lots of trees and forestry. Kayla would have never been able to find the address without it.

Joel lived on a country road with large houses on huge acres of land. Neighboring homes were spaciously separated, with at least ten to twenty or more acres of land between them. Joel lived toward the end of the country road, having at least thirty acres of land.

"Wow!" Kayla was impressed with the three-story brick home that had a wraparound porch. "Joel's done well for himself!" Steering her BMW up the long driveway, Kayla admired the white Cadillac SUV parked in the driveway. *Must be Joel's. Jonah wants the same car. Lord, let his heart be opened to receiving Jonah back into his life. Jonah needs him, and I am fairly certain Joel does as well. Give me favor, Lord!*

Kayla rang the doorbell.

No answer.

She rang it several times before returning to her car. She

ripped out a piece of paper in her tablet and scribbled out a quick note for the woman of the house.

> *Mrs. Bates,*
>
> *My name is Kayla Lovett. I am the fiancé of Jonah Bates. I found your address information in a box given to Jonah by his Aunt Alice. Jonah doesn't know I came to visit, but I feel in my spirit that the twin brothers need to reunite. Jonah is a different man; he's changed and he's a Christian. Actually, his witness brought me to Christ. If you think that Joel is open to seeing his brother, please contact me. However, if you think that Joel wants nothing to do with Jonah, then throw away my name and number. I don't want Jonah to suffer anymore. I love him dearly.*
>
> *God bless you and Joel. Kayla (555.1212)*

Well, Lord, I am disappointed that no one is home.

Have faith in My perfect timing!

Driving the three-hour drive to Greenville, Kayla felt joyful thinking about her doctor's visit. True to his word, although Jonah was not there, putting him on the speakerphone while the doctor examined her was the next best thing to being there. Jonah encouraged Kayla, and was just as excited as she was when Kayla put the phone to the monitor so he could hear the baby's heartbeat.

"It sounds like horses galloping in a race!" Jonah choked up on the phone.

He is going to make a great father, Lord. Too bad we could not find out the sex of the baby. I really want to know.

I wish my mother…

Kayla shook off the melancholy. She had not been able to reach her mother. Kathryn had not returned any of her calls.

Well, I guess father got to her. She chose him over me, as usual! It does not matter, Lord. As long as I have You, Jonah, and the baby, I will be all right.

❈❈❈

Meanwhile, Yasha was at the hospital visiting with her husband. Joel was not having a good day. His health was rapidly declining.

"I have a doctor's appointment today. I hate you're going to miss the ultrasound to determine the sex of the baby," Yasha held his hand.

"It's a girl," his tone was low. "She's going to have big brown eyes, high cheekbones, full perfect lips, natural curly hair and a smooth, flawless skin complexion like her mother. From me, she will inherit my super-duper IQ," Joel chuckled. "But everything good, she'll get from her mother."

"She will also inherit your kindness, gentleness, compassion, hopefulness, and unshakeable faith," Yasha spoke through unshed tears, her eyes glistening. "She's going to be a daddy's girl."

"With the title of PK, preacher's kid," Joel added. "Poor baby!"

"What if she's really a boy? A little Joel Bates, Jr.?"

"I'd love whoever God gives us because he or she was birthed in love."

"We still haven't selected a girl's name. Name her after my mother, Lillian or after your mother, Patrina, or Trina." Yasha suggested again.

"I don't want her to be named after my mom," Joel had been against the suggestion from the start. "She might end up being like her. In the Bible, names shaped a person's life. And, well, Lillian doesn't feel right either."

"What about Faith?"

"I like that," Joel smiled. "Faith Lillian Bates."

"That sounds perfect when you say it." Yasha squeezed his hand.

"I'm ready to go home, Yasha. It is no need for me to just lie here…and well…wait indefinitely. I rather be at home. I want to go to church tonight."

"Joel, you can't go to church tonight," Yasha chided. "Your body needs rest."

"My soul needs the Word."

"You can read your Bible or watch a sermon on television, but that's about all you're going to get right now." Yasha put her foot down. "Faith needs you," she already claimed the child's name. "I need you." Yasha broke down, covering her face with her hands.

"Shhhh," Joel mustered strength and gently removed her hands, wiping at her tears. "I'm not going anywhere. I'm going to walk Faith Lillian Bates down the aisle and we both know that's going to be when she is in her forties."

"Forty, Joel!" She grinned. "We are not claiming an old maid for our daughter, unless she wants it."

"Hey, she's not going to date until she in her thirties."

"Joel."

"I just wanted to see you smile." His heart ached for his wife. He knew that this all was taking a toll on Yasha. She was trying to be strong for him and their unborn child. "God still has work for me to do."

"Please, Joel, let me find Jonah," Yasha pleaded with him again.

"Not this way. They will find me another kidney donor."

"But what if God wants you to use what you have in your

hand. He gave you a twin, knowing that you two would be perfectly matched. God foreknew your need and provided it at birth."

"Okay, preacher Yasha, I hear you, but I will not ask Jonah for anything. I cannot."

"The message you heard Sunday was for you, Joel. Have you really forgiven your brother?"

Joel closed his eyes, pondering the question that dictated his true Christian walk. Did he actually live out the Bible? Did he walk the walk he talked about to his parishioners every Sunday? Was he exhibiting Christ-like behavior toward his fellowman, which included Jonah?

I did not even tell him about Aunt Alice's death. If I had truly forgiven, how could I have been so heartless then?

"Read Philemon, Joel," Yasha handed her husband his Bible. "Let the Holy Spirit guide you to the light, so that there will be no darkness in any place of your life."

Opening his eyes, Joel saw nothing but pure love radiating in his wife's eyes. God had blessed him with such a great woman, someone who deserved a whole man. Joel felt like half a man. Here he was in the hospital, yet again—sick—unto death unless God wrought a miracle. He had carried tons of baggage into their marriage, holding onto the hurts/pains of his past and his dissension against his brother.

"I will read it *My Love*," Joel promised, even knowing what Philemon was all about. It is the third shortest books in the Bible, yet the most convicting for Joel.

"Don't just read it Joel," Yasha cautioned. "Apply it."

"I will."

"It's time for freedom, Joel," Yasha leaned over and kissed his forehead. "You've been captive too long by your past."

"Has it been that bad, Yasha?"

"Not for me, Joel, but for you. You cannot fake happiness, not true happiness. I know you are happy with me and that God is using you greatly in the church. But, life is more than that Joel. Yes, Joel you love me, you love the church family, and you even love strangers to Christ. But, where is your love for your brother?" Yasha hit him in the gut with that question. "How can you love Me, who you have not seen and you do not love your brother, whom you do see? But you don't see Jonah, do you Joel? You don't."

Yasha walked out, her spirit broken. She loved Joel wholeheartedly and wanted him to be free. She saw the glimmer of sadness in his eyes and she knew it stemmed from being separated from his other half, from his twin brother. Joel needed Jonah, not just for a kidney transplant, but also for completion. God connected them at birth. Jonah's choices separated them. Now, Joel had the power to reconnect them.

Lord, heal Joel, physically and spiritually. Free him before it is too late! Yasha wept.

Joel turned his Bible to Philemon. The book only had one chapter with twenty-five verses. But in those twenty-five verses, there was a message of love, healing and forgiveness. A message of restitution and restoration.

Reading it the first time, Joel felt his spirit pricked with longing. The second time, the pleading to forgive. And thirdly, the cry of his soul to be free!

"...I appeal to you for my son Onesimus, whom I have begotten while in my chains, who once was unprofitable to you, but now is profitable to you and to me. I am sending him back. You therefore receive him, that is, my own heart. For perhaps he departed for a while for this purpose, that you

might receive him forever, no longer as a slave but more than a slave—a beloved brother. If he has wronged you or owes anything, put that on my account..."

Several verses Joel reread repeatedly and mediated on them. The story of Philemon became alive to Joel, in his spirit. Paul's personal letter to Philemon, master of a runaway slave, Onesimus, stirred Joel with conviction. God had somehow orchestrated Onesimus, a runaway slave, to encounter Paul. The encounter changed Onesimus' life. He became a Christian, and now he was free in Jesus. Onesimus faithfully served Paul while he was in prison. Paul called him his beloved brother.

Beloved brother! Joel thought to himself. *Onesimus had done wrong. He had stolen. He had run away. He was not an innocent man. And yet, God saw fit to have him encounter Paul, which caused him to have an encounter with Jesus. God hates the sin, but loves the sinner!*

I hate what Jonah did to me, but I love him.

Joel's heart was opened for the Surgeon to remove all bitterness, all un-forgiveness and all infectious hurts. Joel wanted to be free. But in order to do that completely, Joel had to free his brother. He had to forgive him. *Father God, I want Your forgiveness. Please forgive me for holding onto the anger, the bitterness and harboring an unforgiving heart toward Jonah. Yes, he betrayed me...*

My people betrayed me. Shouting Hosanna in the highest one minute and crucify Him in the next.

He took from me over and over again. He even took my fiancé and slept with her.

Just as Paul told Philemon, charge it to my account, so have I for you. Your sins were charged to my account on the cross. Jonah's sins were charged to my account on the cross.

Just as I forgive you, I have forgiven Jonah.
Joel wept.

And wept some more.

And wept even the more.

Past tears of hurt, pain and anguish flooded his soul. He was releasing inner poison that had bound him for so many years, physically, emotionally, and spiritually. "I forgive Jonah!"

You must tell him.
"I will, Lord. I will."

❦❦❦

"Joel," Yasha called him on the way home, after leaving the doctor's office.

"Hi, Yasha," he could barely talk. He was physically and emotionally washed out after bearing his soul to the Father.

"Are you okay?" she worried.

"Yes. How about you? What did the doctor say?"

"She says that our baby girl is healthy and should be gracing us with her presence in about four months."

"Little Faith," he whispered. "I knew it was a girl."

"Oh, Joel, I'm so happy and sad at the same time."

"Me too. Our Little Faith is going to be a..." Joel tried to catch his breath.

"Joel!"

"I'm fine, Yasha. I just need to rest now. I just had another dialysis treatment." Joel was in pain, but did not want his wife to know as he pressed the nurse's button. "Call me later tonight. I'm going to sleep now."

"Ok, Joel. I love you."

"Love you, too, Honey. Give Faith a big rub for me." He hung up the phone.

"Oh, God, Joel sounds weak! Please let him live to see Faith and to walk her down the aisle in matrimony. I need him, Lord. Please do not take him away from me. Show me what to do to help him," Yasha cried out.

Arriving home, she, too, was tired. This had been a long day. Retrieving the note on her door, she went inside and plopped down on the couch. Her heart raced, as she read the simple notecard. "Thank You, God! Thank you for showing me what to do!" Yasha immediately dialed the number on the phone.

CHAPTER 18

Onesimus

As soon as Kayla arrived at Jonah's duplex, she went straight to the bedroom. Feeling nauseous, all Kayla wanted to do was go take a nap until Jonah returned home from working a double-shift. Wanting to rest without interruption, Kayla turned her cell phone off.

Around nine-thirty, Jonah came home to a sleeping beauty, snuggled under the blanket in his bed. She was breathtaking, with her long locks cascading all over the pillow. Jonah could never get tired of seeing her like this. He did not have the heart to wake her, even though he wanted so much to spend some quality time with Kayla. *We have the rest of our lives to enjoy each other!* He tucked her in and left the room. Exhausted himself, Jonah took a shower and slept in the extra bedroom. His body couldn't take another night of sleeping on the couch.

I will be glad when we are married!

In the early morning hours, Kayla found herself glued to the bathroom. Going to bed on an empty stomach, Kayla woke up famished. She fixed herself a cheese and toast sandwich and large bowl of ice cream at three o'clock in the morning. Apparently, her baby was not a fan of either, forcing the food back up. Kayla was heaving and vomiting on and off for about an hour before Jonah entered the restroom.

"Oh, Baby." He scooted on the floor next to her, "Sick again?"

She nodded.

"How long did the doctor say this is going to last?"

"She didn't," Kayla answered. "I forgot to ask. But I wish I could just skip this phase all together."

"Me too," Jonah coddled her. "Do you feel any better?"

"I do. I don't think there is anything left to come out."

Jonah assisted her upward. "You feel like going back to bed?"

"No. I think I slept too much. I didn't even hear you when you came home."

"I know. You were sleeping so peacefully when I got here, I didn't want to wake you."

"I missed you," Kayla hugged him.

"Not half as much as I missed you," Jonah kissed her on the cheek.

"Let me brush my teeth and I'll meet you in the living room."

"Let us both brush our teeth and go to the living room together," Jonah winked.

Looking at the small bathroom, Kayla wondered how was that going to work, but it did not matter. She needed to get comfortable being around Jonah anyway. In one more week, they would be husband and wife. After freshening up, they went into the den.

"So, tell me how you're doing Kayla. I know it hurt that your mother did not show up. Did you ever hear from her?"

"No," Kayla sighed, shrugging her shoulders. "I called her repeatedly, but she never answered." Refusing to shed another tear, Kayla wiped the one tear that had escaped her eye. "Drew got to her. He threatened to leave her or put her out, I am sure. I cannot imagine my mother ever letting that happen. Her entire life revolves around him. She lives and moves according to what Drew wants. It has always been that way."

"It's sad, but you know I will always be here for you, Kayla."

"You proved that today," love was reflected in her eyes. Kayla was head-over-heels in love with Jonah. "Thanks for being there for me at the doctor's office. The doctor said in all her years of practice, she had never seen a husband do that."

"We are in this together." He lightly kissed her forehead.

"Kiss me." Kayla longed for more.

"I think we should avoid kissing on the lips until marriage. I don't think I can refrain myself." He touched her nose with her finger. "You're so beautiful, Kayla, in every way. I want you so badly and I shouldn't be thinking like this, I know."

"Jonah, I feel the same way. I will be glad when this week is over. Next weekend, we'll be married."

"One long week. Tell me about your gown."

"Oh, Jonah, it's so lovely. I know you are going to love it. Mom picked it out and so it is probably too much for our simple wedding, but I felt like a bride in it. It's amazing!"

"You're amazing!" Jonah fought the sharp urge to plant one on her lips. Dressed in a long pink gown with a matching robe, her hair cascading loosely, and her face glowing like the sun, Kayla was so enticing. It was hard to restrain himself. "Steven is wearing a black suit. I hope that's okay."

"Of course. Did you rent the white tuxedo I called about?"

"No need."

"Jonah, I don't won't you wearing just anything for our

wedding day. It may be simple, but I think…"

"Don't stress your pretty little head about it," Jonah pecked her nose. "Steven blessed me with a white suit, and it's sharp."

"Really?" Kayla breathed.

"I'm going to make you drool when you see me."

"And I hope my dress knocks you right off your feet," Kayla played along.

"Not the dress," he said seriously. "The beauty inside the dress is going to take my breath away, just like she's doing right now."

"That's so sweet, Jonah," Kayla squeezed his hand. She felt so warm and cozy being near the man she loved. "Jonah, do you want me to keep staying at the Marriott, or should I look for us a place next week? I'm taking Tuesday off, so I can do some last minute things before the wedding."

"Well, Steven says that my transfer should be in about three weeks."

"That's good," Kayla beamed. "So does that mean you are going to move to Macon City sooner?"

"Actually, after the wedding, Steven is giving me two weeks paid vacation. Isn't that crazy? I haven't even worked there long enough to earn any vacation days."

"Jonah, I'm so happy." She snuggled closer.

"Me too. So what I was thinking is that we can marry on Saturday. Spend the night here. Travel back to Macon City Sunday, after service, and then stay at the Marriott. I know it's not a real honeymoon, but I promise you, I will take you somewhere to have a real honeymoon in the future."

"Oh, Jonah, a honeymoon isn't a place, it's a purpose. The purpose of two people coming together as one, consummating the union and solidifying the oneness. We'll have a honeymoon, for sure."

"That we will, but..."

"What's wrong?"

"Kayla, I don't have much. How am I going to afford a down payment for a place?"

"Jonah, we're in this together, right?"

He nodded resignedly.

"Well, I have money."

"Kayla, I'm not..."

"Jonah, what's mine is yours, and yours mine. Please, do not spoil this. I want us to have a home. It does not have to be anything huge or fancy. Just a place that we can call ours. I lived in a big house, but it was a lonely place, not a home. I want a home with you, and for our baby." Kayla placed his hand on her small stomach. "Will you accept all of me, Jonah, which includes my money?"

He sighed. "I want to take care of you, Kayla, not you taking care of me."

"How about we both take care of each other?" She held up her hand to high-five him. Jonah looked at her as if she was crazy.

"That's old-school, Kayla."

She shrugged. "So are you just *gonna* leave me hanging?"

Resignedly, Jonah high-fived her back. "You got yourself a deal."

"Oh, Jonah, I just want to kiss you so badly. Just one kiss."

"Nope!" He stood and reached for her hand. "I'm going to escort my pretty lady back to bed so she can rest a little. We have to meet Pastor Goodwin in a few short hours. We don't want to look like we both didn't get any sleep."

"Jonah, I'm looking forward to being your wife."

"And I your husband."

✕✕✕✕

The three-hour counseling session with Pastor Goodwin was intense and straightforward. Pastor Reggie did not bite his tongue or mince words about the seriousness of being unified in holy matrimony.

"Couples bring baggage into a marriage. Past mistakes, sometimes abuse, promiscuous relationships, lingering hurts and un-forgiveness, insecurities and inflated egos. However, in a marriage, when two people come together as one, they must deal with all of the baggage. You cannot just sweep it under a rug and think that it is going to just stay there. No, trust me, it shows up one way or the other. Take me, for example," Pastor Goodwin folded his hands and looked directly at Jonah and Kayla, "I came in the marriage with a huge chip on my shoulder. I was an angry man, but I concealed it for many years. I concealed it from my wife. She had no idea that she was marrying a man who was angry and had a temper. I would never hit her, but our first apartment had holes in every room. After a rough day, I would put my fist through the wall to relieve the pressure I was feeling. It scared Lauren. It got so bad that Lauren had her bags packed and was ready to leave me."

"Why were you so angry?" Kayla asked.

"My father was a very abusive man, to my mother and to me and my siblings. Even after leaving that abusive environment, going to college and giving my life to Christ, inwardly, I battled with anger issues," Pastor Reggie confessed. "I thought once I became a saved man and worked in the church, prayed and read my Bible, the anger would just go away, but not so. You

190

have to deal with your issues. Just like a drug addict or an alcoholic, I had to first admit that I had a problem. I told my pastor about it and he helped me work through it. Eventually, I learned how to let go and let God deliver me from all the anger I had inside of me. He helped me through it. It wasn't an instant miracle; it was a process of healing and forgiving. Eventually, the anger dissipated and I forgave my father."

"Is he still alive?" Jonah asked.

"Yes, and he's a changed man, I'm proud to say." Pastor Reggie still felt honored about leading his father to Christ. "I said all of that to say this: you can't hide skeletons in the closet forever. Sooner or later, they will come out and show up in all sorts of ways. Have you two been totally honest with each other? Are you showing your true selves to one another? Is there something that affects you now, individually, that can possibly affect your marriage later? Are you tackling your issues together, or are you avoiding dealing with them? These are serious questions that require serious and honest answers."

Jonah looked at Kayla. His conscious was tugging at him to be truthful about his past, all of it. Shame engulfed him. He feared the truth would run her off for good. The risk of losing Kayla was too great for him to take.

"Jonah has a twin brother, who he hasn't seen in over five years," Kayla timidly began. "Joel told Jonah he wanted nothing to do with him and that he no longer considered him a brother. That was five years ago, and Jonah still suffers from it as if it happened yesterday. He—he's not whole, Pastor Reggie." Kayla turned to Jonah, her eyes watering. "He loves his brother and needs him, but Jonah refuses to reach out to him."

"Jonah," Pastor Reggie knew this issue had to be dealt

with. "Have you ever read the story of Philemon?"

Jonah shook his head.

"It's a short book, but a very powerful one. It deals with forgiveness and restoration. It shows God's amazing ability to look beyond our faults and see our need to be loved, forgiven, and restored." Pastor Reggie opened his Bible and read a few verses. Jonah's heart pounded in his chest, beating wildly. Surely, both Pastor Reggie and Kayla could hear its thundering sound.

Closing the Bible, Pastor Reggie synopsized the message. "Paul was sending Onesimus back to his owner, Philemon, even though it could mean the death penalty for him. Paul made an earnest plea to Philemon to have mercy and to show love to Onesimus, just as Christ had shown love to him. To ensure that Onesimus would be okay, Paul offered to pay Onesimus' debt, just as Jesus paid our debt on the cross. Onesimus did wrong. You did wrong. Onesimus ran away from his problem and found Christ Jesus through Paul. You were sent away to prison, where you found Christ Jesus. After some time, Paul sent Onesimus back to deal with his issue. But Onesimus was not going back the same way he left. He was a changed man. He was loved by Paul and loved by God. Just as I believe it is time for you to go back to your brother. Face the issues. Be like Onesimus and go back. Joel will see that you are not the same man. And if, by chance, he does not, then that is on him. Jonah, you cannot keep running from it. You cannot allow this hole in your heart to bleed continuously. I know you hurt for your brother. It is time to let go of it all. It's time to forgive, heal, and move forward."

Jonah could not hold back any longer. His strong resolve crumbled and he buried his face in his hands and cried. His body trembled with agony. Kayla gently rubbed his back in a soothing motion to comfort him.

Pastor Reggie felt God's presence and knew He was working on Jonah's heart. "Jesus already paid the debt for your sin on the cross. You cannot recompense your brother for your wrongs. All you can do is ask him to forgive you. And all I am asking of you today is that you forgive yourself. Christ Jesus expects you to. Confront your past. Face your brother. If you don't, Jonah, you will not be a whole man, and neither will your marriage be whole."

"I hurt my brother," Jonah sobbed. "I betrayed him and…I don't think he'll ever forgive me for that."

"Onesimus stole from his master and was deserving of death, and yet he went back to face the man who could have him killed. Paul said," Pastor Reggie opened his Bible and read, "For perhaps he departed for a while for this purpose, that you might receive him forever, no longer as a slave but more than a slave—a beloved brother, especially to me but how much more to you, both in the flesh and in the Lord. You and Joel were separated for a while, for this purpose—that he will see you no longer as a sinner, or a man who wronged him, but as his beloved brother."

Jonah looked up at the pastor, his heart hopeful and his spirit broken. *Beloved Brother! Oh how I want that Father God! Oh, how I desperately long to be a brother, a beloved brother!*

"Pastor Reggie, I have been having nightmares about my brother. I think Joel is in trouble. I do not know what kind, but we used to sense when the other was hurting or something was not right. He was always sickly. As a baby, his kidneys never fully developed. The doctors said he would always need medical care, but that never happened. We were poor and Aunt Alice couldn't afford taking him back and forth to doctors. She did the best she could. But Joel seemed fine, other than being so tired all the time. I want to reach out to him, but he asked me to stay away from him."

"I understand, Jonah," Pastor Reggie stated. "I also understand there is a season for everything. There was a season for you two to separate, but now I believe this is the season for restoration. Jonah, you can do this. You need to do this."

"And I'll be with you every step of the way," Kayla assured.

"I know," he swallowed, grateful for Kayla being by his side, both physically and emotionally.

Pastor Reggie witnessed the evident love between the twosome. He had no doubt that their marriage would be strong enough to survive both of their pasts.

"Pastor Reggie," Kayla turned to him. "My parents, mainly my father, don't accept my Christianity. He is an atheist. He does not want anything to do with me now that I am a believer. Do you think this issue will cause us problems down the road?"

"Not as long as you both are upfront about it. If you are feeling lonely for your parents, then talk about it with Jonah, and Jonah you listen and support her. Validate her feelings because they are real," Pastor Reggie counseled. "But we will all pray that God will save your parents, Kayla. Remember, God saved Paul. Surely, He can save your father and mother. What are their names? I want to keep them on our prayer list."

"Drew and Kathryn Lovett."

"Well, we've been at this a long time, so I think we will end this session with prayer."

"Will you marry us next Saturday?" Jonah held his breath. He still had issues to deal with. Demons to tackle. Moreover, his brother to face. Not to mention nightmares about Nixon.

Pastor Reggie came from behind his desk and held out his hands for the both of them. Kayla and Jonah seized the offered hands, as they stood in a circle. "It is my honor to marry you, Jonah and Kayla."

Kayla and Jonah happily hugged him.

"You both are good people, with good hearts. You have endured much and have learned even more," Pastor Reggie began. "As long as you keep God first in your individual lives and in your marriage, your marriage will be blessed. Pray together, hurt together, love together, be real together, and face your problems together. Jonah, make amends if at all possible with your brother. Kayla, pray for your parents. You both, rear this baby to know Christ Jesus and to serve Him. Remember, a true dad is one who loves his child, unconditionally, and raises him in the right way. One who stands by him or her and is physically and emotionally there for the child. Jonah, you may not be the biological father, but you are the dad."

"Thanks, Pastor Reggie. I'm going to love our baby no matter what."

"I know," Pastor Reggie clasped their hands again. "Let us pray."

CHAPTER 19

Moving Forward

While Jonah was picking up dinner, Kayla was resting in the apartment. It was then that she realized that her phone was still turned off. Unfortunately, she had missed several calls and text messages.

Lisa left a message, reminding Kayla to pick her up from airport on Friday morning. A message from the hospital, informing that she had been approved for two weeks' vacation. Nevertheless, the message that curled her toes was the one from Yasha Bates.

"Hi I'm Yasha, Joel Bates' wife. I got your note. Please call me as soon as possible." That was left on Friday. There was a text message on Saturday morning.

I am anxious to hear from you. Please call me.

"Thank You, Lord!" Immediately Kayla dialed the number, before Jonah returned.

"Hello!" Yasha answered on the first ring.

"Hi Yasha. This is Kayla."

"Kayla, I'm so glad you returned my call."

"I forgot that my phone was turned off," Kayla was so excited and out of breath. "How are you?"

"I'm great now that you called. How is Jonah?"

"He's wonderful!" Kayla exclaimed. "We're getting married on Saturday. I am marrying the man of my dreams. He's so good to me."

"That's great," Yasha was a little skeptical after all the negative things she had heard about him from Joel. "Umm Kayla, do you know the history of Joel and Jonah?"

"I know some things. I am sure not everything. Jonah is tightlipped about his brother."

"Joel, as well."

"I know that Jonah did some horrible things to Joel. He said something about sleeping with his fiancé."

"Yes, that was unbelievable."

"I know." Awkward silence followed.

"Joel is a pastor."

"I think Jonah mentioned that. So you're a First Lady?"

"Yes, nowhere near being like the former First Lady of the church. I am a First Lady in training. I don't know the first thing about being anybody's First Lady," Yasha laughed. "But, if it means standing by my husband's side, I think I have that covered."

"I'm sure you do."

"We're expecting our first child in about five months. It's a girl!"

"Oh that's wonderful! I'm three months, pregnant," Kayla said timidly, not wanting Yasha to unduly judge her.

"Oh…congratulations!"

"It's not what you think?" Kayla jumped to conclusions.

"I'm not thinking anything," Yasha assured. "I don't know you well enough to think anything. I sincerely congratulate you. Our babies will hopefully grow up, close."

"I hope so."

"So, you said that Jonah was a changed man. He's a Christian."

"Yes, and Pastor Reggie is training him in the ministry, as well. Jonah believes he is called to be a youth pastor."

"Amazing!"

"Do you think Joel would want to see Jonah?"

"I'm not sure," Yasha honestly answered. "Joel...is sick, really sick."

"Oh my goodness!" Kayla sat upward. "Jonah's been having dreams about him and fervently praying for Joel's wellbeing. He sensed that something wasn't right with Joel."

"Twin brothers do that," Yasha sighed. "The thing is Joel doesn't want Jonah to think he wants anything from him. I believe he forgives him...but, there is still a lot of hurt there."

"Rightly so," Kayla understood. "Is Joel going to get better?"

"He needs a kidney transplant...immediately. His been on the list for the past four years, but...with his rare blood type... he hasn't had a kidney match."

"I see." Suddenly, the light bulb clicked on. Kayla understood the urgency now. "And Jonah is probably a perfect match."

"Joel doesn't want Jonah to know...even if it can save his life. He does not want them to reunite out of obligation. It is a debt he does not want to owe to Jonah. I know it's prideful, but Joel is stubborn."

"So, is Jonah. What do you want me to do, Yasha? Do you want me to tell Jonah about his brother's sickness?"

"Maybe after your wedding on Saturday," she was thinking aloud. "You two can come to my house. Joel will probably still be in the hospital and maybe I can talk to Jonah myself. Don't tell him that you spoke to me just yet. Let's do this in person."

"I'm not sure I can keep this from, Jonah," Kayla did not feel good about keeping secrets, especially after the counseling session with Pastor Reggie.

"You're not lying to him, Kayla. I just do not want him to get cold feet and not come. Joel…is dying, Kayla."

"I'm so sorry," Kayla ached. "God is a Healer."

"I know," she sniffed. "Nevertheless, God uses man to make the healing possible, sometimes. I feel that is what God is doing now. But we are dealing with two stubborn men."

"God knows that's the truth," Kayla agreed. "We will be there…uh…Wednesday. Is that soon enough?"

The sooner the better! "It is!"

"I wish I could come to your wedding, but I can't leave Joel."

"That's sweet of you to even want to come. It's going to be a small ceremony with just the bride and groom, my best friend, Jonah's friends, Pastor Reggie and First Lady Lauren."

"What about family, your parents?"

"My parents are atheists," Kayla began to explain. "At least my father is and my mother does whatever my father says. My parents are wealthy and they really would not approve of Jonah. It doesn't matter," she sighed. "As long as I have Jonah, that's all the family I need."

"My parents died in a plane crash, right after my high school graduation," Yasha stated. "I miss them dearly and no matter how much you say it doesn't matter, I know it does, Kayla. Your parents should support you and stand by you, even if they do not agree with your decision to marry. You are grown and can make your own decisions. Regardless, they should be there. I'll pray for them."

"Thanks," Kayla swallowed the lump in her throat.

"It's been good talking to you, Kayla. I feel like we're going to be close friends, close sisters-in-law."

"Me too!"

"Bring pictures of the wedding on Wednesday."

"I will do my best."

"Good."

"I'll be praying for Joel, faithfully."

"Thank you."

"God bless you!" Kayla saluted, closing her cell phone. Instantly, she dropped to her knees and interceded for Joel's healing. She prayed fervently for God to spare his life and for Jonah to be a perfect match for the kidney transplant Joel needed.

"God, touch Jonah's heart, not to hesitate to do the right thing by Joel. Heal both brothers' hearts and heal Joel's body. In Jesus' Name, I pray and believe. Amen.

❧❧❧

Sunday after church, Jonah and Kayla had dinner with Steven and his family. Kayla and Paula, Steven's wife, instantly clicked. The three boys, Kent, Kirt, and Keith, kept the family gathering lively. The boys were eleven, nine, and seven, and were well-mannered, but boys all the same. They couldn't keep still, played rough, and pestered each other relentlessly.

"You see Keith?" Paula pointed to the middle child. "He is the quiet one. He likes reading and writing, while his brothers like playing outdoors. Look at him, trying to fit in with his brother playing basketball," Paula chuckled. "He has two left feet."

Kayla smiled, looking at the proud mother. "Do you want

any more children?"

"I sure do," Paula looked at Kayla. "Steven isn't the boys' biological parent. Their father died. They are from my previous marriage. We want a big family, at least six children. Steven is from a family of eleven and I'm from a family of eight."

"Wow! I would have never known he wasn't their father." Witnessing the love between father and sons validated that Jonah was going to love their baby as his very own.

"Steven adores them, and they adore him. What about you?" Paula asked.

"I'm an only child," Kayla envied the little boys, who had built-in playmates for life. "Jonah has a twin brother. I guess you can say we both have small families."

"How many months are you?"

"Three."

"You aren't showing a bit. At three months, I was a whale," Paula laughed again. "I gained over fifty pounds with each pregnancy."

"I'm showing a little," Kayla pulled her dress tighter. "I lost weight recently, so my clothes are a little big."

"Are you feeling okay?"

"I'm having a lot of nausea, besides that I'm fine."

"Usually during your second trimester, the nausea fades. Just hang in there."

✕✪✕

Meanwhile, Steven was showing Jonah Shane's pictures and trinkets that delved into the history of his deceased brother. "Shane was such an athlete." Steven showed a display case containing numerous trophies of Shane's athletic accomplishments in track, basketball, soccer and football. "He could play any sport. Kent and Kirt have the same ability. Now, Keith, he's my scholar. He's smart like his momma."

Jonah admired the way Steven openly showed affection. He wore his sentiments on his sleeve, not too macho to openly show affection for his family. Jonah wanted to be the same way.

"Shane would be proud of you, Jonah," Steven turned to him. "You're doing great. You took the lemons life handed you and made pretty good lemonade. You are a great worker and I can tell you are going to be a great husband and father."

"How? I feel so inadequate for both tasks."

"My man," Steven rested his hand on Jonah's shoulder, "we all feel inadequate at times. However, the key is allowing God to mold you and shape you into a great husband and great father. Only with Him can we become the men God created us to be. Without God, I would suck at taking care of my family the right way. But because of God, I have a happy home and a happy family."

"I think I am going to reach out to Joel, my twin brother."

"Good. I've been praying for that."

"I'm not going to lie, I'm scared that Joel is going to kick me to the curb when he sees me," Jonah opened up. "I have to at least try. Pastor Reggie encouraged me to read Philemon and to let the story get in my spirit. That's been helpful."

"Good Book! God restores, Jonah!" Steven praised. "He surely can restore your relationship with Joel. You've got to keep the faith."

"It's a daily fight."

"Yes," Steven chuckled. "That's exactly what it is, a fight of faith. So how are you doing with the dreams?"

"Still having them," Jonah admitted. "Sometimes they are

intense, and I wake up in a full sweat, and other times Nixon isn't so powerful." Jonah didn't mention the dreams about his twin.

"That means your spirit man is fighting back. Jonah, God wants you free from all of it. Just keep trusting Him and before you know it you'll sleep in perfect peace."

"I quote Psalms 4:8 every night, 'I will lie down in peace and sleep, for you alone, O Lord, make me dwell in safety.'"

"You're doing good, Jonah. I say the Word is your medicine. Take it daily and watch the symptoms, the dreams disappear."

"I'm counting on it."

"I tell you what, Jonah, my brother, Shane, is smiling from heaven. You just got to keep moving forward and pay-it-forward."

"I will, Steven. You can count on it!"

You got three choices. Live in the past, stay where you are, or keep it moving! Aunt Alice's words came to mind.

I'm going to keep it moving!

CHAPTER 20

The Wedding

Jonah frowned at the haggard-looking face staring back at him in the bathroom mirror. His eyes were red and puffy. His face wet with sweat. His curly hair was damp and in total disarray. His shoulders slumped with defeat. Jonah looked and felt old. This was his wedding day; he should not feel so worn out! Wasn't this supposed to be one of the happiest days of his life?

"Oh, God, look at me! I'm a mess!"

He ran his fingers through his hair. "I can't endure these dreams anymore, Father! Please make them stop! How can I escape my past? How can I escape Nixon? How am I going to be a real man to Kayla? Oh, if she only knew the truth about Nixon, she would probably run as far away from me as she could."

Jonah, let go! Softly, the whispering in his soul pleaded. *Just let go!*

How?

Forgive!

Oh, God, forgive Nixon? He tortured me! He—

You are a prisoner to Nixon. Forgive him and you will be free!

Oh, God! I do not think I can.

You can and you must. Remember, I forgave you.

Tears cascaded down his cheeks. "I want Joel at my wedding. I miss him. I need him." Jonah was heartsick. "Please help me, God. Please take away all this hurt."

Give it to me. Stop holding on to it. Let go, Jonah. Let go of all of it.

Broken, crushed, and humbled, Jonah at last surrendered.

"Take it all Lord! I give it all to You!"

Meanwhile, Kayla and Lisa were at the beauty salon, pampering themselves before Kayla's wedding.

"I can't believe you're getting married," Lisa began. "I feel like it is the right thing, and yet I'm cautiously wondering if things are going just a little too fast."

"Lisa, I love him," Kayla beamed. "Can't you tell? You know me more than anyone does. Can't you see how happy I am? I can't wait to be Mrs. Kayla Bates. Jonah makes me happy! He's like no other man I have ever known."

"What about Isaac?" Lisa asked. "You seemed happy with him."

"As I said before, I was content with him, Lisa. He was a good man. But there was never real chemistry, like with Jonah. What I feel for Jonah can't compare to what I shared with Isaac. I wasn't in love with Isaac. I was lonely and I wanted to please Isaac. He was so good to me, and he was leaving for Iraq. It just seemed like the right thing to do."

"I want to ask you something, but I want you to promise not to get upset with me?" Lisa's straight-faced expression exposed her seriousness.

"Lisa, this is my wedding day. I don't want anything to upset that. So if…"

"Do you think you would be marrying Jonah if you weren't

pregnant?"

"Absolutely! I think my pregnancy might have rushed things a little, which I'm glad. I have no doubt in my mind that I would have agreed to marry Jonah, no matter what. God caused our paths to meet for this reason. To unite us as one!"

Lisa gazed at her friend. In all their years of friendship, Lisa had to admit, she had never witnessed such joy exuding from Kayla.

"Kayla, I am happy for you," Lisa embraced her. "You deserve to be happy. It's about time!"

"Thanks!"

"We better stop all this crying," Lisa wiped at her eyes. "This is a happy day!"

"These are happy tears. I can't wait to marry Jonah! I can't wait!"

"I know the feeling," Lisa giggled. "My goodness, we need to hurry up or you will be late for your wedding."

Kayla's phone vibrated.

"Who is texting you?" Lisa asked.

"It's Yasha, Joel's wife, you know, Jonah's twin brother I told you about. Anyhow, she texted: May God richly bless you and Jonah on this very special day. May your marriage be filled with love, joy, peace, good health and an abundance of wealth. I wish Joel and I could be there. I'm praying for you. Love, your sister-in-law and friend, Yasha."

"That was sweet of her."

"I can't wait to meet her."

✖✖✖

In the meantime, Kathryn was sitting at her dressing table on Saturday morning, feeling extremely melancholy.

My daughter is getting married today! I should be there! She ached inside. Her heart was torn. Ever since Drew had found out about her seeing Kayla, her once secure, stable, posh world was falling apart all around her. She missed Kayla dearly. Also, she missed her intimacy with her husband. He hadn't touched her or slept in the same room with her since Kayla left.

He's trying to teach me a lesson!

What lesson? That I need him. That I cannot make it without him. That if I ever cross him, he'll strip me of everything I have.

Some lesson!

Where is the love? What happened to the man I married?

Kathryn sat in silence. Retrieving a picture she kept in the top drawer of the vanity in her room, Kathryn admired the portrait of her parents. Both of her parents were God-fearing Christians. Her father was strict, but a compassionate man, sometimes working two and three jobs, providing for his wife and three children. No, she didn't grow up in a big, fancy home like the one she lived in now, but their home was always filled with laughter and love. Her mother was the kindest, most giving woman. She would give her last dime to help somebody, often doing without so that she could meet the needs of others. She never raised her voice, but always had such a meek, mild, tender spirit. Being raised in the church, with strict rules and expectations, Kathryn couldn't wait to leave home and all that went along with it, including her parents' religion.

Kathryn went to college in hopes of finding a profession that would secure financial prosperity. She didn't want to struggle with money like her parents. She wanted to live life and live it to the fullest. Wear the finest clothes. Live in the grandest house and drive the finest cars that money could buy. Kathryn threw herself into her studies and made an academic choice of focusing on the sciences, in pursuit of becoming a plastic surgeon. She wanted to help people look better and feel better about themselves since she didn't. After almost completing her medical degree, Kathryn started working at a small clinic that specialized in plastic surgery. That's when she met Drew. He was an intern there, six years younger than her. Right away, the two started seeing each other. Drew became Kathryn's entire world. She believed what he believed. Regrettably, Kathryn never completed her medical degree. She did whatever he wanted her to do. The Kathryn that once was, was no more. She was the woman Drew created. And now, peeling back the onion, layer by layer, Kathryn didn't recognize the face in the mirror. Her daughter was right; she no longer looked like herself. She was Drew's creation. Tears resurfaced. "I miss you so much," she uttered, viewing the picture of her parents. "I wish you were both alive. I would tell you that I am sorry I didn't visit you often. Sorry that I let my marriage keep us apart. Drew wanted nothing to do with religion and so he didn't want me to be around you. What happened to the daughter you raised? I don't know her anymore." Kathryn sobbed. "My daughter is getting married, and I'm not even going to be there."

Why not?

Kathryn looked around startled. *Where did that come from?*

She placed the portrait down and picked up another one. This one was a picture of her and her siblings, Lewis and Daisy. At the time of the photo, she had almost completed her doctorate, and the three were celebrating her sister's wedding. It was a happy day, and the last time they were all together. Regret consumed her.

I wonder how Lewis and Daisy are doing. I wish...

Spontaneously, Kathryn took out her cell phone, searching

for Daisy's old number. Feeling blue, Kathryn dialed the unfamiliar number. She was about to hang up, when finally the phone was answered.

"Hello."

"Daisy?"

"Yes."

"Daisy, this is Kathryn," her voice cracked as she spoke.

"Katie!" she exclaimed. "Glory be to God! You're alive!"

Kathryn hadn't heard that nickname in over twenty years. It was the last time she had spoken with Daisy, ending in a very heated argument. "I'm alive," Kathryn sniffed.

"Lewis isn't going to believe this."

"How is Lewis?"

"He's doing good."

"How are you?"

"I'm great, better than ever now that I'm talking to you. It's so good to hear your voice." There was no bitterness, no anger, and no malice. All Daisy felt was gratitude. "I have two wonderful sons, Lance and Troy, and I'm a proud grandmother of four. And Lewis, he has six grandchildren and three girls: Sylvia, Julian, and Fran. What about you?"

"I have a daughter and…." Kathryn sobbed, "she's getting married today."

"How wonderful, I think." Daisy was thrown off kilter by her sister's sniveling.

"I'm not going to be there."

"Why in the world not? That's crazy. Are you ill?"

"No, I'm fine."

"Well, excuse me, sister, but what in the world is wrong with you? What would keep a mother from attending her daughter's wedding?"

"Drew."

"Oh, Drew," Daisy scoffed. "Your daughter must be a Christian."

"She is."

"Katie, when are you going to grow a backbone?" Frustration was evident in Daisy's tone. "Drew kept you from your parents. You didn't even attend your own parents' funerals. Drew kept you from having a relationship with your own brother and sister. You haven't even seen my children. And I didn't know you had a child! This is crazy. Grow a backbone! Tell Drew to go fly a kite! Don't let him keep you from your daughter! Are you going to walk away from…from…."

"Her name is Kayla."

"Kayla, like you walked away from all of us?" Daisy sniffed, trying to hold it all together. Years of pain threatened to surface. "All these years, not one word from you. We thought that surely something bad had happened to you."

"I'm so sorry, Daisy. Please forgive me."

"Of course I forgive you. But, Katie, you will never forgive yourself if you don't attend Kayla's wedding. Never!"

"I know."

"Then do something about it!"

Thirty minutes later, Kathryn was driving towards Holly Hill! She'd arrive just in time for the wedding, if she didn't make any stops. *It's time for me to get the old Katie back! Not the old, stuffy, fake Kathryn, who looks like a fake. I don't even recognize me anymore.* She knew that by driving to Holly Hill she had all but signed her divorce papers. Drew certainly would not hesitate to divorce her now. She had made her choice—freedom!

Jonah took deep breaths as he waited for his bride to make her grand entrance. Pastor Goodwin smiled at him, encouraging him to relax.

Relax! I'm nervous as a cat on a hot tin roof, as my Aunt Alice would say.

Steven, his best man, leaned over. "Man, you look like you're about to run out of here. You okay?"

"I'm fine. Just anxious...to see...my bride!"

His heart skipped a few beats as Jonah beheld his future wife standing in the doorway of the church. Naturally beautiful, never had he imagined that Kayla could look any more beautiful. Oh, but she most certainly was! Her splendor was angelic! *She's gorgeous! Her gown is absolutely amazing! She looks like a princess—my princess!* Jonah's chest puffed out a bit more. At his request, Kayla's long, curly locks cascaded freely down her back. Complete calmness engulfed Jonah. His eyes were glossy, his smile wide, and his heart overflowing with an indescribable sensation. Truly, Jonah's cup ran over.

Their eyes locked from afar.

Hurry up here, Kayla! I've been waiting for you all my life.

Kayla couldn't believe the time had finally arrived to marry her soul mate. Walking slowly up the aisle, alone, she shook off the melancholy feeling. Sure, what daughter didn't want to hold the arm of her father as he walked her down the aisle? And what daughter didn't want to have her mother help her to dress and prepare for this special day? At least she had Lisa to help her. Kayla looked to her friend, her matron of honor standing at the altar, wearing a beautiful lavender gown. Then, fixing her eyes on her husband-to-be, Kayla felt overwhelmingly blessed. God was surely smiling down on her. Dressed in a white suit, Jonah was smashingly handsome. Even though it wasn't tailor made, it fit his muscular body perfectly. *Be still, my heart!*

Granted, Kayla's family wasn't there to witness this momentous occasion, but the fact that she was creating a new family, this very day, overrode any negativity. God was giving her a new family, someone to love her, unconditionally, for who she was. Jonah would be a great father to her child, not expecting him/her to be perfect, but allowing the child room to grow, spread wings, and soar. He would lead their family in their Christian walk.

Kayla smiled at First Lady Lauren, and Paula, Steven's wife, and then Patrick. It was a small affair, not what she had dreamed of as a girl, but perfect all the same. All that mattered was that she was happy and in love. As she stepped closer to Jonah, he hastily seized her hand, kissing her palm.

"You're stunning, taking my very breath away."

Her heart leaped. "Thank you. You are so handsome, Jonah."

Kayla's hazelnut eyes drew him in, hypnotizing him. Jonah was a goner! His heart wholly belonged to Kayla.

"Um, Kayla," Lisa apologetically interrupted them.

Kayla looked at her friend.

"Look!" Lisa glanced over in the audience.

She couldn't believe her eyes. Kathryn Lovett had just sat down in the first row, next to First Lady Lauren.

Jonah squeezed her hands.

"It's my mother."

"God answers prayers." Jonah felt Kayla's bliss.

She looked at Pastor Goodwin. "Excuse me one minute,"

In two strides, Kayla was in the arms of her mother. "Oh,

Momma, thank you!"

"I wouldn't miss this for the world!" Kathryn reluctantly pulled away. "You are so beautiful, Kayla. So very beautiful!"

"Thank you," she wiped at her eyes.

"Here," Kathryn said, removing a kerchief from her purse and dabbing gently at Kayla's face. "No more tears. Now go, marry that handsome man."

"He is handsome, isn't he?" With her heart in her eyes, Kayla looked at her eager husband-to-be. "Love you, Momma, so much." Kayla kissed her cheeks and rushed back to the altar.

"Now where were we?" Kayla captured her husband's hands.

As the two recited their vows and went through the short but sweet ceremony, Kayla and Jonah never once took their eyes off of each other. Everything was perfect! At last, the bride and groom heard the acknowledgment they had been waiting for. "I now pronounce you husband and wife. Jonah, you may salute your bride," Pastor Reggie Goodwin advocated.

Jonah kissed Kayla with such sweetness that she melted in his embrace, her breath jammed in her chest. In their minds, the people around them vanished. Temporarily, Jonah and Kayla were in their own little world. They were irrevocably drawn together by an unseen force. Love had brought them together, and it would keep them together. Today, their different worlds joined, becoming one – a marriage of endless possibilities.

CHAPTER 21

Haunted Honeymoon

A small reception was held in the church's dining hall, courtesy of First Lady Lauren. A party of nine people, including the bride and groom, sat at a large oval table as the food was served to them by caterers.

"Father doesn't know you're here, does he?" Kayla whispered to her mother.

"He probably does by now," Kathryn shrugged. "It really doesn't matter. All that matters is that I am here. I would have never forgiven myself otherwise."

"I'm so glad you're here," Kayla touched her mother's hand. "You being here made this day perfect."

"You look so happy, Kayla."

"I am."

"And the baby?" Kathryn looked around making sure no one was listening.

"Mom, everyone at this table knows I'm pregnant," Kayla replied. "And it doesn't matter. They accept us for who we are," Kayla said, turning briefly to her husband.

"I love you." Jonah pecked her cheek.

"I love you." Kayla replied back, slowly turning back to her mother. "What are you going to do, Momma?"

"I'm going to visit my sister, Daisy."

"Sister?" Kayla never knew her mother had any siblings. Kathryn's childhood was a closed subject, thanks to dear *old* father.

"Yes, I have an older sister, Daisy, and an older brother, Lewis. They both live in Kentucky. I'm going to fly out tonight."

"Really?"

"Really!" Kathryn had never felt lighter. Albeit, she was frighten by it all, there was also an excitement in the air. Kathryn missed her family immensely, more than she had allowed herself to admit before. Though her parents were no longer living, she still had time to reconnect with Daisy and Lewis.

"I'm happy for you, Momma. I haven't seen you like this before."

"Like what?"

"Genuinely excited, almost like a kid."

"I am excited. I cannot wait to see my family."

"How much longer do we have to stay here?" Jonah whispered in Kayla's ear, his eyes twinkling flirtatiously.

"We have all night, my love. All night," Kayla teased with a wink.

It seemed that nothing could ruin this day for Kayla and Jonah.

✖✖✖

After dropping both Kathryn and Lisa off at the airport, Jonah followed behind Kayla's rental, driving Kathryn's Mercedes Benz. Today had been a royal day, and Jonah felt even more royal behind the wheels of his mother-in-law's luxury vehicle. Surprisingly, he and Kathryn had hit it off pretty well. Obviously, she was still skeptical about her only daughter marrying beneath their expectations. Nevertheless, Kathryn had kept a pleasant attitude the entire day, and had even entrusted her car to Jonah. *That must have a hurt a little!* Jonah smiled as he parked next to his wife's vehicle.

My wife! His heart swelled.

Rushing to open Kayla's car door, Jonah scooped her up in his arms.

"Jonah! I'm too heavy!"

"Please, you probably weigh less than a hundred pounds soaking wet."

"I'm pregnant, Jonah. I weigh more than that."

"Yeah, right." He opened the door and carried her over the threshold. "Here we are, Mrs. Bates."

"I like the sound of that, Mr. Bates."

Gently putting her down, Jonah weaved his fingers through her curly hair, unclipping the barrette that held her hair back on the sides. His eye contact spoke a love language only lovers would understand. Jonah's heartbeats were erratic. "I love you so much, Kayla," he mumbled, his breath delicate on her neck. Softly, his lips glazed her neck, then her cheeks, forehead, and the tip of her nose. Their eyes locked. Kayla's pulse quickened at his touch. Her breathing was unsteady, her heart mounting. Life was good!

At last, his lips claimed hers in complete oneness. Her lips tasted like sweetness, Jonah could not get enough of them. The kisses intensified. He kissed Kayla like she had never been kissed before, so full of passion and desire. Kayla thought surely that she was in heaven.

Breaking, Jonah looked at Kayla with a lengthy pause.

And then…

It happened….

Jonah's worst nightmare became reality. As he leaned over and kissed her again, visions of ugliness danced in his head. He no longer saw Kayla. Instead, he saw Nixon. Instantly, the kisses turned bitter as tart!

Abruptly, Jonah pulled away, a look of disdain on his face.

"What's wrong?" Kayla worried, feeling slighted. She had never seen such a disgusting look on his face.

He could not speak.

"Jonah! What is it?" Kayla became flustered, her cheeks reddened.

"I….I can't do this!" He freaked and fled out the door as if he were being chased.

"Jonah!" Kayla yelled, following him out the door. "Jonah come back! Please come back!" Closing the door, Kayla ran to the bedroom, dropped on the bed, and began to cry. *I'm too fat!* Kayla pulled her wedding dress on both sides, revealing a little pudgy tummy. *Jonah must find me undesirable. But I thought*—the floodgates burst. Eventually, she cried herself to sleep.

Meanwhile, Jonah ran until his legs would not go another step. Instinctively getting on the bus, the demons of the past chased Jonah all the way back to Aunt Alice's. He entered the dark, musky home and sat on the couch. "Oh, God! I've messed up!" He envisioned the unsettled look on Kayla's face. He had hurt her. Like a coward, he ran from her. Instead of staying and dealing with those horrid demons, Jonah let them hold him back from the one thing he wanted more than anything else, to become fully one with Kayla.

"Stupid! Idiot!" He paced the floor. "Forgive Nixon! I hate

him! I hate what he did to me! I hate what he is doing to me now! How can You expect me to forgive him, God? How?"

I forgave you!

The same answer as always.

But God…

Forgiveness will lead to your freedom! Forgive him! Not for him, but for you!

Jonah dropped to his knees and whimpered like a wounded animal. Truly, Jonah was suffering. His soul mourned. His spirit groaned. Jonah was a broken man.

There Jonah slept on his honeymoon night, on the floor.

✖✖✖✖

The following morning, with his head tucked between his legs, Jonah entered the duplex and found Kayla sitting at the kitchen table, dallying over a bowl of cereal.

Her red, swollen eyes locked with his. Guilt and shame knocked the wind out of him, and he felt he deserved it.

"I'm sorry," Jonah knelt beside her.

"What did I do, Jonah?" the tears started all over again.

"Nothing. It is not you, Kayla. It's me," he gently wiped her tears with his fingers. "Kayla, I don't deserve you."

"Please don't say that, Jonah. I thought we were passed that."

"Me too." Jonah laid his head on her lap. "But I don't know if I can ever get past my past, Kayla."

Kayla cupped her hands under his chin, and pushed it upward, so he could face her. "Jonah, together we can overcome anything, but not if you run away or keep me in the dark. I cannot bear you leaving me like that. I was alone, and worried…and…"

"Shush," he touched her lips. "I apologize, sincerely. Please forgive me, Baby."

"I forgive you, Jonah," she said easily. "But I still don't understand what happened last night."

Jonah got off the floor and sat next to her. "You need to eat." Jonah frowned at her untouched bowl. "You have to eat for you and our baby."

"Don't change the subject, Jonah."

"I'm not," he smiled. "I just want you to eat, that's all."

Obediently, she consumed her cereal, not wanting anything to get in the way of the much-needed conversation with her husband. "Now are you satisfied?" She shoved the emptied bowl away from her. "Let's talk. What happened last night?"

Jonah struggled with what to say. He could be totally upfront and tell her the entire truth about Nixon, or he could shove it on the back burner of his mind and pray that it would never happen again. Jonah chose to put it on the back burner. "I was scared." He was playing with fire and somebody was bound to get burn if he did not come clean with the truth soon.

"Scared?" her forehead creased with confusion. "Scared of me?"

"Scared of not living up to your expectations."

"My only expectation is to be your wife and to make you happy. But obviously...I didn't last night."

"Oh, I was very, very happy," Jonah held her hands in his. "I was just a fool, Kayla. A big fool! Can we please take this slow?"

"What do you mean, Jonah?" Kayla stood. "You don't want me? Is that it? You don't find me attractive?" She closed her robe, feeling portly. "It's because I'm carrying another man's baby."

"This is our baby!" Jonah emphasized. "And Kayla, yes, I want you," he pulled her into her arms. "I just think, well, we need to take our time. Get to really know each other. We have a lifetime of intimacy. We don't have to rush into it."

"Jonah!" She pulled away. "What is going on here? I am not stupid! I know something else is going on! You're a man and I'm a woman, and we both love each other. It doesn't make sense!"

"Kayla, I love you."

"If you really loved me, you wouldn't be running from me, but to me!" The unhappy newlywed marched out of the kitchen and into the bedroom, slamming the door as hard as she could.

Lord, help me!

Forgive!

They did not speak the entire day. Late in the evening, Kayla finally came out of the bedroom. Jonah was sitting in the living area, flipping channels. Kayla sat next to him. His heart ached when he saw the redness around her eyes. He felt like such a heel. After all, he was the reason for her hurt.

"I don't want to fight, Jonah," Kayla began.

"Me either."

She turned to him. "I don't understand any of this, Jonah. But as your wife, I am going to do my best to make this work. I know that you have endured a lot of hurts in your past. I just wish you would let me in here," Kayla laid her hands on his chest. "I love you and I'll wait as long as you want me to wait."

"Kayla, please don't doubt my love for you. I really do love you." Her sacrificial words had penetrated his being.

"I know you do, Jonah."

Hugging her to his chest, Jonah did not want to let go. He

pecked her lips several times before leaning back. "I don't want to lose you, Kayla."

"You will never lose me. I'm not going anywhere."

"You promise?"

"I promise."

"Are we still traveling to Macon City tomorrow?"

"I think we should," Kayla replied.

"Are you hungry?"

"Starving."

"Let's go out to dinner?" he suggested.

"Fine," she forced a smile. "Let me go change out of these sweatpants and this t-shirt."

She had never look prettier to Jonah. Reaching for her hand, he gently pivoted her around into his arms. His lips captured hers for a real kiss. It felt so right being with Kayla and kissing her. Why couldn't he just—but he could not. Again, Nixon's face appeared. Fear gripped Jonah like a noose around his neck.

Kayla's witnessed his sudden transformation, but tried to move passed it. "I'll be ready in a few," she said, offering a smile as she left the room.

✠✠✠

After returning from dinner, the married couple slept cuddled together in the same bed without becoming totally intimate. The closeness was somewhat satisfying for Kayla, but left Jonah longing for something more.

Two times, Kayla awakened her husband from tossing and turning in his sleep. *Whatever secret Jonah is keeping from me, it is obviously taking a toll on him and playing out in his dreams.*

Early the following morning, after returning Kayla's

rental, the couple drove to Macon City in Kathryn's car. The three-hour drive seemed longer, due to the underlying tension between Jonah and Kayla. Endeavoring to reassure Kayla of his love for her, continuously, Jonah sent smiles her way and squeezed her hand. Still, neither of them could deny that an elephant was riding in the car with them. Jonah carried guilt, while Kayla harbored insecurities, both infiltrating the atmosphere with confusion.

God is not the author of confusion.

Arriving at the Marriott, Kayla unpacked and helped her husband get settled before leaving to stop by her office. She needed to pick up a few files from Lovett's Restoration Plastic Surgery Center and check on a patient at the hospital before taking the rest of the week off. Attempting to go behind the building in order to avoid running into her father, Kayla could not unlock the back door. Irritated, Kayla walked around the front and went inside.

"Good morning, Ms. Kayla," Tiffany, the receptionist, greeted. "Can I help you?"

"Yes, Tiffany. I used my key to unlock the back door, but my key didn't work," Kayla explained.

"Dr. Lovett had all the locks changed yesterday," Tiffany stated.

Kayla was dumfounded. "Does my office key work?"

"No, I'm sorry. He changed all the locks and he said if anyone needs a new key that they would need to see him first. No exceptions."

"Is he around?" Kayla felt sick. *How can he be so mean-spirited? He is heartless, that is how!*

Tiffany checked his schedule. "Actually, he has about fifteen minutes before his next client. Let me check to make sure it's okay." Tiffany felt bad. Dr. Lovett made it perfectly clear that Kayla and his wife had no authority at the Center anymore, and had to go through him to get anything.

"You can go back," Tiffany replied after getting Dr. Lovett's approval for Kayla to see him. "Ms. Kayla, it's so good to see you. I missed seeing your smiling face."

"Thanks, Tiffany." Kayla walked away with dread resting upon her petite shoulders.

Lord, give me the strength to face the lion!

I am with you. Walk in love!

"Dr. Lovett," Kayla greeted.

"Miss Lovett," Drew stared at her. "Or is it Mrs. Bates?"

Kayla wasn't the least bit surprised that her father already knew of her marriage. "Yes, it's Mrs. Bates," her voice trembled.

"You're a disgrace to the family!" he lashed out. "Marrying a criminal! Marrying beneath you! You never were a Lovett! I tried to make you into something! You have greatly disappointed me!"

"And you, Dr. Lovett, have greatly disappointed me!" Kayla found the courage to stand up for herself. "Yes, you tried to make me into something, just like mother. Why couldn't you just accept us and love us the way we are. I feel sorry for you."

"For me!" Drew scoffed. "Don't feel sorry for me. I have everything I need."

"Everything but a heart! You're a heartless man," Kayla turned to go.

"Your former office has been cleared. You are no longer an employee here," he said with disdain. "See Tiffany on your way out and she will have your things brought to you. And if you see that mother of yours, tell her she is not welcome here or in my home."

Walk in love!

Taking deep breaths, Kayla turned and walked to her father's desk so that she could face him eye to eye. "I am going to pray for you, Dr. Lovett. I am going to ask God to soften your stony heart with His love. I thank God for you raising me as your daughter, and even though you don't want anything to do with me now, I still love you." Kayla meant every word. "I will always love you."

Drew stared at Kayla. She was brave, facing him that way. Where did she get the courage? And how could she still say she loved him after the way he treated her?

"Get out!" he yelled.

"Goodbye." Kayla walked away with dignity, though she hurt deeply. Closing the door, she stood for a minute, allowing the tears to fall. She ached something fierce. Even though Drew did not deserve her love, she still loved him, and always would. Kayla could not turn love off like a faucet.

God, I cast this care on You. You know my heart is heavy! I have no earthly father anymore, and I have no job with the family. Through it all, I still have You, and I have Jonah and our baby! I know I can make it.

All things are working together for your good.

CHAPTER 22

Jonah and Kayla went house hunting the following day. After seeing six houses in one day, both of them felt deflated. The prices were too extravagant for Jonah, and none of them felt homey to Kayla. The large, empty homes resembled the emptiness Kayla felt. The inability to provide Kayla with what she deserved, and was accustomed to, diminished Jonah's sense of manhood.

He did his best to make up for their lack of intimacy by lavishing Kayla with attention and affection during the day. He was sensitive to her every need. Making sure she rested. Making sure she ate. Making sure, he held her hand and frequently spoke sentiments of adoration. It was not something Jonah had to force himself to do, for he found it easy to love her. Making Kayla happy was all he wanted to do, but the fact that Jonah had not completely given her all of him gnawed at him relentlessly. He was trying, though.

Nevertheless, there comes a time when one must stop trying and just do! That is faith in action!

Faith without works is dead!

Wednesday, while having lunch at Sandy's deli, Kayla broached the subject of contacting Yasha Bates.

"Jonah, there is something I have to tell you," she began nervously. "I, uh…"

"Go head, Kayla. You can talk to me about anything." Jonah had no idea what Kayla was about to tell him, but inwardly, he knew that it was going to be a doozy.

"I contacted Yasha Bates."

He swallowed, unsure of what he was feeling. A range of emotions submerged him. All Jonah knew was that Kayla's revelation was about to shake his world—either for the better or the worse. Since seeing the wedding photos of his brother and wife, Jonah had not ceased praying for them.

"Say something," Kayla fretted. "Are you mad at me?"

He shook his head, still speechless.

"You were so down, and having those dreams about Joel, and I just wanted to help. So, I went to see her when I was here last."

"You saw her?" Jonah forced out the words.

"No, she wasn't home. I left her a note, and I told her if she thought Joel was ready to see you, to contact me; but if she felt he wasn't ready, then don't respond to my note." She paused, and then said, "She called me."

Jonah gasped, finding it hard to breathe. It felt like his airway was blocked. Abruptly, he leapt up.

"Jonah!"

"I have to get some air." Jonah took twenty dollars out of his wallet for Kayla to pay the bill.

Quickly, Kayla went to the cashier. *Oh God, help Jonah. Please let him consent to go see Yasha this evening.*

"Jonah," Kayla called as she caught up with him. He had

walked quite a distance, trying to digest the information his wife had just shared with him.

"She called you back." His lips quivered as his eyes began to water.

She nodded.

"That means Joel wants to see me." Hope had taken wings in his heart, ready to fly to wherever Joel was now.

"Jonah, there is something else…"

Jonah stopped in his tracks, his heart rate elevating to an abnormal level.

"Joel is sick. Very sick."

"Oh no!" Jonah's knees buckled. Kayla hugged him to herself. "What is wrong with him, Kayla?"

"Yasha wants to tell you. I promised her that I would let her talk to you about it."

"Please tell me, Kayla," he begged. "It probably has something to do with his kidneys."

"I want to Jonah," she caressed his face, "but I promised. She's waiting to see us."

"Now?"

"She should be home now. I will call her and let her know we are on the way. Is that okay?"

He nodded. "Oh, Kayla, I'm afraid. What if, after all this time, I lose my brother?" he asked through choked sobs.

"You will not lose him." Kayla held him tighter. "God is a Healer and a Deliverer. He did not bring you all this way to lose Joel! I don't believe that."

"I pray so," Jonah said, worried.

"Let's pray, Jonah. Right now." Kayla took over. "God, you know all about Joel. You know his illness and You know how to heal him. Your Word says that by Your stripes we are already healed and that Jesus took our infirmities and bore our sickness. Therefore, on the cross, any sickness and disease that the enemy tries to attack us with, we are already healed from. It was finished on the cross. Touch Joel and touch Jonah. Reunite them in love and let them live a long life together, rekindling their love for one another. We surrender this all to you. We cast this care on You, knowing that You have already answered and that You have already healed Joel's body and healed Jonah's heart. And Father, forgive us our sins as we forgive those who have sinned against us and hurt us. In Jesus' name, amen."

"Amen." Jonah stared at Kayla. She had prayed such a sweet prayer. Kayla had the biggest heart, just like Aunt Alice. She put his needs above her own needs. He loved her more and more each day. She walked in forgiveness, even after the way her father treated her, even after the way her husband withheld himself from her. God was definitely trying to reach Jonah. His wife was breathtaking. In his arms, with her hair pulled back in a ponytail and her eyes moistened, cheeks glowing, Jonah was in awe that God had so blessed him. Leaning over, Jonah tenderly kissed his wife, tasting her tears and his own. Together, they could face anything. Together, they could walk in forgiveness.

❈❈❈

"Lot of land," Jonah admired Joel's property as he opened his wife's door to escort her to the front door. "My brother has done well for himself."

"He has," Kayla took his sweaty hand. "They have a beautiful home. It's going to be all right, Jonah," Kayla smiled at him.

Her smile lit up his world, pushing the darkness back.

230

"I have you and God," he said. "It has to be all right, one way or the other."

"I love you, Jonah."

"I love you, too," he said and kissed her cheek. "Now let's go face this together."

Yasha immediately answered the doorbell. "I'm glad you are both here." She hugged Kayla first, and then Jonah. Her heart lurched as she took a good like a Jonah. He was a carbon copy of Joel, but her husband was not built with the same muscular frame. Jonah had at least twenty pounds on Joel. They both had the same dimple on the right cheek. And those eyes, identical, with the same hollowness overshadowing them. And that good grain of hair, curly and soft. Albeit, Joel's hair was much thinner as a result of the various medications he was on. Yasha still relished its softness. "Please come in." She escorted them into the large family area.

"Kayla didn't tell me you were expecting, as well," Jonah grinned. "Congratulations."

"Faith will be here in five months." Yasha rubbed her belly. "Kayla and I are going to be first time mothers."

"It's exciting!" Kayla beamed, looking at her husband. Their eyes spoke volumes.

Yasha was observant, and knew immediately that they were in love. It brought back the look in her husband's eye for her. Oh, how she missed him. She wanted so badly for him to come home, healthy and whole.

"Congratulations to you both on your marriage," Yasha happily acknowledged.

"Thank you," the couple replied in unison.

"Kayla told me that my brother was sick, but she wouldn't say what's wrong with him." Jonah jumped right in.

"First, I want to ask you something." Yasha fixed her eyes on Jonah, unblinking.

"Please, go ahead," Jonah said as Kayla squeezed his hand for support.

"There have been years of separation between you and Joel. He told me a little about it, but I want to hear it from you. What happened?"

Jonah did not expect this, and yet he should have. "I was a fool. My Aunt Alice said I had a hard head and just would not listen. She was right. Joel and I had a rough childhood. Mom was a drug addict. Dad left us. The only good thing about our lives was that we had Aunt Alice. But, we lived in such a rough area. You either did what others did to survive, or you lived like an outcast. Joel was sickly and stayed inside all the time. He was the outcast. I was with the in-crowd. Joel lived by the Bible; I disobeyed everything in the Bible. Joel forgave, I hated. Joel had a compassionate, forgiving heart, and I was angry all the time. I got into trouble all the time. Joel was good and honest, but he stuck with me. Growing up, we had each other's back. But the tables turned." Jonah buried his face in his hands, trying to find the strength to go on.

"It's okay, sweetheart," Kayla consoled him.

He smiled at her, his eyes wet. "Joel had my back, but I no longer had his back. I lied to him. I stole from him. I rejected him and then…I slept with his fiancé." Jonah looked at Yasha. "She was no good for him, but still, that was wrong. I had been locked up several times and Joel would bail me out. But the last time, he said that was it! He had washed his hands clean of me and wanted nothing to do with me. I did not blame him. He was right. I deserved to be locked up and I deserved him walking away from me and never looking back."

"I guess I should thank you for breaking up Joel and his ex-fiancé," Yasha said as she came over and took his hand, "because I love Joel with all my heart. He is the best thing that has ever happened to me, besides Jesus Christ."

"Joel has always been a good man."

"And so are you." Yasha's voice held an even tone. "You may have messed up, but who hasn't? God forgives and He forgets. Joel has hurt for many years over you, and I pray that now—now restoration will surely come to the both of you."

"Thank you," Jonah embraced his sister-in-law. "Thank you, so much."

"Before we talk about Joel's illness, I want to see your wedding pictures." Yasha needed something to change the mood, momentarily, before discussing her husband's health.

"I have a few," Kayla took out the small photo album. "My mom came."

"Praise God! I prayed that she would," Yasha exclaimed. "Won't God do it every time?"

"Yes, He will!"

"Wow, these are beautiful. Kayla, your gown was amazing! You are so beautiful." Yasha smiled at Kayla. "And you're just as handsome as your brother." Yasha looked to Jonah. "So very handsome." Her heart swelled with pride as Yasha's mind drifted to her husband. "Joel wore a white suit, similar to yours at our wedding."

"I know. Aunt Alice left me an album of your wedding pictures."

"She was such a sweet woman," Yasha said. "I miss her. She talked about you a lot with me. She told me about your salvation. She never stopped praying for you. You made her so very happy."

Fresh tears sprung forth in Jonah's eyes. "I miss her so much. Aunt Alice was the greatest."

Yasha closed the photo and tried to hand it back to Kayla.

"It's for you to keep. We want you and Joel to have it."

"Thank you," Yasha hugged it to her bosom before putting it down. "Well, let me tell you about your brother." She again looked at Jonah, worry in her eyes. "He has kidney failure. Dialysis is no longer working."

Jonah's heart dropped, having no idea Joel was even on dialysis. He expected bad, but not this bad. He struggled not to go into panic mode. Jonah was heartsick for his brother. It was as if he was feeling the physical symptoms of his brother within himself. In all truthfulness, he had been feeling this way for some time now.

"He's really ill. He is in the end stage of kidney failure. He has been sick for a long time during our marriage. But you know Joel, he was stubborn. He would not go to the doctor for a while. Said he was tired of being pricked by doctors. He had endured enough. By the time Joel finally went, well you know the diagnosis. He's been on dialysis two to three times a week for years. It seemed that everything was fine, just a little inconvenience with the treatments. But now, the dialysis is not doing the job it once did. Joel's health is declining, rapidly. Every day is a miracle for Joel. The only thing that can save him is a kidney transplant, unless God Almighty hurries up and performs a miracle, which we know He can."

"I'll do it!" Jonah did not wait to be asked. "Whatever Joel needs, I'll do it."

"Thank you!" Yasha rushed to him and hugged. "Oh God, thank you!"

"God is faithful!" Kayla joined the hug.

"But Joel mustn't know." Yasha stepped back. "He wants to see you, but not like this. He does not want to ask you to do this, because he does not want recompense."

"I don't care. I do not want Joel to die. I will do it anonymously. Tell me, who do I need to call? What do I need to do? Anything, I'll do it if it will save my brother!"

"I have already spoken to his doctor, Dr. Thomasina Benson. She said if you agree to do it, she will not be in tomorrow, but she wants you to come by Friday morning and be tested." Yasha retrieved the card from her purse. "Here is the address of the hospital and her number."

"Is Joel in this hospital?"

"He is, but you can't see him just yet, or he'll know."

"I promise, I won't let him see me," Jonah assured. "But somehow, I've just got to see him."

"I understand."

"Thank you for calling my wife back. Joel has always been there for me, and now I can be there for him." It was a privilege and an honor to give Joel a part of him. "He's half of me. I haven't been complete without him."

"I know it's the same with Joel," Yasha replied. "I am so thankful that Kayla found us. God will never put on us more than we can bear. And with every temptation, He will make a way of escape so that we can bear it."

God, thank You for making me the way of escape for Joel! Thank You!

CHAPTER 23

Let Go and Let God!

Around three o'clock in the morning, Jonah awakened from a terrible nightmare. The worst yet. Thankfully, he hadn't woke Kayla this time. Tiptoeing to the bathroom, Jonah wiped his face with a cold rag. His reflection appalled him. Dark circles under his eyes, face haggard and pale-looking. All attested to the fact that Jonah had experienced another restless, torturous night of sleeping. He felt less than a man. His wife had practically threw herself at him last night, and he couldn't perform his duties as a husband. He wanted Kayla, badly, but the past haunted him. The secret was driving a wedge between them. And every day the wedge grew bigger and wider. If he didn't do something soon, it would surely drive them apart.

For years, Jonah had been a pro at masquerading his feelings in prison. However, now Jonah found it too hard to fake it anymore. He couldn't just smile and pretend that everything was going to be alright. He couldn't just kiss his wife passionately one minute and then reject her the next. Something had to give. Something had to change.

"Live in the now!" He could hear his Aunt Alice's voice booming in his ear. "Stop living in the past. Stop being mad at your mother. Stop being mad at your father. Stop blaming

Joel! Stop blaming everybody about your past. Your past is just that…your past. And don't worry about the future; it may not come. All you have Jonah, is right now. Live in the now. Live it to the fullest. Let go and let God!"

Oh God! I want to be free! I want to live in the now! But I don't know how.

Forgive! Forgive! Forgive!

Dropping to his knees in the bathroom, finally Jonah sincerely surrendered everything. "Father forgive my trespasses as I forgive those who trespass against me. I forgive momma. I forgive my dad. I forgive Joel. I forgive…Nixon. I forgive Nixon!" Jonah's entire body shook with emotion. "I forgive Nixon, for everything he did to me!"

Forgive yourself.

Jonah rocked back and forth, releasing all to God. "Father God, I forgive myself. I messed up. I hurt people. I did my best to defend myself against Nixon. I was young and stupid. I let go and let God!"

That's freedom, son! You shall know the truth and the Truth shall make you free! Be free!

Unable to go back to bed, Jonah put on his sweatpants and a t-shirt. After peeping in on his sleeping wife, he left. He needed to see his brother. Even if the hospital was closed, Jonah would find a way to somehow be near Joel.

✖✖✖

Entering through the emergency room, Jonah stopped at the front desk.

"I know visiting hours aren't for another four hours, but I really must see my twin brother. He's suffering and, well, I'm giving him my kidney," Jonah rambled.

238

"Sir, I'm sorry, but you won't be able to visit him until 7:00 a.m." the elderly lady replied.

"Please Ma'am. I haven't seen my brother in five years and I need to see him. I beg your mercy to help me," Jonah pleaded, while praying inwardly for God's favor. "Tomorrow may be too late. All I have is now, Ma'am. All I have is now."

She gazed into his eyes, sensing his deep-seated pain. "What's your brother's name?"

"Joel Bates," he uttered.

She looked the information up on the computer. "He's on the seventh floor, room 7227. I'll contact my son; he works on the seventh floor. He'll let you in."

"Thank you, Ma'am! Thank you so much!" Jonah took the elevator she pointed to. Her son met him at the Elevator.

"My mom said you were coming," he strolled with him to Joel's room. "Your brother had a rough night. He was in a lot of pain. The nurse had to give him something strong, so he is sleeping now. He'll probably sleep for most of the morning."

Jonah felt disheartened by the news that his brother had been in so much pain. "Thank you."

"This is his room. You can't stay long or I'll get in trouble."

"I won't. Thanks!"

Taking a deep breath, Jonah entered his brother's hospital room. Peering down at his sleeping brother, who appeared so fragile and lifeless, shocked him, as if a lightning bolt had struck his chest, stopping his heart. Joel looked so different. Physically, he had deteriorated. His face was thin and pale. He blended in with the white sheet and pillowcase. He looked older and deathly sick.

Silent tears escaped Jonah's eyes. If he could trade places with his brother, Jonah would not hesitate. Joel had always been the good one, the one who gave of himself freely to others, never expecting anything in return. He was the one who had obeyed his aunt and never talked back, had good grades and did not cut school. He was the one who loved the Lord God with all his being when he was young and at no time in the past or future turned his back on God. Even now, with this dreadful illness, Yasha had acknowledged Joel's unwavering faith in God.

"Oh Joel, you must live and not die and declare the works of the Lord," he mumbled under his breath.

Suddenly, Joel's head slowly moved from side to side. Jonah flinched, fearful Joel would wake up. Standing still as a board, Jonah held his breath.

Joel became motionless again.

God, bless Joel. Heal him. Let him be used even more so to bring people into the Kingdom of God. Thank You for bringing us back together again.

✺✺✺

Kayla sat nervously on the couch with her hands tightly folded. She had been up for over an hour. Waking up and not finding Jonah in the bed, or in the hotel suite, she feared the worst.

Jonah's left me! I was too pushy last night! He doesn't find me attractive! He's regretting marrying me! Her mind raced form one thing to the other. Peace eluded her, fear engulfed her. She leaped from the chair when she heard the door opened.

"Jonah!"

He met her halfway and hugged her.

"You're back!" Her shoulders shook with elation and fear.

"Of course!" Jonah held her tight. Kayla crumpled in his

240

arms. Repressed feelings emerged as she cried.

"Where were you?"

"I went to see Joel."

"At this time in the morning?" Kayla was skeptical. "I thought the visiting hours weren't until seven or eight."

"God gave me favor. I just had to see him, Kayla. I woke up feeling pretty bad after another nightmare. I just felt like I needed my brother."

"And you don't need me." Hurting, Kayla turned her back to him. Gently, Jonah put his hands on her shoulders and spun her around to face him.

"What's really wrong, Baby?" He ran his fingers through her tousled hair.

"When I woke up, you weren't there. I thought you left me."

"I would never leave you! I love you, Kayla, so much." Jonah knew that for the past few days, Kayla had been irritable and moody. He was sure some of it was hormonal, but something else was going on.

"What's troubling you, Kayla?"

"Last night…" tears were near the surface as she began to speak.

"I'm sorry about last night. It was all my fault, not yours."

"We are married, but you avoid intimacy. I know you want to take things slow, but—and I know I'm fat and...."

Jonah laughed. "You are not fat, Kayla. If I didn't know you were pregnant, I couldn't tell. You are beautiful." Jonah drew her back in his arms. "It's not you, Kayla. It's me."

"Don't you desire me?"

"I do, greatly. I want you badly, Kayla. My heart cries for you, but my head…it's all messed up," he confessed. "I want to do what's right. I want to do the noble thing."

"I think you have been noble long enough," she said boldly.

"Kayla," he said her name softly, "I have to tell you something. I want to come totally clean. I'm not sure how to say this without sounding like a punk," he hesitated. "Let's just say I was forced to give up my manhood."

Kayla's mind battled to find the meaning.

"In prison, I was tortured by this guy named Nixon…"

"I know, Jonah. You told me that at the park."

"I didn't tell you everything, Kayla," he took in a deep breath. "Nixon ran the prison. He liked me…and…forced me…" He bore his soul, laying all the raw, sordid details out in the open. Jonah told Kayla everything.

"Oh, Jonah! I'm so sorry. Please don't say anymore. I can't bear to hear it!" Like a child, she put her hands over her ears.

Jonah pried her hands away and just held them. "Kayla, do you understand what I am saying to you?"

With wet eyes, she nodded.

"I was raped." Finally, Jonah said aloud the painful truth. His fists were clenched tightly, fingernails digging into his palms. "I was forced to do things with a man that killed something inside of me. I was stripped of my manhood in prison! I became a punk!"

"You're not a punk, Jonah."

"Kayla," he hesitated, looking away briefly, "people looked at me in prison and called me Nixon's Sweetie. I couldn't free myself of him. Everywhere I turned, he was there. I prayed and asked God to help me, but it still happened. Then, when I truly gave my heart to Christ, for the right reason, Nixon became meaner. He tortured me. He nearly killed my spirit."

"But he didn't, Jonah," Kayla assured. "You're still here.

Moreover, he's still there, locked up. You're a free man!"

"Kayla, I'm not gay. I don't want to be with a man." Jonah felt the need to say it.

"I know that, Jonah."

"I'm a man, in spite of what happened to me."

"Jonah, you are all man and I love you!"

"Even after all that, you still love me?"

"Nothing can separate us, Jonah. Not your past. Not what happened to you with Nixon, unless you let it. My love for you is unconditional." Kayla cupped his chin and fixed her eyes on him. "What you had to endure in prison was wrong, degrading and callous, but it doesn't define the man you are right now. You are my husband. You are the father of our child. You are a bold soldier in the Army of God. You are a warrior, Jonah. A true warrior! You are my Lover."

A weight was lifting from Jonah's heart. Kayla's endearing words squeezed his heart with so much love he could barely breathe. Her words were like fresh, cold water to a thirsty soul. Jonah hugged her, feeling safe and loved, as Kayla nestled her head on his chest. Looking down at her, Jonah beheld such warmth brimming from her eyes.

Jonah stepped back and thoroughly looked at his wife. There she stood, barefoot, pregnant, and beautiful as ever. Jonah's heart soared. He had a family. He wasn't physically alone anymore.

"We will get through this Jonah, together. Now, I understand why intimacy is an issue with you. I promise I'll be patient. Maybe counseling will help," Kayla suggested. "I will stand by you, Jonah, no matter what."

"Thank you, Baby," he pulled her closer. "But, I don't think we are going to need counseling."

243

"Why not?"

"Because, as of this very moment, I think I can stop playing the noble part." Jonah winked his eye.

Kayla detected a sensual connotation in his tone. "Oh, do you?" She blushed, butterflies churning in her stomach.

"I most certainly do." Jonah picked Kayla up, carried her into the bedroom, and shut the door. Like a gazelle freed from the hands of a hunter, Jonah had found freedom from the past to a promised future with God.

That morning, the two became one in every way.

CHAPTER 24

Mercy Hospital

Early Friday morning, Jonah met with Dr. Benson.

"I should have the lab results back by this evening. I'm putting a rush on it," Dr. Benson explained. "The other test results may not be back until Wednesday. As I said earlier, without a kidney transplant, unless God miraculously heals him, Joel won't make it through this month, if that long."

The truth sickened Jonah. "It's unbelievable that I'm his twin, with the same DNA, and yet I don't have any kidney problems."

"Joel was born with this defect and it's been undiagnosed for years. You said he suffered a lot as a kid, unable to play because he was tired all the time, and that he was such a sickly child, without proper medical care. And although he went to the clinic, they were unequipped to help him. With the lack of resources, some clinics are like Band-Aids; they patch you up and send you back out with the same problem. As an adult, Joel was finally diagnosed, and eventually given dialysis. It worked for years."

"I know I'm going to be a match. So, when do you think we can do the surgery?"

"After we get all the tests back from EKG, the chest x-ray,

blood work, and urine test, the goal is to shoot for Friday or the following Monday, here at Mercy Hospital. The earlier, the better."

"Friday," Jonah repeated. "I'm ready, Doc! Let's do this. I don't want to wait an extra day."

"You're a Godsend, Jonah." Dr. Benson praised the Almighty. "Joel never told me about you and I don't understand it. But, it doesn't matter. God foreknew Joel's need and provided a *ram in the bush* at birth." "Dr. Benson, remember, you can't tell Joel I'm the donor. He'll never agree to it. He has to believe it's an anonymous donor."

"Understood."

"I love my brother," Jonah choked, suddenly overwhelmed with the possibility that he could help save his brother's life. "I made some mistakes in the past and, well, Joel had a right to disown me."

"There is no need to explain this to me," Dr. Benson interrupted. "God forgives and forgets. Sometimes it takes longer for humans to do the same, to follow in the Master's footsteps."

"I just don't want you thinking badly of Joel. He had good reasons for not talking about me. Joel has a big, loving heart, always has. He deserves a second chance at life."

"And so do you," Dr. Benson rested her hand on Jonah's shoulder. "So do you."

Six hours later, after going through all the tests and being prodded and stuck with needle after needle, Jonah felt like a jaded porcupine. Leaving the last examination room, Jonah waited in the lobby for Dr. Benson to give him an update.

"Jonah!"

He turned to see his wife and Yasha.

"Are you okay?" Kayla worried. "You look peaked."

"From all those exams." Jonah kissed Kayla's cheek. "What are you two doing here?"

"We couldn't wait," Yasha answered. "And we figured you needed the support. How did it go?"

"I feel like a porcupine, being stuck and prodded and x-rayed. I didn't know there were so many tests."

"Me either. I thought since you're twins, you'd automatically be a match."

"I know I am. Nevertheless, they have to make sure I'm healthy in other areas for the surgery. Like my heart, my blood, all sorts of things."

"That's understandable," Kayla replied.

"Have you seen Joel?" Yasha asked.

"I peeped in earlier. He was still sleeping. I think they sedated him to keep him from experiencing so much pain."

"Yes," Yasha nodded, her eyes tearing up. "I'll just be glad when this is all over and I can have my husband back…with me."

"It won't be long. God's got this." Jonah gave Yasha a much needed hug. "He's the Great Physician, who heals and delivers."

"I'm just glad He is using you to be a part of the healing process," Yasha smiled up him. "I just know that God is working this all out for both you and Joel's good."

"Me too."

Dr. Benson entered the waiting area. All eyes were glued on her as she spoke.

"Jonah, I went ahead and scheduled you to do the psychosocial assessment on Monday at 9:00 a.m. here at Mercy Hospital."

"Good!"

"The surgery is tentatively scheduled for next Friday morning at seven o'clock, pending the final test and assessment. You'll have to be here at 5:30 a.m. If you go see my receptionist, she'll give you all the details."

"Thank you, Doc!" Jonah gave her a hearty hug. "I know I'm in good hands."

"We are!" Dr. Benson pointed upwards. "He holds us in the palms of His hands. The Master will lead and guide us every step of the way."

"Amen," Jonah agreed.

"When are you going to tell Joel about the transplant?" Yasha inquired. "I want to be there when you tell him."

"Let's do it right now."

"Now?" Yasha covered her mouth with her hand, overwhelmed and happy at the same time. "Shouldn't we wait to be sure?"

"I have it on good authority that the surgery will take place on Friday." Being led by the Holy Spirit enabled Dr. Benson to be one of the greatest in her profession. Dr. Benson's faith never wavered when it came to the things of God. The surgery was one of those divine appointments set up by Jehovah Ropha.

"I'll be right back." Yasha hugged Kayla first, and then Jonah.

"I wish I could see his face," Jonah spoke his heart aloud.

"I know," Yasha squeezed his hands.

"Go," Jonah fought back his raw feelings as he watched Dr. Benson and Yasha walk away. Jonah wanted to be there.

"It's all right, Baby," Kayla embraced him, resting her head upon his chest. "You're with him in spirit."

"I just want my brother back. I want us to be whole again."

"You will be," Kayla encouraged. "All in God's perfect timing."

✂✂✂✂

"Joel," Dr. Benson called his name again, "Joel wake up."

"Huh," Joel stirred.

"Honey, wake up," Yasha leaned over and kissed him on the lips.

His lips conformed, softly kissing her back. "Hey, beautiful." Joel's eyes opened, revealing his mannish side.

Dr. Benson cleared her throat, letting Jonah know she was in the room.

"Doc! I didn't know you were here."

"Obviously," Dr. Benson smiled. "How are you feeling?"

"Tired, real tired of all the drugs. They are making me sleep. I'm sleeping my way through life. I can't stand that."

"It helps with the pain."

"I'd rather have the pain, so I can talk to my wife." Joel reached up and put his hand on the side of Yasha's face. It took all his strength and then some to do that for even a moment.

Yasha place her hands over his. "I miss you."

"I miss you so much, Yasha. More than you can ever know."

"Joel," Dr. Benson addressed him again. "I have some really good news."

"You got me a kidney!" Joel beat her to the punch.

"How did you know?" Dr. Benson asked.

"I dreamed I walked out of this hospital, with my wife by my side." His eyes locked with Yasha. "I knew God was telling me that I was healed. Have you found a donor match?" Joel once again looked to the doctor.

"A perfect match," Dr. Benson boasted. "Surgery is

249

scheduled for next Friday morning."

"How did it happen, Doc? I mean, did somebody die or something? We haven't had any success all this time."

"God gets the credit."

"I know, but…who?" Joel was anxious. "I just want to know the person that is saving my life."

"In most cases, the information is confidential and the donor anonymous. So it is with you," Dr. Benson informed. "Instead of asking who, just be thankful that God provided *a ram in the bush*."

"Yes, Joel!" Yasha was beside herself. "This is an answer to our prayer, for us and for our baby."

"I thank God, truly," Joel spoke, his voice weak. "I just…"

"Enough talk," Dr. Benson warned. "You're wearing yourself out, and we need for you to be strong for the surgery. This is a serious operation, Joel, as you know. It will probably take four to six hours."

"God brought me this far, Doc. I know He won't leave me now."

"No, He won't," Yasha agreed.

"It's a miracle!" Joel exclaimed, all of it finally sinking in. "A true miracle!"

"God is a miracle worker!" Dr. Benson admonished. "I'll leave you two alone, but I will see you later tonight, Joel, before going home."

"Thanks, Doc, for everything." Joel acclaimed genuinely. "Thanks!"

"Thank Him!" Dr. Benson didn't take the credit. "All glory goes to Him, and Him alone."

✕✕✕

That night, Kayla fretted over her husband's upcoming

surgery. "I know you're doing the right thing Jonah, but it's a serious operation. Things can go wrong."

"Kayla, Baby, I'm not worried," Jonah turned over in bed and wrapped his arms securely around his wife. "And I don't want you to worry; it's not good for our baby. God is in control. This is all orchestrated by God. Joel is going to pull through the surgery, and so am I."

"I love you, Jonah and I don't want anything to happen to you. You mean so much to me and…" she couldn't go on.

"Hush now," he turned her to face him. "Nothing is going to happen to me. You have to have faith in God, Kayla." He kissed her. "You think something is going to happen to me now, now that I have you? That's crazy! Me and God got this understanding, you see."

"What kind of understanding?"

"That I'm going to be a great father to our baby." Jonah rubbed her tummy. "So, I have to make it through this surgery in order to do that, right?"

She nodded.

"So we have nothing to worry about. We are just going to trust God and believe He will bring us all through it. No doubts whatsoever."

"No doubts." Kayla felt better.

"Now, let's get some sleep. Yasha wants us to come over early to help get some things fixed up in the house before surgery next week."

"I'm so glad we're going to move in with them temporarily," Kayla beamed. "I hope Joel will be fine with it."

"Me too," Jonah admitted. "But if not, we can always come back here."

"Do you think Joel will sell us some land? Yasha really

thinks he will so that we can all be close."

"Joel has a big heart. We'll see where God leads us. We will just have to take one day at a time with Joel. First, he has to heal physically and emotionally. There's a lot between us and…"

Kayla's cell phone rang. "It's eleven thirty. Who could be calling this late?"

"Kayla," Kathryn Lovett sounded panicky.

"Mom, what's wrong?"

"It's you father?"

"What happened?" Kayla's pulse raced, heart pounding in her chest. She expected the worst.

"He's was hit by a truck on the way home, a four-wheeler."

"Huh?" Kayla couldn't process it all. Jonah held her, deducing that the news was terrible.

"The ambulance is transporting Drew to Mercy Hospital. He's in bad shape, from what the doctor said over the phone. I can't be there until tomorrow. Please go check on him, Kayla," Kathryn rambled. "I know he's been terrible to the both of us, but Drew needs us now."

"I know, Momma. I'm going now," Kayla didn't hesitate. No matter how bullheaded Drew could be, he was still her father and she loved him. "I'll call you when I get to the hospital."

"Please do, Kayla," Kathryn choked, "I love him, Kayla. Drew is still my husband, and I love him."

"Me too, Momma. We'll get through this together."

"Tell Jonah hello, and I'll see you two tomorrow."

"What's wrong Baby?" Jonah got out of the bed with his wife, allowing her to cry in his arms.

"My father was hit by a four-wheeler. He's in bad shape. They're taking him to Mercy Hospital."

"Same hospital as Joel."

"Oh Jonah, what if he…." She buried her head in his chest.

"Let's pray," Jonah quickly countered. "Father God, you know what's going on. Right now, Kayla's father Drew is in bad shape, fighting for his life. I know he's not a Believer, but God please give him a chance to make it right with You. Bless him with Your healing balm and touch every doctor and every nurse that comes in contact with him. Anoint them and give them wisdom in dealing with him. Save Drew, Lord. Heal Drew, Lord, and heal their family in Jesus' name, amen."

"Amen." Kayla looked up at him. "Thank you."

"Let's dress and get to Mercy Hospital.

CHAPTER 25

Second Chances

"Wow, you're better!" The nurse was stunned, seeing Jonah in the emergency room waiting area. "You look good, Mr. Bates."

Jonah eyed her suspiciously, as he stood. "Thank you." *I think.*

Kayla immediately stood beside him, bitten by the jealousy bug. "Hello."

The nurse frowned. She remembered all too well Yasha Bates, her patients' wife, and this woman was not her. *I thought he was a pastor. Hypocrite! No wonder he is so sick. Playing with fire, he ought to get burned.*

"I'm Nurse Brianna Patten," she greeted through tight lips.

"Nice to meet you," Jonah replied.

"Well, I'm glad you're feeling better, Mr. Bates. I thought—well, never mind!" She waved her hands and turned to leave.

"Do I know you, um, Nurse Patten?"

"Excuse me?" Brianna wasn't about to play games with him. "I've been your morning nurse for over two weeks. I know I haven't been here for a week, but—"

"Oh, you must mean my twin, Joel," Jonah smiled widely. "He's in room 7227."

"Twin," she chuckled. "Well glory be to God! I thought...I

thought something was not quite clean in the milk. So glad to know you are his twin. Didn't know he had a twin."

"He doesn't know I'm here. I'm visiting my father-in-law." Jonah wrapped his arms around Kayla. "This is my wife, Kayla."

"Nice to meet you," Brianna heartily shook her hand. "I'm sorry about your father. He isn't the one involved in the accident with the four-wheeler, is he?"

Kayla nodded, her eyes misty again. "No one will tell me anything."

"Stay put, I'll find out something and be right back."

"Thank you," Kayla called after her.

Shortly, Nurse Patten returned. "Your father is getting prepped for surgery. There's a lot going on with him. What I know for sure is that both of his legs are broken. He has fractured ribs, collarbone, and I am afraid he may lose his eyesight in the right eye. He's really banged up, but it's a miracle he's even alive."

Kayla did not know what to say. It was a lot to take in. "Can I see him?"

"Yes, I can take you both in before they wheel him down to surgery." Brianna escorted them to the area where Dr. Drew Lovett was lying flat on his back.

"Dr. Lovett," the nurse spoke softly, "your daughter is here."

Drew's eyes opened, almost in alarm as his eyes fixated on the nurse. Something about her was familiar. He frowned, racking his brain to figure out how he knew this lady. Obviously, they had met before. However, she didn't appear to be one of his clients. Everything about this lady was natural—including her long braid. Quietly, the nurse left the room.

"Oh," Kayla covered her mouth, as she beheld her father. His face was swollen and bloodstains were still visible all over his body. Tubes were everywhere. He looked like a different man. The usually squeaky-clean Drew was a bloody mess.

"It's okay Baby," Jonah whispered. "He's alive. That's a blessing."

She nodded, walking slowly to his bedside. "Daddy," Kayla had not called him that since she was a little girl.

Immediately, Drew's eyes opened again. Their eyes locked. No words were spoken. Then Drew looked at Jonah, who was holding his baby girl in his arms, protectively.

"Daddy, I'm so sorry," Kayla cried. "I want you to…be alright."

Drew was in so much pain, he could not even move. His head hurt. His arms hurt. His chest burned. His legs went through excruciating spasms of pain. However, all he wanted to do at that very moment was hold his baby girl.

"Please don't die," Kayla went on. "I need you, Daddy. I love you." Cautiously, Kayla kissed his forehead.

"I'm so-o-o sorry." Drew mumbled, his words barely above a whisper.

"Me too, Daddy." Kayla never thought in a million years that she would ever hear those words coming from her father lips. "I love you."

"I love you, Kay, and…Kath…ryn." Big, fat teardrops slid through his eyelids. "Please…tell her…"

"You can tell her yourself, Daddy. She'll be here tomorrow," Kayla feared he was giving up. "Fight Daddy! Please fight."

"Take care of…my…little girl," Drew stared at Jonah. He drew in a long breath, experiencing chest pains. "And my… grandbaby."

Kayla gasped. She did not know her father knew she was with child. "Oh Daddy, please fight. God can heal you."

Drew's eyes fastened on her as she declared God's ability to heal him. "God...."

"Yes, God," Kayla assured. "He loves you, Daddy."

"Not me...Kay...I...am a sin...ner." Suddenly, thoughts of his father popped in his mind. The man who he adored, until he realized he was not who he thought he was. He wasn't an upright pastor, nor a faithful husband or father. *He was a sinner. He was a hypocrite!* The thoughts shot through his head. He wanted to find a tidbit of hope, something he could digest in such a hopeless situation. Drew knew in his heart he was dying. Death was knocking at his door, and he wasn't ready to answer.

The remembrance of the four-wheeler coming towards him spooked Drew. There was no way he should have survived. He should not be alive. He should not be here talking to his daughter, who obviously loved him, in spite of how horrible he treated her. Could God be real? Could He love him, even though Drew had walked away from Him years ago, professing to be an atheist? Drew, who walked away from his sister, not even going to her funeral. He didn't deserve God's help now.

"Oh Daddy," Kayla was overcome.

"Don't cry, Kay." Her pain was his. "I...have made my bed...so I must lie in it. I deserve....to...be here."

"Dr. Lovett, we are all sinners, saved by God's grace," Jonah intervened. "Don't go into surgery without knowing Jesus. All you have to do is ask Him to come into your heart, right now."

"It's..." he squirmed in pain. Closing his eyes, trying to block out the pain, Drew went on. "It's too late."

"It's never too late," Jonah exclaimed. "As long as there is breath in your body, there is time. Do you want to know him, Dr. Lovett? He loves you, and God is waiting on you. It's that simple."

Drew wanted to accept the lifeline that was being thrown to him, but it couldn't be that simple.

No one comes to the Father, unless the Spirit draws him.

Where did that come from? From his childhood days in church, that verse popped in his spirit.

I am drawing you back to me, Drew. Come, my son. Drink from the fountain that never runs dry. There will be no more dry places in your heart. I will fill your hurt with my love.

But, God...my father...he was a liar!

The truth shall be revealed. Only believe in Him, and the darkness will flee when Light has come in you.

I believe, Lord, but help my unbelief.

"I'm ready," Drew affirmed.

"Dr. Lovett," Jonah began, "The Bible says that if you confess with your mouth the Lord Jesus, and believe in your heart that God raised Him from the dead, you shall be saved. Everyone that calls on the name of the Lord shall be saved. Repeat after me. Lord Jesus I am a sinner and I need a Savior."

"Lord Jesus...I am a sinner...and I need...a Savior," Drew repeated, painstakingly.

"Forgive me of my sins and come live in my heart. I want You to be Lord and Savior of my life. I confess with my mouth and believe with my heart that God raised Jesus from the dead. I am Yours now. I need You, and I ask that You heal me heart and my physical body. In Jesus' name, amen."

"In Jesus' name, amen," Drew repeated, his eyes wet, his heart free. "Thank you," he looked at Jonah, and then Kayla.

"Thank you."

A male nurse entered with a hospital gurney. "I'm sorry, but we must take him to surgery now."

"We'll be waiting, Daddy." Kayla touched his hand lightly and blew him a kiss.

Drew smiled, feeling lighter than he had felt in years. His physical body may be all banged up and a mess, but inwardly, Drew felt like a new man.

"Tell Kathryn....I love her."

"I will, but she wants to hear it from you."

Whether Drew survived the surgery or not did not matter. His soul was free. Free from years of anger, bitterness, and hatred toward his father and all that represented the religious world where Jesus Christ was proclaimed Lord and Savior.

Watching Drew being rolled away, Kayla could not believe it. Her father, a professed atheist, had given his heart to Jesus.

"It's a miracle, Jonah!"

"I know," Jonah stammered. "A fool says in his heart that there is no God. Only God could spare your father's life, so that He could give Him real life in Jesus Christ! Only God! Praise You, Jesus!"

"I have to call momma," Kayla took out her cell. "She's not going to believe it!"

"All things work together for our good."

"Amen."

⟨⟩⟨⟩⟨⟩

"Good afternoon, Mr. Bates," Dr. Benson said over the phone to Jonah on Tuesday.

"Hi Doc." Jonah braced himself for the news about the surgery.

"All is good. The tests confirmed that you're a perfect match for Joel. The surgery is scheduled for Friday morning."

"Praise God!"

"He deserves all the praise," Dr. Benson admonished. "I'm going to let you talk to my secretary and she'll give you all the details. Do you have any questions for me?"

"No, Doc. I am just grateful God is giving me the chance to bless my brother. Joel deserves this and so much more."

"So do you, Jonah. Do not forget that. God is pleased with both of you."

"Thanks Doc!"

"Hold on while I transfer you to my secretary."

After Jonah obtained all the details from the secretary, he went to the hospital chapel to pray. Kayla and her mother were visiting with Drew, who had not only survived the surgery, but was healing rapidly. Though bruises and cuts showed that he was involved in some kind of accident, no one would have ever believed how sick Drew was the night before. The doctors did not think he would survive the surgery. But God is always in control.

"I can't believe how great you look," Kathryn said as she held her husband's hand. "The officer who called me didn't think you would make it to the hospital. He said you were in really bad shape." She wiped her eyes. "But look at you now. You look good, Drew."

"I feel good." Drew kissed his wife's hand, something he had not done in a very long time. "God has given us another chance to make things right between us." Glancing at Kayla, he said, "God gave me a second chance with you. I'm a blessed man."

Tears rolled down Kayla's face as she witnessed the love

in her father's eyes. At last, she felt she had a dad and a mom. She did not feel like an outsider. These were her parents and she loved them both dearly.

"God has given us both second chances," Kathryn professed. "I gave my heart to Jesus. My sister, Daisy, led me to the Lord."

"God is so faithful!" Kayla hugged her mom and then leaned over and kissed her dad on the cheek. "My prayers have been answered."

"Where is my son-in-law?" Drew asked.

"He's sitting in the waiting area," Kayla answered.

"Go get him."

"Sure Daddy."

"Kay!" Drew called after her. "I'm so glad you're calling me daddy again."

"Well, you are my Daddy." Kayla smiled and left the room.

Jonah wasn't waiting outside. Kayla found out from one of the nurses at the nurses' station that her husband had went to the chapel.

Entering the chapel, Kayla found Jonah at the altar on bended knees with his head bowed. Kayla quietly slipped in a middle pew and prayed silently.

Father God, my heart is bursting with joy, joy unspeakable and full of glory. Only You God could mend my broken family. Only You could snatch my father, a proclaimed atheist, from the hands of the enemy and free him from sin and save his soul. Only You God could bless me with such a loving husband, like Jonah, who willingly accepts my unborn baby as his own. Oh, God I do not deserve such grace and mercy, but I am thankful. I love You because You first loved me. Now I believe You have freed my husband from his past and opened a door for him and Joel to reconnect. I know You will bring them both safely through their upcoming surgeries. God, I am Yours. I will do what You want me to do. I will go where You want me to go and be who You want me to be.

In the interim, Jonah felt God's presence cloaking him like a warm blanket, keeping the elements of life far from him. Peace engulfed Jonah's very soul. God's unconditional love soothed him, like a balm removing the fragments of his painful past. While on his knees, Jonah was not alone. God was with Him. God had led him to Macon City to bring the pieces of the puzzle of his life together again. To bridge the gap between he and Joel. To make amends for his wrongdoings, and to discover new beginnings with Joel.

Thank You, God, for my freedom in You. Thank You for not giving up on me. Whether Joel has given up me or not, it does not matter. Finally, I get to do something for him. Finally, I get to express my love for him by giving him a part of me. Thank You God for the chance to do so.

I am pleased, my son.

Getting up from his knees, Jonah turned and saw the loveliest human creature walking toward him.

I am so blessed.

"Are you okay, Jonah?"

Jonah gazed at his wife, elated that she belonged to him. He pulled her into his arms, needing to hold her, to feel her next to him. "I'm a blessed man," he said, happy tears burning behind his eyes. "The surgery is scheduled for Friday. Everything is going to be alright."

"Oh, that's great!" Kayla clung to him.

"I'm ready."

"Me too," her lower lip trembled.

"Is everything alright?'

"Yes. Daddy wants to see you."

"Really?"

"Really! Jonah it's so hard to believe that he's a changed man, but he is."

Jonah put his hand on Kayla's back and led her out of the chapel. "He's not going to act like the overprotective father with me now? I mean, we married without his permission and all."

"I don't think so, Jonah. But it doesn't matter," she said and clasped his hand. "We're one; nothing and no one can separate us."

"You're right," he said. They exchanged a tender kiss in the hallway.

"Let's go face Papa Bear," Jonah laughed.

"And Momma Bear," Kayla played along. "They seem to be mating rather well."

"Come closer," Drew commanded Jonah. Kayla and Kathryn had left at Drew's request. He needed to speak with his son-in-law privately.

Jonah obeyed, observantly sizing up Kayla's father. There was an air of arrogance about him. He appeared much younger than his age. Jonah wondered if it was good genetics or cosmetically enhanced. Looking past the scars, Dr. Lovett was a good-looking man.

"So, you married my daughter, my *only* daughter," Drew emphasized, "without my blessing."

Jonah nodded, unflinchingly locking eyes with the father.

"How are you going to provide for her? Kayla is

accustomed to living a good life. We made sure she had the best of everything."

Jonah stood tall and strong. He had endured Manchester; surely, he could endure anything this man had to say to him. Jonah was not going to let this man run him off from Kayla. It would take much more than that.

Clearing his throat, Jonah answered. "Kayla will be taken care of, Sir. I assure you that I will provide for her and our baby."

"How?"

"I have a job. I work at Hutto's Department Store. Eventually, I will work my way up to supervisor. It may take some time, but I will do right by your daughter and grandchild."

"What about your criminal record?" Drew did not hold back. "Are you truly finished with that lifestyle?"

"I am, Sir," Jonah's jaw tightened. "God has changed me, just like He has changed you, Sir. I am a new person."

Drew eyed him long and hard before speaking again. "I owe you my life, Son."

His comment took Jonah aback. "Sir?"

"You were bold enough to share Jesus with me," Drew went on to explain, "and I could have died—should have died —without knowing Jesus. I thank you for being a bold soldier in God's army." Drew extended his hand as a peace offering.

Stunned, Jonah shook it.

"Now, since I was too stubborn to be at my only child's wedding, I want to have a wedding reception. I want it to be grand, celebrating the union that God put together."

Not wanting anything elaborate, Jonah stifled his feelings. Besides, he perceived that somehow Drew needed to do this for his daughter. "Thank you, Sir."

"Stop calling me Sir," Drew requested, a hint of amusement displayed in his eyes. "Call me Dad. I have always wanted a son."

"Thanks, uh, dad," Jonah awkwardly complied.

"Now, I know you are working at Hutto's, which is a respected job choice. However, our family practice could use someone like you to manage the office."

"Manage," Jonah frowned. "I don't know the first thing about plastic surgery."

"Of course you don't," Drew agreed. "But you can learn. I want to expand the center. I want to help children whose faces have been scarred by abuse. Young people who cannot afford to have plastic surgery to fix their problems. We can look into grants and other outreach sources to provide free services to them. I want you to research it. I have a few contacts that I want you to talk to and learn everything you can from." Early in the morning, this idea came to him while praying. Drew believed God wanted to take Lovett's Restoration Plastic Surgery Center to another level and a new direction. He did not just want it to be about cosmetic surgery, although he would still do that. Drew felt propelled to help the less fortunate. Thus, a new vision was placed in his spirit. "I will get you all the training you need. I just want the Lovett Center to stay in the family. Of course, Kathryn can teach you everything she knows about management. The added pro bono services will be called Second Chances. I want you to run it. Find resources. Find children who need plastic surgery and cannot afford it. What do you think?"

"I'm honored," Jonah was floored. This was definitely something new, but exciting. Helping the less fortunate, especially children, was right up his alley.

"And your salary will be six figures."

"Sir, I'm not…"

"You will earn every bit of it Jonah, every bit of it," Drew smiled. "Do we have a deal?"

Jonah heartily shook his hand. "It's a deal."

"Excuse me," Nurse Brianna Patten said as she entered. "I need to check your bandages."

"I'll step out," Jonah replied. "See you in few."

"I'm not going anywhere," Drew chucked. Focusing his attention back on the nurse, he couldn't shake the feeling that he knew her. "Do we know each other?"

Brianna smiled. "I don't think so."

Drew closed his eyes and allowed the nurse to change his bandages. His mind was going a mile a minute, endeavoring to dredge up the familiar face. Then it hit him like a ton of bricks, as his eyes popped opened. "My father…you knew my father!"

"I don't think so." She frowned.

"Pastor Lovett…Nathaniel Lovett," Drew was convinced. "I saw you with him at a hotel."

"Pastor Nate," she couldn't believe it. "You're Pastor Nate's son?"

Drew nodded, unsure of his feelings. A baby in Christ, he tried to push back the hatred he felt for the home-wrecker, who now stood before him.

"Oh blessed Jesus! Your father was an angel," she began. "He would come to the hotel once a week and hold Bible Studies with me and a several women, all former prostitutes. Not only did he teach us the Bible, Pastor Nate taught us how to read. Because of him, I went on to college and got my nursing degree. I can't believe it! You're Pastor's Nate's son!"

Tears welled up in her eyes.

Drew's heart dropped. All those years, he blamed his father, pointed a finger at him for being a hypocrite, when in fact, his father was practicing what he had preached for years. He had helped those who were less fortunate than himself. Years wasted of turning his back on his family and on God, for nothing. He judged the book by its cover, never opening it up to see what was inside. *Forgive me, Father God! Forgive me father!* "My dad was a good man," tears of old collided down his cheeks.

"Yes, he was," Brianna touched his hands. "Just like his son."

CHAPTER 26

Confront and Conquer

"**Y**ou look well rested, Honey," Yasha leaned over and pecked Joel's parched lips.

"I should be," he grunted. "That's all I've been doing for weeks. I'm so ready to get this surgery over and go home."

"It won't be long. Two more days," Yasha chimed. "And you'll be on your road to recovery, with a new kidney."

"I'm still amazed at how that happened. I've been on the waiting list for a long time, and all of a sudden," he paused, "suddenly the perfect kidney shows up."

"Suddenly miracles happen all the time," Yasha replied. "You of all people should know that. I remember you preaching one of your sermons about *Suddenly Miracles*."

"I remember, but it's just that…"

"Stop it, Joel. Stop trying to figure things out when God has already worked it out. Just be grateful and thankful."

"I am, Honey," his words were soft and coming out slower. Talking overexerted Joel. "God's timing is always perfect."

"It is." Yasha reached for his hand and placed it over her rounded tummy. "Faith is moving a lot this morning. I believe it's because she hears her daddy's voice."

"More like cartwheels," Joel chuckled. "We may have a

gymnast in the family."

"Oh, Joel, I can't wait until we are all home again," she said. "We're going to be one big happy family now that God has answered our prayers."

"You never doubted, Yasha," Joel said seriously, caressing her face gently with his hand, briefly. The simple gesture wore him out. "You had unwavering faith. I know I'm the pastor, but so many times I felt like giving up, but your steadfast faith wouldn't let me quit. I appreciate you and love you so much, Yasha."

"I know," she smiled. "We have always been there for each other and we will always be that way. We're one."

"Absolutely."

"Hi, Mr. Bates," Nurse Brianna Patten said as she walked in. "I need to check your vital signs." She began by taking his temperature. "I tell you what, Mr. Bates, your twin sure had me fooled."

"What?" Joel's eyes bulged.

Yasha shook her head, trying to get the nurse to be quiet. Fear festered in her soul.

"Your twin," the nurse rattled on. "I think he said his name was Jo...Jonah. When I saw him in the emergency room, I thought I was looking at a miracle. I was blown away. Although he is slightly bigger than you are, you two look just alike. I guess that's how it is with identical twins," she laughed. "Anyhow, he seems like a nice guy. I…"

"Excuse me, Nurse," Joel was beside himself as he looked at his wife. "I really need a moment alone with my wife."

"Well, I'm finished anyway," the nurse put up her instruments. "I'll come back later to change your IV bag."

Joel nodded, waiting for the nurse to disappear.

"What have you done, Yasha?" Anger echoed in his shaky voice.

Yasha lifted her eyes to meet his intense gaze. "I haven't done anything."

"How could you?" His jaw tightened. "You promised me you would not get in touch with Jonah."

"And I didn't."

"Ah, come on, Yasha." Joel leaned back down, feeling somewhat fainthearted. "How is it that Jonah is here at Mercy Hospital? How? Huh?" Hurt lingered in his voice.

"I didn't contact Jonah," Yasha began to explain. "His wife, Kayla, came by the house."

"Wife?" Joel was shocked. "Jonah is married? That's hard to believe."

"He's a newlywed, married just last week. Anyhow, Kayla lives in Macon City and she found our address through some things Aunt Alice left Jonah, which included our wedding book."

Joel remained silent, trying to digest it all.

"While I was visiting you at the hospital, she left a note on the door and asked for me to please call her. Joel, you're really sick and your health was rapidly declining, so I called the number. I felt like God was making it possible for you and Jonah to meet, and for Jonah to help his brother out."

"By giving me his kidney," he said.

"Yes, if it could save your life!" Yasha stood with her hands on her hips, annoyed by Joel's self-righteous attitude. "I'm tired of feeling like the bad guy about this. I want you to live! So the door opened and I let him in! You should be thanking me not scolding me like I'm some child!"

"You were wrong, Yasha." He finally looked at her. "You

went against my wishes."

"Bump your wishes, Joel! If your wish is to die…well, I'm not going to just stand by and let that happen, not if there is a chance for you to live."

"You don't know that I wouldn't live without his kidney."

"Joel, you had one foot in the grave and one foot in heaven," she spoke the harsh truth. "You said that you have forgiven Jonah."

"I have. Forgiveness has nothing to do with this."

"Oh, I think it has everything to do with it," Yasha countered. "If you truly have forgiven him, then why won't you let him help you?"

"The Bible says owe no one anything except to love one another. I don't want to owe Jonah anything."

"Don't make the scripture work for your benefit, Joel. That is beneath you. Love reaches out to the lost, to the hurting, and to the unlovable." Yasha picked up her purse. "That's what Jonah's doing. He's reaching out to the hurting. I wish I could say the same about you."

"I want to see him," Joel mustered the strength to shout at his wife before she walked out.

Yasha turned and looked at him, surprised by his request.

"I want to see him before surgery," Joel's eyes were glossy. "Please, Yasha."

"Okay."

"Alone," he added.

"Okay. I love you."

"I love you, too," Joel concluded.

Left alone in his room, Joel felt discombobulated. He was not prepared for an encounter with his brother. Talk about a blast from the past. The possibility of seeing Jonah again, soon, caused his heart to beat erratically. His wife was right. He had forgiven Jonah with his lips, but something was still lurking in Joel's heart. The truth stung like a bee. Yasha was also right about his brother reaching out to him, an act of love. While he, a pastor, was still hiding behind the locked door, refusing to let Jonah in. Joel was keeping him at a distance, controlling the situation, so his twin could not hurt him again. Fear kept them apart. It was time for Joel to confront and conquer his fears and his inability to forgive.

⊱⊰⊱

While Kayla and Yasha waited in prayer in the waiting area, Jonah hugged the wall outside Joel's hospital room. A mixture of emotions warred within him. Faith against fear. Hope against regret. Rejection against acceptance. Love against past iniquity.

Lord, help me! I am about to face my brother. There is a gulf between us—fill it with Your love. I feel like a little boy about to face punishment for my wrongs. Please, let Joel be forgiving. Keep my feelings under subjection. Joel had a justifiable reason to put a roadblock between us. There was no denying the horrible sins that Jonah committed against his twin.

I betrayed him.
I lied to him, repeatedly.
I treated him unkindly and inhumane.
I stole from him.
I slept with his fiancé.
I was evil back then!
Lord, You have forgiven me. I am forgiving myself, slowly. Now, Lord, let Joel forgive me. Not just for me, but for himself.

So that we both can be free.

Fear not, Jonah. For I am with you and I am with Joel.

Taking a deep breath, trying to calm his nerves, Jonah took a step toward the closed door. *Here it goes Lord!*

Slowly, opening the door, Jonah's eyes met Joel's as he entered the room. His hands were clammy, sweat was seeping out of his pores like a faucet, he could barely suck in enough air to breathe. Everything was still. Tension filled the atmosphere.

Joel's face was pensive, no emotions displayed.

Jonah's countenance revealed his joy.

Swallowing hard, endeavoring to dislodge the lump clogging his throat, Jonah spoke first. "Hello, Joel."

"Jonah," Joel acknowledged, both emotionally and physically drained.

"It's good to see you."

"It's good to be alive."

"You have a lovely wife," he regretted his words, thoughts of the past plummeted before him. "I mean, she, uh, seems to be a-a…good, Christian woman," Jonah stuttered.

Joel was amused by his brother's awkwardness. "Yasha is the best thing that has happened to me, second to God of course." Joel spoke above a whisper. Jonah had to come closer to hear him.

"That's how I feel about Kayla. Truly she is a Godsend."

"Newlyweds, I hear."

"Yep." Jonah's smile widened. "Who would have ever thought? Right?"

"Not me, for sure."

Strained silence followed.

"Yasha says you live in Macon City now?" Joel attempted to keep the small talk going.

"For now," Jonah fidgeted with his hands. "We're looking for a place. I am going to be working at the Center with Kayla and her family. Her father is going to train me to be the office manager."

"That's good," Joel looked at his brother more closely. "What's that?" Joel pointed to the scar on the side of Jonah's face.

"Oh, it's nothing," he shrugged. "Prison scar."

"Sorry," Joel frowned. "What happened?"

"Trying to stay alive," he said, giving the short, safe answer.

"Aunt Alice said prison was hard on you," Joel recalled, remembering her pleading for him to go see him. He swallowed, as if to push back the painful remembrance of Aunt Alice's tears when she begged Joel to forgive Jonah. "She said prison was not for every man, it could break a man's spirit, like it was breaking Jonah."

"Prison is not supposed to be a vacation," Jonah said and faked a laugh. "You do hard time for the crime. I deserved what I got. You reap what you sow. And surely, I sowed a lot of bad seeds." Jonah looked his brother in the eye, a twinge of sadness exposed itself. "I should have listened to Aunt Alice, and to you."

Joel saw sincerity in his eyes and heard it in his voice. Lingering minutes passed before he finally responded. "Why are you doing this, Jonah? Is this payback or something?"

"I can never payback the debt I owe you," Jonah quickly replied. "Never."

"Then why?" Joel drew in a long breath. He was experiencing chest pain.

Jonah's brow furrowed, revealing signs of worry. He knew Joel was in physical agony. "Joel, do I need to get you something, or go get a nurse?"

Their eyes locked.

"I'm fine," he mumbled. "Answer my question."

Jonah thoroughly looked him over before speaking. "Why? Because we are brothers, and brothers are supposed to have each other's back. I admit I was young and stupid, and never had your back in our teenage to adult years. But I am a man now, Joel. I want to do this for you. I want to give you a part of me. I want…." His emotions surfaced, making it difficult to go on. "I want for us to somehow build a relationship again. I love you, man. I love you with my whole heart. Forgive me, Joel. Please forgive me," Jonah began to shed tears. "I was so wrong for everything. Please forgive me."

Tears trickled down Joel's face, matching the tears of his twin. Regret started in the pit of Joel's stomach and worked its way to his heart, squeezing dear life out of him. He ached for his brother, deeply. His strength evaporated like the dew in the morning. Joel could barely lift his hand to reach for his brother.

Quickly, Jonah was by his side, clinging to his hand. This entire experience was surreal for both of them. Feelings of old, mixed with the newness of what could be engulfed them, like a soothing ointment in the depths of their parched souls.

"I forgive you." Joel uttered the three words that freed both him and his brother. "Now, I need you to forgive me."

"Forgive you?" Jonah thought that was ludicrous. "Forgive you for what?"

"For not telling you about Aunt Alice." The wrongdoing had eaten at Joel for years.

Likewise, Jonah had been angry at his brother for not telling him about their Aunt's death. "Forgiven."

"And for…letting things come between us. For shutting

you out of my life completely," Joel added.

"I would have done the same thing, Joel. I deserved it."

"No one deserves that," Joel corrected. "I turned my back on you when you needed me the most. I should have been there for you when you were locked up."

His words moved Jonah. He hadn't expected this from Joel. He was the one who should be apologizing and groveling for forgiveness. Not the other way around. "It's all water under the bridge."

"It'll take time for us to mend the bridge, but with God all things are possible," Joel replied.

"Thank you, El," Jonah said, a sigh of relief released from the pit of his gut.

Hearing his nickname produced a smile on Joel's thin lips. "Thank you, Jo."

"I should let you go," Jonah said, fearing his brother was overdoing it. He needed rest for the following day. "We both have a big day tomorrow."

"Thank you." Fresh tears spilled from Joel's eyes. "For saving my life."

"We're brothers. That's what brothers do," Jonah said as he leaned over and hugged Joel.

"If something happens to me," Joel began, "please look after my wife and daughter. Promise me you will be there for them."

"Nothing is going to happen to you." Jonah wasn't hearing it. They had come too far for anything to separate them now.

"Only God knows for sure," Joel replied. "Either way, my life is in His hand. Just promise me, Jo. I need you to promise me."

"I promise. But God will bring you out of this surgery."

Joel smiled, closing his eyes.

"Aunt Alice wanted me to give this to you at the right time." Jonah retrieved a folded envelope from his back pocket. "She left me a letter, as well."

"Aunt Alice always had the final word," Joel smiled again. "She sure did."

"Thanks, I'll read this later." Joel held onto the letter tightly. "I'm going to rest now."

"Do you want me to get Yasha? She's waiting outside with Kayla."

"Nah, I'm really tired. Can you tell her to go home and rest, and I'll see her early tomorrow morning?"

"I sure will. See you soon, El," Jonah replied, reluctantly walking toward the door. "I love you, El."

"I love you, Jo," Joel whispered back.

The minute the door closed, too curious to wait, Joel opened the envelope, surprised at the lovely necklace that was folded in the letter. Putting it aside, he began to read the last words from his beloved Aunt Alice.

Dear Joel,

Praise God! If you are reading this letter, you and Jonah have united. Oh, this has been my prayer since the day you two separated. Joel, God is pleased. You are a Messenger for Christ, sharing the good news of Jesus Christ. Jesus represented love, unconditional love. You have shared love with countless others, now you must share it with your brother. Jonah made mistakes and caused you a great deal of pain. Of this, he was greatly wrong. But God has forgiven him and I believe you have forgiven him, or are on the path of forgiveness. Jonah endured some horrible things in prison. Things he will probably carry to the grave, for shame of the things that happened to him, which he could not help. Oh, Jonah has told me nothing, but God has revealed many things to me. Love Jonah through the healing process. It is going to take some time, but I know God is a healer. Jonah is a changed man. So Joel, let the past be the past. Now is all you have. Live, love, and laugh with your brother. Enjoy your family. Thank God for your brother's kidney. Yes, I know this too. God always had a plan, Joel. And in His Perfect Plan was creating twins, to help each other along the way. You have helped Jonah, and now Jonah has helped you by giving you his kidney. That is what love does. Love gives and keeps on giving. Keep on giving your love, Joel. You have the biggest heart I know. Give love and watch how God gives it back to you in abundance. You cannot out-give God. I gave Jonah our family ring. I am leaving you the enclosed cross necklace. It belonged to your mother. Another heirloom passed down from generations. Give it to your wife or your firstborn. Just keep it in the family. It is priceless. And so are you and Jonah. I could not have children, but God blessed me with two beautiful boys to raise and to love as if they were my very own. I am forever grateful for that. I know how a mother feels when she has to say goodbye to her children. It is bittersweet. I am excited to be going home to see Jesus. But my flesh longs for a little more time with you and Jonah. Take care of each other. I love you, Joel. I am so proud of you.

Love, Aunt Alice

Aunt Alice's beautiful face was etched in Joel's memory. There was not another kind soul like hers. He missed her greatly, and wished he could just sit by her feet just once again and listened to her tell stories of old, from memory, which prepared him for life more than any book had. *Oh Aunt Alice, you were so wise!* Joel held the unique cross necklace in his hand. *Faith is going to love this, someday, after Yasha passes it on to her.*

Thank You, Lord God, for this special day. I am free! **"I will restore you to health and heal your wounds, declares the Lord, because you are called an outcast, Zion, for whom no one cares."**

CHAPTER 27

Kidney Transplant

Jonah's gaze darted to the woman standing at the door, his true love. Standing there in an off-white sundress, with her cute baby bump, Kayla was radiant. Jonah loved seeing her hair hanging loose. Everything about Kayla was exquisite. Nonetheless, Jonah could not overlook the puffiness and worry in her eyes, which revealed she did not sleep well. He had held her late into the night, until she had finally fallen asleep in his arms.

Today was the day. Jonah would give a part of himself to save his twin.

"Come on in," Jonah motioned as he lay in the hospital bed, waiting for his surgery.

"You're such a handsome man," Kayla said and kissed his lips. "I'm a blessed woman." Kayla's finger traced the scar on the right side of his face. She admired her husband greatly. His sacrifice of love was going to save a life. Kayla knew the tender side of her husband. Though he could have a gruff exterior, inwardly he was a soft teddy bear.

"You love my beauty mark, don't you?"

"It's distinguishing," she nodded. "As a matter of fact, it distinguishes you from your brother."

"My battle scar," Jonah flaunted. "Can't come through a battle without any battle scars."

"Mom is checking dad out of the hospital now. It's amazing how he's changed overnight."

"Staring death right smack in the eyeballs will do that to you." Jonah understood that all too well. "Only God could convert an atheist to a Believer. Only God."

"And Mom, she's different, too. Visiting her sister and brother awakened her sleepy spirit. She's so, so…" Kayla could not find the right word to depict her mother's new identity.

"Real, not so fake like before," Jonah filled in. "I mean, with all those plastic surgeries, she lost her identity and her values."

"Absolutely. I feel like we are all going to be a family now—with you included. Dad likes you. I can tell."

"I think I'll grow on him. Besides, who can resist my charm?" Jonah winked.

"I think someone's got the big head," Kayla played along with him. Anything to get her mind off the upcoming surgery.

Jonah pushed Kayla's hair behind her ear, and then covered his hand over hers. "Don't worry about me, Kayla. Just keep the prayers going up for Joel. He is weak and this surgery is going to take a toll on his body. He has a long way out of the woods and he needs constant prayer."

"I will pray for Joel, but my prayers are with you, as well," Kayla's stomach fluttered. "I just want this all to be over and for us to enjoy being newlyweds."

"We will," Jonah kissed her hand. "Doc says I will need to take it easy for two to four weeks, after leaving the hospital in a couple of days. We'll make up for lost time, you can bank on that," Jonah's eyes harmonized with his underlining thoughts.

"You're a mess," Kayla felt heat rise to her cheeks.

"And you're beautiful." Jonah pushed upward, his lips capturing hers.

"Excuse me," the orderly with the gurney entered. "It's time to go, Mr. Bates."

"I love you," Kayla pecked his lips, her eyes misting. "God bless you and keep you. God make His face shine upon you and be gracious to you. May God lift up His countenance before you and give you peace. And may the Lord guide this surgery and the hands of the surgeon and bring you back to me, healthy and whole, in Jesus' name, amen."

"Amen. Thank you, I love you."

Kayla watched her husband being wheeled away and felt such a peace. God had heard her prayer; therefore, she knew that God had already granted the petition that she had asked of Him.

Jonah is in God's hands now! There is no better place to be!

❃❃❃

Meanwhile, Yasha was saying her sendoffs to Joel. Inwardly, she struggled to keep her emotions intact. The paleness in Joel's countenance alarmed her. Joel was paler than she had ever seen him before. Yasha fretted that he was not strong enough to handle the transplant. All the same, it was his only hope of surviving.

"The church is doing a round the clock prayer chain for you," Yasha spoke, anxiety shadowing her eyes. "Every moment of the day someone will be praying for you. Pastor Jerry and Doris organized the prayer vigils."

"They are so faithful," Joel weakly responded, every breath coming out slow and painful.

"Yes, they are." Yasha fought to be strong for her husband. "I spoke with Jonah before coming here. He wanted me to make sure to tell you," Yasha began reading from a sticky note, "El, as the big brother, you have got to set the example and come out of this surgery. I am depending on you to get well quickly, so that we can make up for lost time. El, what happened in our past does not determine who we are now or who we will become. We will be even better men of God and better brothers after our surgeries. And remember what Aunt Alice always said, you got three choices. Live in the past, stay where you are, or keep it moving. I suggest we get these surgeries over and keep it moving. We've got a lot of catching up to do. And El, I love you."

Joel's vulnerable emotions resurfaced. "Aunt Alice always said that our past does not determine who we are now or who we will become. Jo remembered...and I can't tell you how many times Aunt Alice repeated those three choices... especially to Jo."

"He's a good man, Joel, just like you."

"I am realizing that," Joel mumbled. "He reminds me of Paul. When Paul was of the world, he radically lived that life. When he accepted Jesus, he was just as radical for the things of God. Jo is like that."

"So, you're the oldest," Yasha smiled.

"By eight minutes," Joel boasted. "I never let El forget that. I guess I better pull through so I can show him how big brothers always..." he choked, and a spell of painful coughs followed.

Yasha panicked, quickly giving him a sip of water. *Please Lord, strengthen Joel's body.*

"Thanks." Joel motioned for the cup. "Big brothers always

come out on top."

"You will come out on top," Yasha said confidently. "You will be stronger and healthier after this transplant. Faith is counting on it, and so am I."

Joel stretched his hand to his wife's tummy. "Faith, I'm looking forward to seeing you. Be good to mommy and none of that disliking what she eats," he winked at his wife. "Daddy loves you." Joel locked eyes with his wife. "Yasha, thank you for always standing by me, in the ministry and in our home. I would have never made it this far, without your unconditional, unwavering love. You light up my world, Yasha."

"You light up my life, Joel," Yasha sniffed, squeezing his hand lightly. "All things have worked out for our good, Joel. All things."

"Amen."

Dr. Benson and the nurse entered the room. "Well, it's time, Joel. Are you ready?"

"Yes, I am."

"Let's pray and then we will take you on down to surgery."

❃❃❃❃

Approximately an hour and half later, Jonah was wheeled into the recovery room, where he would be watched closely and vital signs taken frequently as the anesthesia wore off. As expected, there were no complications during Jonah's laparoscopic surgery. The surgeon was now placing Jonah's kidney in Joel's lower belly, leaving his other two kidneys intact.

Kayla waited patiently by his side in the recovery room. She was so relieved that everything went well, and the worst part was over. Later, he would be transitioned to a private room.

Jonah would mostly likely be discharged in two or three days.

Meanwhile Joel's surgery was underway. Seemingly, the routine surgery was going well, and the surgeon was closing the wound. Then, the dreaded sound in an operating room boomed.

Beep….beep…beep…

"We're losing him!" Dr. Benson shouted.

Joel was in cardiac arrest.

"Begin CPR, now!"

Beep…be-e-e-e-e—

"He's *flat-lining*!" Dr. Benson stated, distraught but composed. "Keep doing CPR. The defibrillator will not work for him."

"God save him," Dr. Benson silently prayed. "Bring him back."

Meanwhile, the members of the church were fervently praying in the spirit for Joel. Every second of the day was filled with prayers going up for their pastor. Yasha was in the hospital chapel on bended knees, praying, sensing the need for fervent prayer.

The effectual fervent prayer of the righteous avails much.

⚜⚜⚜

"Jonah," Kayla saw his eyes flickering. Gently, she caressed his hand. "I'm so glad you're all right."

Slowly, his eyes opened. Jonah opened his mouth, trying to say something, but it was so low she could not understand what he was trying to say.

"El," he whispered again.

"Joel," Kayla repeated, unsure.

Jonah nodded.

"He should be out of surgery," Kayla replied, looking at her watch. "I'll go check on him a few."

"Pray...for El," fright was in Jonah's eyes. He thought nothing of himself at the present.

"Jonah, I will, but don't get yourself worked up. You just came through a major surgery, as well," Kayla detected his uneasiness.

"Trouble. El is in trouble," he spoke louder. "We've got to pray."

"Okay."

"Now," he urged.

"Okay," Kayla closed her eyes, her husband's plea tugging at her heartstrings. "Father God, touch Joel with Your healing power. We do not know what is going on right now, but You do. So, Lord, we are standing in the gap for Joel asking that You miraculously touch him, heal Him, and deliver him from the attack of the enemy. Work all things out for his good and his family's good. In Jesus' name we pray, believe, and receive it as done. Amen."

"Amen." Jonah squeezed her hand. "Thanks."

"I'm going to check with Yasha to see what's going on." Kayla stood. "Do you want something before I leave, like ice chips or water?"

He nodded.

Kayla assisted him with drinking the ice chips. "I love you, Jonah."

"Love you."

Kayla leaned over and kissed him on the lips before leaving. "Be right back."

Jonah closed his eyes and silently praised and prayed for Joel in the spirit. "El will live and not die and declare the works of the Lord." Jonah mouthed. "He will live!"

Shortly, Kayla returned with the news that Joel was apparently still in surgery, which had been expected to be over two hours ago. Yasha had not heard anything, but she was anxiously waiting with several church members in the waiting area.

"Go be with her," Jonah encouraged.

"I don't want to leave you."

"I'm not going anywhere. She needs you."

Kayla inwardly struggled. Partly, she wanted to give her support to Yasha, but she also wanted to be there for Jonah. He had just endured surgery, and a wife should be by her husband.

"Please, Kayla," Jonah pleaded.

"All right," she relented. "Are you in pain?"

"A little."

"All you have to do is press this button." Kayla showed him the gadget that would instantly give him morphine to control the pain. "Don't wait until the pain intensifies, but take it as soon you feel it. Don't try to be all macho, either." Kayla knew her husband.

"See," he pressed the button. "Macho is out the window."

"Good!"

"Keep me posted with Joel."

"I will. I'll be back shortly," Kayla grabbed her purse.

"You still don't look pregnant."

"Look," she pulled her dress tight, indicating a small bump in her midsection. "I'm huge."

"Huge?" He chuckled. It hurt to laugh. "You're fine."

"I hope you keep saying that even when I'm waddling." Kayla went to the door. "Rest."

"Resting," Jonah closed his eyes again, feeling exhausted.

Kayla returned to Yasha at the perfect timing. Dr. Benson had just arrived in the waiting area. Yasha extended her hand for Kayla to stand by her.

Yasha was overcome with emotions. He heart raced with anticipation. For support, Kayla wrapped her arm around Yasha. "It's going to be alright."

Yasha nodded.

"Joel survived the surgery," Dr. Benson began.

"Thank God!" Yasha sighed, sensing there was more news.

"His heart stopped during surgery. Twice."

Yasha gasped, her knees buckling. Kayla supported her, bearing her up, not allowing her to fall.

"But God brought him back," Dr. Benson said, giving credit where it was due.

Yasha hugged Kayla, crying tears of joy and relief. "What about the kidney transplant?"

"Everything appears good. Joel's body is not rejecting the kidney. He is in intensive care right now. He's very weak, so we need to monitor him closely."

"Can I see him?"

"Yes, but only briefly. In fact, you can go with me now. He's heavily sedated, because his body needs to rest," Dr. Benson went on to explain. "Joel's not out of the woods yet, but God is definitely with him."

"I know," Yasha agreed, shaking her head. "He is always with him."

CHAPTER 28

Celebration...Redemption

Three days after his surgery, Jonah, slowly walked to his brother's hospital room. No longer in ICU, Joel had his own private room. His rapid recovery was nothing short of a miracle.

"You look good, El," Jonah sat beside him.

"I feel better," Joel gazed at his brother, "thanks to the Man upstairs, and to you."

"God is good."

"All the time."

"So, how long are you going to be here?" Jonah asked.

"They'll probably let me out sometime next week. I'm ready to go home. I miss sleeping in my own bed."

"Least you got a bed," Jonah chuckled. "With all that's been going on, Kayla and I still don't have a place to call home yet. We're staying at the Marriott."

"You're looking for a house to buy or build?"

"To me it doesn't matter, but Kayla wants our home to be built. In the meantime, we're looking for an apartment."

"I have a lot of land. Why don't you build on it?" Joel suggested, not knowing his wife had already mentioned it.

Hearing the proposition from his brother warmed Jonah's heart. Obviously, his brother had forgiven him. "That would be great, El. It will give us a chance to get to know each other again. I would love being close to you again."

"I want that, too. We've got a lot of catching up to do," Joel grinned. "Seriously, Jo, thank you for giving me your kidney. I already feel so much better."

"It's the least I can do. Besides, you would have done the same for me."

"In a heartbeat."

A comfortable silence followed.

"I met our father," Joel professed.

"Really?" Jonah frowned. "When?"

"Before Aunt Alice died. Yasha loves to trace family history, so she searched for our father and found him. She wanted our children to know their grandfather."

"Okay. So what happened?"

"Mom lied to us, Jo."

"Not a shocker. The shock would be that she was telling us the truth about something."

"You are right there. Anyhow, he lived in Georgia."

"Lived? He's not living?"

"He died a week after I met him. He had a heart attack."

"Wow. I don't know how I feel about that," Jonah pondered. "I mean, I should be sad, mad, something…but I feel nothing."

"I know," Joel hesitated. "Guess what?"

"What?"

"He was a pastor."

"Get out of here."

"He was," Joel chuckled.

"Well, why didn't he visit us? Or call us? Or send us a birthday card, anything to let us know he cared? Didn't he know we were dirt poor? He could have supported us and gave us a better life." So many unanswered questions plagued Jonah.

"First things first. Mom told us that when dad got out of the Army he came home and just left us for another woman. Not so. Dad came home for about two weeks before being sent to Germany. While home, mom had packed her things, left him, and took the both of us. For two weeks, he searched for us. At that time, we were living on and off with Aunt Alice and dad did not even know about Aunt Alice. He reported back to military duty and hired a private detective to find us, but the detective could not find us. It was as if we had vanished. For years, dad searched for us. Then he received a letter from mom, revealing that we had been adopted and were happy. And the letter said, please don't bother them. They deserve to be happy."

"I can't believe she did that."

"I saw the letter. All those years, Jesse carried it with him in his wallet. It was in mom's own handwriting. She wrote it before she died and sent it to dad's last post, which forwarded the letter to him. He did not want to disrupt our lives, but he suffered terribly. He prayed that, when we got older, we would find him."

"That's low," Jonah's hidden anger surfaced. "How could she do that? We needed a father, especially since she wasn't a mother."

"For sure," Joel agreed. "Anyhow, he was somehow injured while in the army and had trouble seeing out of his right eye. He was given a medical discharge. After losing us, Jesse practically ran from God, for a long time. He was mad at God about his health and about us. Finally, God got his attention and Jesse accepted the calling upon his life, which was to preach."

"Sounds familiar," Jonah replied, feeling able to relate.

"We look just like him," Joel went on. "I have a picture of him back at the house."

"Did you tell him about me," Jonah hesitated. "About me being locked up?"

"I did, but I also told him that Aunt Alice said you were a Christian now and doing good."

"Thanks, El. Didn't want him to die thinking I was a no-good sinner."

"He didn't."

"So, I guess we are truly orphans now."

"We've got each other."

"That's all that matters," Jonah stood. "Let's leave the past in the past. Today is a new day."

"It's a new season for us, Jo," Joel spoke with confidence. "I missed having my twin in my life. No matter how hard I tried to be happy, something was always missing …you."

"Exactly. Now I feel whole," Jonah confessed.

"Exactly!"

"Nothing like freedom!"

❀❀❀

After getting out of the hospital, Yasha and Joel insisted that Jonah and Kayla move into their home until they could build their new home on the land. Kayla's father would be paying for their new two-story home. It was a wedding present.

A month after their surgeries, the twins were home and having a family gathering to celebrate their reunion. It was a happy time for both extensions of the family. Kayla sat next to her husband, and Jonah sat next to Joel, with his wife on the opposite side. Also seated at the table were Kayla's parents, Drew and Kathryn Lovett. Pastor Jerry and Doris Mack, Dr. Benson and her husband attended. Kathryn's siblings, Lewis and Daisy, along with their spouses, were thrilled to be included in the celebration. Drew paid for their first class tickets. Also, from Holly Hill and Moncks Corner, were Pastor Reggie and Lauren Goodwin, and Steven and Paula Hutto. Kayla's best friend, Lisa Walsh, and her husband, Dan Walsh, were also present.

After enjoying a great meal inside, family and friends gathered outside by the pool. It was a lovely day for a lovely celebration. Joel and Jonah had reunited as if nothing had ever come between them. Love heals all wounds and forgives all wrongs. As the twins splashed in the pool, enjoying a game of water volleyball against Steven and Dan, the others mingled, enjoying the fellowship.

Everyone was staying in town so that they could witness Jonah preach his first sermon at the request of his brother, Joel, who had not yet recovered enough to preach.

"Shane is smiling down from heaven, for sure," Steven said to Jonah before leaving to return to hotel. "You've done him proud."

"Thanks, Steven. That means a lot."

"We surely miss you at Hutto's, but God had a better plan. I know you're excited about spearheading the Second Chances Project."

"I'm looking forward to the challenge," Jonah said proudly. "Working with the Lovett family means a lot to me. Kayla's father accepting me like this is an honor. I'm a blessed man."

"They are blessed to have you," Steven responded. "Don't ever forget that. You're a blessing, Jonah."

✖✖✖

After embracing his brother, Jonah went to the podium to minister his first sermon. There was no fear, only anticipation of what God was going to do through him. The message that God had placed in his heart was dear and personal.

"Brothers and Sisters, I want to talk to you about freedom, true freedom in Jesus Christ. The Word of God says, 'Where the Spirit of the Lord is, there is liberty,'" Jonah began. "Liberty means freedom. When you are baptized in God's spirit, the Spirit of the Lord abides within you. Therefore, there should be freedom. Yet, many of us today are not walking in true freedom. We are in bondage. Not a physical bondage that others can see, no. Physical bondage was when I was locked up in Manchester. People could see my bondage. However, that bondage was a piece of cake when compared to my inner captivity—the secret, private pain that was hidden behind my smiles and laughter once I became "a free man".

"In prison, I accepted Jesus Christ as my Lord and Savior. God freed me from my sins. Praise God for that. But I wasn't free in here," he pointed to his head. "You see, the accuser of the brethren, satan himself, held me as a prisoner—and I let him. My mind was a playground for him, for sure. My mind and heart were imprisoned; my life was in chains. I was in total bondage. I was not free, even though I was saved.

"The Bibles says, in Isaiah 61, verses one and two,

The Spirit of the Lord GOD is upon Me,
    because the LORD has anointed Me
    to preach good tidings to the poor.
He has sent Me to heal the brokenhearted,
    to proclaim liberty to the captives,
    and the opening of the prison to those who are
bound,
    to proclaim the acceptable year of the LORD,
    and the day of vengeance of our God.

"I have come to proclaim liberty to you today. Freedom from whatever has you bound. To open the prisons of your heart, so that you can experience true freedom in Jesus. The devil is the accuser. He is constantly accusing you of things. His goal is to keep you in bondage. He knows that once you are totally free he cannot keep you from walking in your full God-given purpose. As long as he has you bound, then you cannot fully give yourself one hundred percent to spreading the gospel, to sharing Jesus with others, to healing the brokenhearted and so forth. His goal is to keep the wool over your eyes so that you cannot see all the great blessings that God has in store for you…because you do not feel you deserve it. I know, I've been there," Jonah paused, taking a good look at his captivated audience. He had there undivided attention. God's anointing was upon Jonah, to bring deliverance to His people.

"He accuses you by constantly bringing up your past mistakes. Whispering in your heart that you are not good enough because so and so said so, or because such and such happened to you. He hounds you like a dog in pursuit of its victim, dogging you about past abuse, past trauma, past lies, past indiscretions, past failed relationships, and past secret sins that no one knows about but you and God. That is how he torments us. That is how the enemy keeps us in bondage, prisoners of our past. He keeps you in bondage through fear. Fear that someone will find out what happened to you, what you did, your secrets—fear that you will fail, yet again. Through fear, he punishes you and keeps tormenting you. However, the devil is a liar, and there is no truth in him. Praise God!

"I had a problem," Jonah confessed. "I was being tormented by the devil in my dreams. He constantly accused me and brought up my past. I suffered daily. I had to fight back.

I cried out to God and He heard my cry and sent my answer. The answer was in the Word. I started quoting the Word over my situation. I quoted Proverbs 3:24, 'When you lie down, you will not be afraid. Yes, you will lie down and your sleep will be sweet.' And Psalms 4:8 'I will lie down in peace and sleep, for you alone, O Lord, make me dwell in safety.' Nightly, I prayed these Scriptures before going to bed. The dreams didn't stop overnight. It was a process. However, the process started with forgiveness. I had to forgive my abuser. And that was a hard thing to do in the flesh, but the grace of God is sufficient. With much prayer and faith in God, He delivered me. I am no longer a prisoner of the devil. I took back what he had stolen from me, which was my peace and joy. Oh, yeah, he still tries to come and whisper lies in my heart even now, but I do not accept it!

"Today, God wants to set you free and make you fully whole in Him. If you find yourself being a prisoner of past pains, hurt, trauma, abuse, relationships, or anything that holds you back from being truly free, I want you to come to this altar for prayer. God wants to set you free, not just from your sins, but also from your bondage. He wants to open the prison doors of your heart and give your true freedom today."

Jonah paused, watching as many parishioners came forward to the altar. Jonah motioned for Joel and Pastor Mack to join him at the altar. "We're going to lay our hands on you for healing. For the Bible says that we can lay our hands on the sick and they shall be healed. Healed from your past hurts and pain. Healed from your guilt and shame. Healed from *anything* that has you bound today. All we ask is that by faith you receive it. But first, if anyone has wronged you, abused you, hurt you, disappointed or betrayed you, and you're still holding onto un-forgiveness, I want you to forgive that person.

If you don't, you'll never be free. If you're serious about being free, you must forgive.

"Let's take a moment here to forgive. You know the person who wronged you and you're still harboring bitterness, anger and un-forgiveness in your heart. What he or she did to you was wrong, but you have to let it go. You have to forgive him or her. Release them so that God can release you, so that you can be free. Repeat after me...

"Father God, right now I forgive... (say that name or those names)...I forgive (say the name(s)) for what they did to me (confess what they did). I forgive (say the name(s)) as You have forgiven me. I release (say the name(s)) to You right now in Jesus' name." Jonah paused. "Praise God for forgiveness. Now repeat after me this prayer of freedom. Pray it from your heart and not your mind.

"Dear Father God, I want to thank You in advance for my total freedom today. Your word says You came to proclaim liberty to the captives and open the prison to those that are bound. I am bound Lord, and I want to be free. I have been held captive and I want liberty. Free me Lord. Heal me. Deliver me from (say whatever it is)," Jonah paused. "Deliver me from (whatever it is) today. I bind up the devil. I resist his lies. I denounce his authority over my life, over that past situation. He has no place in my life because the Kingdom of God is within me. Today I accept my freedom because Jesus has given it to me. In the name of Jesus, I curse the spirit of fear, depression, rejection, abandonment, past failures, past mistakes, worthlessness and command all to go in Jesus' name. I speak love, joy, hope, and peace to my body, my mind and my spirit. Fill me God with your love. Fill me with more of You. Thank You, Lord. I am free in Jesus' name, amen."

The three ministers went about laying hands on everyone, standing in agreement with them. It was a day of victory for so many people. God came to set them free. He came to deliver them from their bondages. He came because He loved them.

After service, Jonah and Joel recapped on the message and the goodness of the Lord.

"Joel, I need to go see Nixon and I want you to go with me," Jonah proposed.

Jonah had revealed his ongoing torture from Nixon in prison, leaving out no details to his brother. "Are you sure?"

He nodded. "I feel God wants me to face him and to forgive him."

"Let's do it."

✄✄✄

A week later, Jonah and Joel waited in the Manchester visiting room for Nixon. Jonah's heart was beating wildly, his body perspiring form head to toe, and his face was ashen. Maybe this wasn't such a good idea. Jonah wanted to hall tail and get out of this place that contained so many painful reminders.

"You're not alone," Joel whispered, looking his brother in the eye. "God is with you, and I'm here. I've got your back."

Immediately, Jonah felt strengthened.

Sitting with his back straightened, head high and feeling more confident, Jonah watched as the big, bulky Nixon entered the room, feet chained and hands chained, until the guard removed the chains on his hands. Nixon looked around, confused at who would be visiting him. He had no family and no friends left on the outside. Then he laid eyes on Jonah and smiled the biggest, crooked, sinister smile he could muster up.

Walking near, with the guard right behind him, it wasn't until he got right up on them that he noticed Joel.

"There's two of you," he sat down, separated by a window with bars.

"Nixon," Jonah greeted.

"Hi, Sweet *Thang!*" Nixon drooled. "Guess you missed me. I knew you couldn't stay away. And then you brought me doubles."

"Nixon, this is my twin, Joel."

"Hello, Nixon," Joel spoke. "Jonah's description of you didn't do you justice. You're rather puny to me."

"Puny!" Nixon's voice went from zero to ten in a split second. The guard quickly came over.

"Nixon," the guard firmly called his name.

Nixon calmed down.

"Listen, Nixon, I just came here to tell you two things."

"Oh yeah, and what's that?"

"One, I forgive you."

"Forgive me," he scoffed. "I don't need your forgiveness."

"Regardless, I forgive you for everything. For assaulting me and for making me do things that were totally against my wishes. You beat me, you pushed me around, your tortured me, but I still forgive you."

Nixon watched him, confounded by Jonah's willingness to let bygones be bygones.

Joel looked to his brother, making sure he was okay, and said, "Go ahead, Jonah."

"Secondly, God loves you Nixon, and so do I."

Floored for sure, Nixon didn't have a comeback. How could this man, whom he did all those things he had just confessed and so much more, love him?

"God so loved the world that He gave His only Son," Joel took up where his brother left off. "That whosoever believes in Him, should not perish, but have everlasting life. Further, the Bible says that we have all sinned and fallen short of the glory of God. And then, while we were yet sinners, Christ died for us," Joel paused. "You see, Nixon, Jonah and I have both sinned and messed up, but God loved us so much He sent Jesus to die for us. Jesus died for you, too.

"There is no way you can do what you do and keep doing what you're doing and find happiness—true happiness—in that. I imagine that you are always looking over your back, trying to stay one step ahead of the next victim. You probably sleep with one eye opened, paranoid that someone is going to kill you in your sleep or something. Nixon, you will never stay on top. Someone bigger than you, stronger than you, wiser than you, younger than you, is going to take your spot. One day. And then what?"

Nixon had no idea that today he was going to confront the man in the invisible mirror. Today, he had a choice that could make his life better or worse. Either way, he knew he was soon to be dethroned with the fresh new inmates coming in, looking to dismantle his domain. His life was meaningless. What he saw in Jonah and Joel sparked his interest.

"If you want peace," Jonah started, "real peace comes from God. Look at me, Nixon. I'm no longer messed up, or walking around with hatred in my heart, sucking the life out of me. I have the peace of God. You can have it, too. God wants to give it to you."

"I've done too many horrible things," Nixon finally spoke. "You of all people should know."

"So have I, but God forgave me, and better yet, He doesn't

remember my sins *no* more!"

"He forgives and forgets," Joel added.

"How do I get this peace?"

Jonah and Joel looked at each other, feeling that God was about to snatch another one from the kingdom of darkness into His marvelous light. It was the greatest feeling!

"It's easy," they both answered.

"You do the honors," Joel said to his brother.

"Gladly," he intensely fixed his eyes on Nixon. "You need Jesus. Do you want Him today? Do you want Him to be your Lord and Savior?"

"I do."

"Good. Just repeat this prayer after me...Father God, I am a sinner in need of a Savior. I confess with my mouth the Lord Jesus, and believe in my heart that God raised Him from the dead. I accept your gift of salvation by accepting Jesus Christ as my Lord and Savior. Forgive me for all of my sins. Fill me with Your Spirit, so that I may walk in the path you have for me to walk. I surrender my heart, my mind, my soul to you. I am Yours, Lord. Thank You for making my heart Your home. In Jesus' name, amen."

"Amen." Nixon opened his eyes, spilling forth fresh tears of peace, joy, love, and forgiveness.

Epilogue

One year later.

A lot had happened in a year. Jonah and Kayla's home had been built on the ten acres of land that Joel had deeded to him. In between the properties, a guesthouse had been built which Drew and Kathryn Lovett often occupied during the weekends. Drew and Kathryn were more than just Kayla's parents; they had become parents to Jonah, Joel, and Yasha, all whose parents were deceased. Unable to have children of their own, Drew and Kathryn had adopted them all into their hearts. God had blessed them by extending their family, with the added bonus of two lovely grandchildren.

Little Faith and Little Mariah had been born a week a part. Little Mariah couldn't wait a full month longer to be born. Now the eight-month-old girls captured the hearts of everyone around them. They were a bundle of blessings, reminders of how the gift of love keeps on giving and growing.

"I think the burgers are about ready," Drew said as he flipped the burger on the outside grill. This had become a second Saturday of the month tradition, when the weather was good. The three families would come together to barbecue and eat outside on the patio at Joel's home, and enjoy the pool. Then they would head over to Jonah's, where the kids could play on the swings and play area, especially built so that as their family expanded, there would always be pool time and outdoor playtime activities at both homes.

"Good, I'm hungry, Pops," Joel had christened him.

"Me too, Dad," Jonah chimed in with bun in hand. "I want one hot off the grill."

"Son, I do believe you have tapeworms or something," Drew teased. "Didn't I just see you eat two hotdogs? We are supposed to wait and eat at the picnic table together."

"Don't worry, I've saved plenty of room," Jonah played along. "Besides, after being worked by a slave-driver, five days a week, I've skipped many meals, so I have to make up for it on the weekends."

"Skipped meals..." Kayla came over, holding Mariah on her hip. "You never skip meals. If you didn't exercise, you would surely be overweight, Jonah."

"Hey, I thought you were on my side," Jonah nibbled his wife's ear.

"Stop that," Kayla shooed him, "I'm always on your side." She winked and headed to the table to assist Yasha with the tablecloth.

"Doesn't Joel look great?" Yasha whispered. The girls were put in the highchairs. "He's come a long way. Dr. Benson says he thinks Joel will not have to keep taking the preventive medicine to keep his body from rejecting the kidney. He's gaining weight. It's hard to tell the two apart now...except for Jonah's scar."

"I know what you mean," Kayla chuckled. "*Poor* Mariah was looking at them both trying to figure out which one was her daddy."

"Faith as well," Yasha smiled.

"It's so good to see that Jonah and Joel have put their past behind them. They are so close, like twins should be."

"Joel told me about Jonah's torment in prison. How is he doing with nightmares?"

"So much better, Yasha. He hardly ever has them now. God truly can heal, restore, and redeem the time. Jonah is taking night classes in Health Administration, because he loves managing the new Lovett's Second Chances Foundation. He and mom are working diligently in finding more resources to help children who have been abused or born with facial deformities and cannot afford plastic surgery."

"It's so wonderful to see young people given a better chance at living whole and complete."

"Yes, and Jonah even found some youth that were headed in the wrong direction, who he has hired to work part-time at the center," Kayla was proud of her husband. "That's his way of paying-it-forward."

"Joel is proud of him, as well," Yasha continued. "He can't stop talking about Jo this and Jo that."

Shortly, everyone sat around the specially made picnic table, made for a large family of twenty or more. As the family expanded, they would have room for everyone to sit, or add on.

As customary, Drew held up his goblet for the family toast. "As we all know, the past year has been a year of tests and trials. Of victories and successes! Kathryn and I are blessed to have two beautiful daughters, two wonderful sons…"

"Hey, you forgot to say two handsome sons," Jonah joshed.

"Okay, two wonderful, handsome sons," Drew emphasized, "and two amazing grandchildren. I lost so much in my life, running away from God and blaming Him for so many things, when all along He was right there, working behind the scenes to give me all of this—all of you," he swallowed. "I was in bondage." Drew looked to his wife, with love and adoration in his eyes. "But now I'm a free man. So, this evening I would like to toast to our freedom! God has freed us from sin and shame. So here's to our freedom!"

In unison, everyone shouted, "Freedom!"

"And we are *No Longer Captive!*" Jonah added.

"Amen, brother," Joel seconded. *"No Longer Captive!"*

Dear Reader,

Every time God leads me to write another book, I get so excited, because there is always a message for me to learn or relearn. Jonah was an amazing character to write about. I like Jonah because he is real. He is not some cookie-cutter Christian. No, he has his flaws, imperfections, and he is messy at times. Yes, he made mistakes. Yes, he did wrong and betrayed even his twin brother. However, he was still worth saving.

God knows that we are but dust. He knows our weaknesses and yet, in Him, we become strong. After being released from prison, having paid the time for his crime, life did not just get easy for Jonah. Why? Because Jonah was still a prisoner. He was imprisoned by his past, in many ways and many faces. However, Glory to God, He never leaves us or forsakes us. Along the way, he met Steven, a wealthy man who wanted to pay it forward in honoring his brother, Shane. Steven gave Jonah another chance. There are not many Steven's out there who will look beyond a person's fault and see his need for redemption. Then God blessed Jonah with Kayla. God used both of their lives to bring healing to one another and to walk in the gift of love, freely.

God has given all of us so many chances to get it right. I know He has for me. Yet, Christians are so quick to judge others and to condemn them for their wrongs. God did not come to condemn us, but to save us. Can't we pay it forward like, Steven?

Joel walked away from his brother. Rightly so, he had a reason to mistrust his brother and to feel the pain of his hurt... but not indefinitely. We must forgive. Joel was a pastor, and yet, he was a prisoner of his past. He was not locked up behind bars like his brother, but he was held captive by bitterness and an unforgiving heart. Captivity is painful and it affects so many people. The symptoms vary. You can be affected physically, emotionally, socially, financially and spiritually. It holds you back from being the real you!

Today, I beseech you to show mercy and love to those who have made mistakes. Give people a chance to get it right. After all, God did the same for you. Help others to discover their true destiny in life. Be forgiving and longsuffering toward others. And forgive yourself, if need be. Every life is worth saving. Everyone needs to be free!

God wants you free, and so do I. Others are depending on you. Please repeat the prayer on page 299, daily if need be, until you have truly released and found relief in forgiving and being forgiven. Remember, Jesus came to set the captives free so that you can say like Jonah and Joel, "I am "No Longer Captive!" I would love to hear from you, please email me at: rlwbooks@gmail.com.

God bless you richly, Rai

PS: Coming soon…No Longer Brokenhearted. Through a journey of healing, Gabe and Queenie discover that after the storms of life the sun will shine again, leaving its footprints of love in the rainbow. For God draws nigh to the brokenhearted… to heal, to deliver and to restore.

Finally Reader,

If you don't know Jesus as your personal Lord and Savior, or if you have backslid, God is waiting on you with open arms to accept you into the family. He loves you and desires to take care of you, from now and into eternity. Accept His gift. Accept Jesus into your heart, today!

"If you confess with your mouth the Lord Jesus and believe in your heart that God has raised Him from the dead, you will be saved. For with the heat one believes unto righteousness, and with the mouth, confession is made unto salvation. For whoever calls on the name of the Lord shall be saved."

-Romans: 10:9-10

Prayer:

Father God, I am a sinner in need of a Savior. I confess with my mouth the Lord Jesus, and believe in my heart that God raised Him from the dead. I accept your gift of salvation, by accepting Jesus Christ as my Lord and Savior. Fill me with Your Spirit, so that I may walk in the path you have for me to walk. I surrender my heart, my mind, my soul to you. I am Yours, Lord. Thank You for making my heart Your home. In Jesus' name, amen.

Discussion Questions:

1. After being incarnated for five years, Jonah was now a "free" man. However, he was still in bondage, captive by his past. What are some ways that people may be in bondage or imprisoned?

2. Jonah realized that he needed to remove himself from his old environment because the temptation to do wrong was constantly knocking on his door. Does changing your environment really help? Or should the change be more inwardly, than outwardly? Explain.

3. Kayla was adopted, but feared that at any moment she would be given back, or disowned for mistakes. Have you ever felt that God would disown you because of your past mistakes, wrongdoings? After all, He adopted us into His family, making us joint-heirs with Christ and Heirs of Him.

4. Everything hidden will be revealed. Do you feel that couples should keep secrets? Why or why not?

5. Jonah betrayed his twin, Joel. Why do you think it was so hard for Joel to truly forgive him and let Jonah back into his life, especially since he was a pastor?

6. Do you feel Joel had a prideful heart in not wanting to ask his brother for his kidney? Explain.

7. Drew was an atheist and hated anything or anyone who claimed to be a Believer. Consequently, Kathryn followed in his footsteps, keeping Kayla from going to church and knowing her relatives. If you were Kathryn what are some

ways she could have stood up for her beliefs, without ending her marriage?

8. Why do you think it was necessary for Jonah to face Nixon and forgive him in person?

9. Kathryn was barren, and deeply desired to have children. Psalms 113:9 says, "He gives the barren woman a home, making her the joyous mother of children. Praise the LORD!" In the end, God had expanded Kathryn and Drew's home with children and grandchildren. God doesn't always answer the way we want, but He always answers. What are some ways that you asked God for something and He gave you something different? In the end, was better?

10. Lisa, Kayla's friend, judged Jonah by the way he looked, which is something we often do without even realizing it. We can become judgmental people. Jonah's story wasn't finished; it was just beginning. What are some ways we can work on being less judgmental about people, based on what we see, or have heard or their past mistakes?

11. As parents, we want the best for our children. However, we must allow them to make their own choices. Drew completely cut Kayla off because she defied him by becoming a Christian. What are some ways parents have to be careful not to stifle our children independence?